A High Courage

GAIL PINER

Publishing Services provided by Paper Raven Books LLC

Printed in the United States of America

First Printing, 2023

Paperback ISBN: 979-8-9881161-1-0
Hardback ISBN: 979-8-9881161-0-3

To the memory of my grandmother, Mary Ellen.

I miss you.

*"[G]o forward…with an unwavering faith, **a high courage**, and a quiet heart…"*

– Princess Elizabeth (later Queen Elizabeth II) on April 21, 1947, her 21st birthday.

Table of Contents

CHAPTER 1

Tom

Southeastern North Carolina
Wednesday, October 3, 1928

For two days, there had been a screaming silence in my head. Then this morning, the silence left, and the thoughts wouldn't stop coming.

I thought I knew what loss was, what strength was. That being a wife for the rest of my days was my future. I thought I knew everything there was to know about loving my children and being a good mother to them.

But I had no idea how much there was left for me to learn.

I'd been kidding myself, along with everyone else, my whole life. Independent and strong, that's what I'd told myself I was. That's what I'd led everyone to believe about me. But now, these thoughts told me I was a fraud. I'd only been able to see myself that way because I'd had my parents and then Tom to catch me if I fell. These mean thoughts told me I was going to be a failure as a mother, and everyone was going to see that. The hardest thought racing through my head was that I wasn't going to be able to take care of my children. That I just couldn't do it on my own. I wasn't smart enough. I wasn't strong enough.

Standing on the back porch, I took a deep breath and gazed over the harvested fields, through the gap in the live oaks hunched over in their Spanish moss shawls. The rising sun was lighting up the waters of the Sound there past the trees and beyond that, the thin strip of Masonboro Island. On the other side of the barrier island was the ocean, although all that was visible this dawn was a tiny band of brilliant sparkles, so glaring it was hard to look at for long.

"Diamonds, Mary Ellen." I could hear my Tom whispering in my ear the first time I'd seen the sunrise from my new home. He'd come up behind me as I was awestruck at the sight. He pulled my back tight against him and held me as we gazed upon the sparkles until the sun rose enough to release some of the magic. "Those are the only kind I reckon I'll ever be able to give you, sweetheart. But you'll have a new batch most every morning."

Even now, I could hear his deep voice from fifteen years ago and feel him kiss my ear. We'd been newly married, and everything had seemed rimmed with diamonds to me then. And he'd been right; there were new diamonds almost every morning for all those years. I'd been a very lucky woman. Luckier than most, I needed to keep telling myself. But there would be no more diamonds for me again. That part of my life was over.

Before panic could completely overtake me, another thought from somewhere else slammed into my head: *Don't you dare feel sorry for yourself, missy. Stop whining. Figure it out. You are already smart enough. If you aren't strong enough, get stronger.*

I fought the urge to walk down to the water and sit on the shore near the broken pilings of our old dock. It was destroyed several years ago by a hurricane that took many of the houses in this area, although our house was spared. I gave birth to our seven children in our little house. We lost one precious daughter at only six months of age to a cough that wasn't helped by the damp, icy drafts, which slipped in from the Sound that hard winter. Yes, I'd thought I already knew all there was to know about loss.

Today, I wanted to sit and listen to the 'lap, lap, lap' of the soft waves of the Sound and let the sun bleach out all the other thoughts. Instead, I took the broom and created my own hypnotic rhythmic sound of the straw swishing across the painted blue-gray porch boards, back and forth, back and forth. Lulled from my earlier panic, once again, I imagined my Tom walking home across the fields, his lanky frame stooping to check the progress of the crops. When my mother saw him for the first time, she took one look at his ears and said, "He looks like a scarecrow with handles on his head." After we were married, my mother always tugged on his ears as she hugged his neck. He would laugh quietly at her teasing.

I thought of running my fingers through his dark, wavy hair. Of his blue eyes and how he usually smiled with his lips close together because he was afraid he had too much of an overbite. I loved it when he forgot himself and just laughed, with his strong white teeth showing and his adorable ears turning red. His eyes watered when he really laughed, and it made them seem bluer than ever.

I smiled at these memories as I dug the broom straw deep into the crevices between the slats. Every errant grain of sand swept back into the yard from which it came. Every rocking chair lined up just so, ready for the friends and family who would arrive in a few hours. For my Tom's funeral. So he could be swept back into the earth from which he came.

I'd already slopped the hogs, fed the chickens, then pumped fresh water for all of them. Finally, I went to the stall in the barn and petted Molly, our old mule, who waited for her breakfast more patiently than the others. I gave Molly her morning ear rub while she ate; then I told her about Tom. She stopped eating and leaned on me as I leaned on her. She didn't mind my shaking body. Sweet girl.

Now I pulled my shoulders back just as a baby's cry came from the kitchen behind me. I had a whole bucket of problems to solve, but first, I had to get us all through today. Best get to it. As I reached for the handle of the screen door, I paused. Now it had started. The rest of my life without Tom had started. I swallowed down the loss, the panic, and the despair that wanted to swamp me. My four girls and two boys were waiting for me. Irene, my oldest, had just turned twelve, and Baby Clarence wasn't quite four months old. In a few weeks, I would have my thirtieth birthday. We were all too young for this. None of us was ready for this.

I opened the screen door and began the longest day of my life.

How on earth had I not heard this commotion going on in the kitchen? Clarence was screaming in the outraged tones that signal an empty belly and a soiled diaper, demanding immediate and simultaneous attention. Irene, whose dark Irish beauty was becoming more pronounced by the day and whose face bore the stains of recent tears, stood at the wood cookstove, adding thick slices of bacon to the hot grease left from the first batch, trying to dodge the painful splatters. A pot of grits was boiling too quickly and threatened to overflow.

Tommy, with his white-blonde hair and who would turn three in less than a week, laughed joyfully as he sprinted away from grimly determined eight-year-old Leah, who was trying to put some clothes on him. "Stop running 'round naked as a jaybird!" she hissed at him, pulling up short when she spied me coming into the kitchen.

Unaware of my return, ten-year-old Celeste was slamming plates and utensils onto our long farm table, miffed again Irene had what Celeste saw as the glamour job of cooking. My youngest daughter, five-year-old Martha, stood by Baby Clarence's basket, trying to soothe him with a little song she learned in Sunday school.

I quickly washed my hands, stepped to the stove, moved the grits off the heat, and took over the frying pan. "Irene, change Clarence, please. You did a real good job getting breakfast started. Celeste, slam one more plate, and you will surely regret it. Tommy! Let Leah get you dressed. You're a big boy, so act like one. You're too big to run around like that. And you know what today is. Martha, sweetie, could you help Irene with Clarence?"

Martha and Irene softly answered, "Yes, ma'am," and moved to deal with the baby.

Leah's "Yes, Mama" held a definite gloating tone as she grabbed Tommy.

"Yes, Mama," Tommy, shoulders hunched, whispered as he glared at Leah.

Finally, Celeste straightened up from the table and crisply bit off, "Yes, Mother." She decided a while back "Mother" sounded so much nicer than "Mama," especially when she was irritated, which was fairly often. I wished that child had a better disposition. And I wished I had a nickel for every time I'd told her so.

Little Clarence stopped crying as he was tended to by his two sisters, and I slid the tray of biscuits I'd made up earlier into the hot oven. I poured most of the bacon grease into the drippings jar, quickly scrambled eggs, and put the butter and muscadine grape preserves on the table. In a few minutes, I'd nurse Clarence while the older children had breakfast. Normally, a pot of coffee would have been made long since, but I couldn't bring myself to do it this morning. Not without Tom here to drink some with me. I couldn't imagine getting any food down, either. Maybe later. Much later.

After breakfast, as the older girls began clearing up the dishes, the front screen door opened. My parents walked in through the sitting room into the kitchen, each carrying two covered dishes. I knew at least one of those dishes would be the fried chicken my mother got up well before dawn to cook. They set the dishes down on the cleared kitchen table and took turns hugging each grandchild and kissing the baby.

My father put his arms around my neck and whispered, "Honey, I'm so sorry."

My mother led me into the bedroom off the kitchen, pulled me to her, and just rocked me for a minute.

I wanted to stay in my mother's embrace, but I knew there was so much to do, so much to get through, so I held onto Mama a moment more and then stepped away.

"I'm not sorry I married him." I needed Mama to know this. "We had a good life together. I'm not sorry."

"I know, sweetness, I know." My mother's eyes filled with tears. "You know we loved that boy. We thought you'd made a fine match, even if you were so young. We'd never have agreed to the two of you getting married, but he was a fine man and had such a good job. We thought you'd always be cared for." My mother's voice broke.

I knew she believed I had made the best marriage of all her children and that I had been better off than the rest of the family, a source of jealousy for some of my sisters. Years after Tom and I married, she told me that after much discussion, she and Daddy had decided Tom was ready to settle down, and I could miss out on a good husband if they didn't let us go ahead and get married. It just seemed too likely Tom might move on rather than wait a few years for me, not quite fifteen at the time, to get to the age my sisters were when they got married. Even Mama had been twenty-one when she and Daddy were wed. But, of course, I was always good at arguing until I got my way, when I really wanted something. I'd been determined to marry Tom.

We startled at the slam of the front screen door. Walking back into the kitchen, I watched as Idella, one of my older sisters, marched in with her husband Frank and their three children. More food, more hugs, more noise as the younger cousins were sent to play on the back porch by Idella, who would now try to be in charge, as she always did.

Idella lifted the cover of one bowl on the table and sniffed. "Well, Frank," addressing her husband, "we stay home and have beans, and we go off and we have beans."

The very nerve of her. I opened my mouth to speak when Mama put her arm around me again and squeezed my shoulder. "I hardly think that's important today, Idella. Mind what you say at such a sad time. It's not about what you get to eat."

"Yes, ma'am. I'm sorry." Idella looked chastened for a moment, but quickly started rearranging the dishes of food and setting out dishware and utensils for later in the day.

Soon, the adults and older cousins were sitting around the kitchen table, and I finally put on a large pot of coffee. Later in the morning, my other three sisters and their husbands and children would come in from their more distant homes and tobacco farms, and we would all meet up at Bellevue Cemetery in Wilmington for the late morning graveside service. I assumed several of Tom's brothers and sisters would be there, although I wasn't sure how many would make it into town from their farms. Yesterday, I had a call from Sis, Tom's sister, to let me know his mother had a turn at hearing of her oldest son's death, and she couldn't travel from Tarboro, well over a hundred miles away, where she lived with Sis and Sis's husband. I was saddened to think Tom's mother and his favorite sister wouldn't be able to be at his funeral. But all the relatives who could attend, along with friends of the family, would travel back to our house afterward for the endless food that would continue to arrive.

Bedtime was so far in the future I could barely hold on to the idea of it. If only I could last until then, maybe I could get through the next day, too.

Finally, the house emptied of all the people who had come back after the funeral. I'd been grateful for the breaks I'd had to take from my chair in the oven-hot parlor when little Clarence would decide it was time to nurse again. I would take the crying baby, go to my bedroom, shut the door, and try to steel myself to endure yet another session of endless kindness and concern, as well as the sly, probing questions put forth by the eternally nosy who wondered what a young, widowed farmwife was going to do with six children to support.

I lost count of the times I had to explain Tom had gone out two mornings ago, apparently healthy, although he'd not slept well the night before. Just before he should have headed back home for his supper, while talking with a sharecropper of one farm he managed for Mr. Garner, the landowner, he had suddenly started sweating profusely and having trouble breathing. By the time the farmer realized something was very wrong, Tom had collapsed. The doctor said it was a massive heart attack. Tom was ten years older than me, but still not even forty years old.

Finally, only my parents remained. My mother made sure the children had supper and got them into bed early. Irene, Celeste, Leah, and Martha were in the room they shared, and little Tommy was on his cot at the foot of my and Tom's bed. Baby Clarence slept in his basket.

Tom had talked about starting to add on two bedrooms to the house as soon as the weather cooled off later in the fall. He was always wanting to improve our home and seemed to have endless energy. I had had mixed feelings about the additional two bedrooms. I knew I had at least another ten years of childbearing before me and foresaw the new rooms filling up only too quickly. I'd had a hard time with the last birth, and I had prayed Clarence would be the last baby I'd have. Last night, as I lay in bed with my four girls crowded in with me for what comfort we could give each other, I had remembered that prayer. My silent sobs shook the bed and my sleeping children as I realized I had got my wish.

Now as I returned to the kitchen from checking on the children, I saw my parents were sitting at the table with elderly Mr. Garner, Tom's employer. He had already expressed his condolences earlier in the day and had gone home, or so I'd thought. Now he stood and said, "Miz Heath, I just wanted to say again how sorry I am about Tom. He was a fine man. I never worried about the farms because I knew he'd be right on any problem. I always depended on him. And he thought the world of you and the children." He had picked up his hat and now nervously turned it in his hands. "I thought I'd drop by tomorrow to talk to you about everything. Don't want to bother you tonight. I'm just on my way out."

I looked at my parents, who seem worried and confused. "Mr. Garner, please go ahead and tell me what you need to say. I'd just as soon hear it now."

"Well, Miz Heath, I hate to bother you today about this, but it does need to be addressed real soon."

I now shared my parents' worry and concern. Tom had always taken care of the money, and I wondered if since he had passed on the first day of the month, Mr. Garner didn't want to pay his salary for October. I thought we would be all right for a while, but that month's pay would surely help until I could figure things out. I had a terrible feeling I was going to need to sell our home and land and move to some place in town. I really had not had time to think about it. Tom had only been gone two days.

"You see," Mr. Garner continued. "I am going to need this house real soon so whoever I hire to take Tom's place can move in."

I stared at him uncomprehendingly. My mother gasped, and my father put his head in his hands. I looked from them back to Mr. Garner.

"But we own this house. And this land, Mr. Garner. What do you mean?" I slowly collapsed onto a kitchen chair.

"No, Miz Heath." Now it was Mr. Garner's turn to look confused. "It just goes with the job. Tom knew that. I have the deed. I'm afraid you and your children will have to move somewhere else." Mr. Garner looked at me with pity. "I'm right sorry. I thought you knew this."

CHAPTER 2

Martha

Thursday, October 4, 1928

Sitting outside the bank manager's office the next morning, I pulled on the tips of my white cotton gloves and then stretched the fabric back down. I'd been doing that for some time now. I was in my second-best dress, the dotted navy one, having worn the best one for Tom's funeral yesterday. Although I hadn't had the chance to purchase a black dress, I looked appropriately somber. I'd removed the small red, pink, and white millinery flowers that had decorated the band and narrow brim of the navy hat. Tom had insisted last spring I should have this new cloche style, and I had been the envy of my sisters. For the first time, I had lowered the small net veil; it reached almost to my lips. My red-rimmed eyes were still visible, I knew, but it gave me the illusion of privacy. And of armor.

My father picked me up in his truck earlier, and now he sat beside me, clutching his hat by the brim, fanning himself, occasionally glancing at me and giving a small smile.

He cleared his throat and murmured, "I think we should get you so you can drive Tom's truck. Help you be more independent." He nodded to himself.

"Tom started teaching me a few years back, but it was hard to find the time, what with the children and all," I responded, watching the manager's door. "But yes, I know you're right. Whenever you have time, Irene can watch the little ones while we practice. She's almost as old as I was when I got married, after all." My voice caught, and I looked down at my gloves again.

The manager's door opened, and he welcomed us to his office, shaking hands with me and Daddy as we walked to the two chairs set in front of his desk. "Miz Heath, I sure was sorry to hear about Tom. He was a fine man and so young. I was with him in the Junior Order. It's a loss to our whole community. I hope you and your family can take some comfort knowing he's gone to a better place."

Squeezing my hands together, I said, "Thank you, Mr. Martin. I appreciate that. My father brought me here today to see what my situation is. With money, that is. Tom took care of all that, and I have to take over, of course. I think my name is on our bank account, but I'm not sure where Tom kept the checkbook or bank book. I'm hoping you can help me out and tell me what I need to know."

Mr. Martin raised his eyebrows and glanced at my father. "Mr. Evans, aren't you going to take over handling financial things for Mary now? Or one of Tom's brothers, maybe? You know women are meant to be pretty. Not be troubled with handling money." He smiled with tobacco-stained teeth and turned back to my father.

I straightened my back and inhaled sharply. What did Mr. Martin mean about having someone else handle my and Tom's money? I turned to my father.

Daddy set his hat on his knee and leaned forward. "Mr. Martin, Mary is a grown woman. She has six children. If she can handle them, I reckon she can handle a bank account."

Mr. Martin blinked. "Yes, sir. Of course…"

"Also," my father continued, "we need to know what you know about who owns the house and land Tom and Mary have been living on ever since they got married fifteen years ago. Mary thought she and Tom owned it. Last night, Mr. Garner said he owns it, and Tom knew that. What do you know about that?"

Mr. Martin cleared his throat and twisted his chair to look out the window. His balding scalp with the thin, oiled strands of hair carefully waved and combed across it glistened even more. Clearing his throat for a second time, he said, "Well, sir, I… I do believe Mr. Garner is indeed the owner. I never heard otherwise. Mr. Garner is a big landowner around here. Very important man. Very honest. But you can check with the Register of Deeds if you want to go down to City Hall, of course. Yes, I think that's your next course of action."

He shifted uncomfortably in his leather swivel chair and reached for the buzzer. We heard it sound in the next room on the secretary's desk. "Now, let me see what we can do to set Miz Heath's mind to rest about the bank account and so forth. We'll get a new checkbook if needs be, but I'm right sure you'll find everything at home wherever Tom did his paperwork. Still, I can give you the information you want and make sure you have a signature card on file."

Two hours later, Daddy and I pulled around to the backyard of my home and stopped. At midday, the black truck was quickly heating up. There was no breeze, and only the motion of the car forcing air into the open windows had made the drive back from town tolerable. Still, we sat together in silence for a moment.

"Daddy, what am I going to do?" I whispered. I was still trying to accept what we had found at the Register of Deeds office. At the end of October, my children and I would be homeless. Mr. Garner had owned the house and land for over twenty-five years, with his father owning it prior to that. It had never been mine and Tom's. Not ever.

I was still fighting bitter thoughts about Tom letting me think it was ours. Had he ever said that outright? I couldn't be certain now, not in the shock and panic I was drowning in. I knew, though, he had certainly implied it and let me think we were the owners. He had let my parents think that when he courted me. I tried to tamp down the sense of betrayal that wanted to rise up and engulf me. I loved Tom so much. I wanted to grieve for him, but I could sense the rage waiting to take the place of the shock. How could he have done this?

My father reached over and patted my hand, finally released from the damp white cotton gloves. "Baby girl, I don't rightly know, but we're goin' figure it out. I think for now, you and the young'uns will have to move in with your mother and me."

I shook my head and leaned it on the window frame, looking away from my father. "You and Mama can't keep all seven of us. You can't feed us and clothe us. You know that." My father's health had made farming impossible for several years now. He and my mother were living on the little savings they had and the rental income from their farmland another farmer was working. At least they owned that and their small house. I was trying to keep my voice level. In a moment, I would be with my children, and I didn't want them to see me in tears.

"We can make do for a while. Just until we can figure everything out. It doesn't mean forever. Tom has his mama and his brothers and his married sisters. You got your parents and four married sisters. You are not all alone. Together we can work this out. First thing is we need to get you out of this house by the end of the month. And get the animals moved. Thank the Lord Mr. Garner agrees they belonged to you and Tom. And you could think about selling Tom's tools."

I snapped my head toward my father. "No, sir, I won't sell his tools. Not his hand tools, anyway. They'll go to Tommy and Clarence when they're big enough. They're so young they won't remember their daddy, but at least they can have his tools."

My father nodded, opened his door, and waved for me to get out of the now sweltering truck. Summer never wanted to leave our coastal area without a fight. "Let's go see what your mother is giving those children for their dinner, and we'll have some, too," he said. "Then we'll all three talk about getting y'all packed up and think about where we can store some of your furniture and things. You're going to want it directly when you get your own place." He glanced sideways at me from under his bushy eyebrows. "And maybe we'll have us a little driving lesson while the young'uns have their afternoon nap."

I sighed, climbed the stairs of the back porch, and opened the screen door.

The cicadas, optimistically ignoring the slightly cooler evening air that hinted of fall's approach, were still calling for mates later that night as I walked out onto the front porch and sat on one of the wooden rocking chairs. The salt air from the nearby ocean had pitted the soft blue paint I had so carefully applied only a few years ago. "Needs doing again," I murmured, only to realize a moment later that painting rocking chairs probably wasn't going to be the kind of work I'd be doing in the near future. "And what about the distant future?" I whispered and hugged my arms around my shoulders, suddenly chilled. Impossible to imagine what the next few months would hold, much less the far future.

"Who you talkin' to, Mama?" a small voice asked from the doorway behind me. I turned in the chair and saw little Martha, her blonde hair in braids rumpled from sleep, as was her rag doll's matching yellow yarn braids. Martha and her doll were dressed in identical nightgowns I had made for them. Tiny blue flowers on soft white cotton, a smocked bodice, and white crocheted lace around the scoop neck and the short cap sleeves.

Many of Martha's clothes were store-bought hand-me-downs from her older sisters, but I had made sure she also had a few brand-new things. With three older sisters myself, I knew what it was like to only have old, worn things come my way. My second, third, and fourth daughters would never wonder if they were only worth castoff clothes from others.

Although I had little enough time to myself, I spent many evenings after the children were asleep sewing for my daughters. I always used the scraps to fashion similar outfits for each girl's favorite doll, although lately twelve-and-a-half-year-old Irene had decided she was too grown up for dolls, and ten-year-old Celeste, who had never seemed to have the attachment to dolls her sisters did, was following her lead.

Tom had told me I was going to ruin my eyes sewing at night, but he always smiled as the girls showed off their new dress or nightgown, holding their matching dolls.

"Now, Martha Marie, what are you and Miss Muffet doing up at this hour? Don't you girls know you need your beauty sleep?" I asked in my pretend-stern voice that let Martha know she wasn't really in any trouble.

"It was Miss Muffet, Mama. She won't let me sleep. She misses Daddy, and she just won't stop cryin' for him." Martha's voice wavered as tears began rolling down her cheeks.

I held out my arms and lifted Martha and Miss Muffet onto my lap. Martha snuggled closer against me. "I miss Daddy, too, sugar." I held my little girl until her breath steadied. Poor little tyke. I had worried in the past that the older children had to make way too soon for the new babies as they came along. That maybe they didn't get enough of the cuddling they still needed. Now I realized I needed to find time to be with each one alone to talk about their daddy's death. But when? Sweet Lord, there were just so many things pulling on me.

At least now I could be with my youngest daughter for a few minutes. My left arm holding Martha, I took Miss Muffet from her with my right hand and looked seriously at the doll. "Miss Muffet, tell me what's making you so sad." I looked at Martha and nodded encouragingly. "I know you can tell me what she's thinking, Martha. I know she tells you all her secrets."

Martha played with the blue ribbon tied about one of the doll's braids. "Well," she drawled out the word slowly. "I think she wants to know where our daddy has gone. Did he want to leave us?"

I sucked in my breath. I knew the younger children wouldn't completely understand even though I had tried to explain things to them, as had their grandparents. Still, I'd never imagined they might think Tom wanted to leave them.

"No, baby, your daddy most certainly did not want to leave us. Not at all. You know he loved you and your brothers and sisters and me, too. But he was such a wonderful, wonderful man that Jesus wanted him to come on up to Heaven and be with him and the angels. The good Lord knows I'm going to take care of you, so don't you worry."

Martha took Miss Muffet from my hand and clutched her doll to her chest. In the glow from the table lamp by the window in the front sitting room behind me, I could see Martha's little forehead wrinkled in thought. She looked up at me and said, "In that case, I'm not going to be so good anymore, so Jesus don't want me too soon. I'd rather stay with you and Miss Muffet."

Despite everything, I had to bite the inside of my cheeks to stop my laugh. Of all my children, Martha had the sweetest nature by far, along with a way of looking at things that took me by surprise all the time. "Well, baby, that's certainly an idea, but I'm not so sure it's a real good one. Just what do you have in mind?"

Martha settled herself more comfortably on my lap and considered. "Well," she finally said with a yawn that threatened to split her little face, "I'm not rightly certain, but I bet Tommy and Celeste could give me some ideas. They're right good at being bad, aren't they?"

My chest shook as Martha's head nodded. Rousing herself, Martha mumbled, "Can Daddy see everything we're doing, just like Jesus now? 'Cause I don't want him or Jesus watching when I go potty. Miss Muffet don't want that neither." She gave a deep sigh, and her eyelids closed.

I bent down to kiss my child's slumbering head, inhaled her sleepy baby-powder scent, and smiled into the darkness. Here I was, in the saddest time of my entire life, and I was sitting on the porch holding my darling little girl and laughing. I shook my head. Life was so much more complicated and unpredictable than I ever thought possible when I was fourteen. Back then, I thought I was all grown up, and talked my parents into letting me get married at such a young age.

Just a week ago, Tom and I had been sitting out here discussing the latest goings-on we'd read about in the newspaper. Martha was right to wonder where he was now. I wondered, too. I knew what anyone would say if I asked, and it was what

I had just told Martha. Comforting words. I had always had a suspicious mind when it came to those. I just couldn't completely trust them, no matter how hard I tried.

Looking up at the dark sky so full of stars, I wondered yet again. One thing I knew for sure, and it was I'd love to have a word with whoever thought it was a good idea to take Tom from me and the children. Yes, I'd definitely like to share my thoughts on that.

I rocked for a while and let Martha sleep in my lap. Tomorrow's troubles would come all too soon. Just for now though, a few minutes of peace.

CHAPTER 3

Elim & Otis

Saturday, October 6, 1928

I looked up from the second pan of biscuits I'd just taken from the cookstove. I always baked enough at breakfast to last for midday dinner and then evening supper during the hot months, in the hopes of not needing to heat up the kitchen more than possible later in the day. After closing the oven door, I turned my head to listen more carefully. Over the chatter of the children just sitting down at the kitchen table, I heard the rattle of more than one truck coming around from the road to park in the backyard. Before I could say anything, the five older children rushed out to see who had come to visit, letting the screen door slam behind them.

Moving the frying pan off the heat, I walked to the back door. Two of Tom's brothers were getting out of their battered old farm trucks. From my higher position, I could see the truck beds were unusually empty, holding only coils of rope, a few empty wooden crates, and what appeared to be canvas tarps. Everything was covered in what looked to be months, maybe years, of grime. They had to have left their neighboring farms in Warsaw, almost seventy miles away, well before dawn, to get here so early.

Elim, at thirty-three, was seven years younger than Tom, and Otis, thirty-one, was nine years younger, although working in the fields had aged their skin far beyond their years. Both men wore their work overalls. It appeared they'd worn the same ones yesterday, too. As they mounted the porch steps, it also smelled like it.

They removed their caps as they approached, after greeting the children with "hey, honey" for the girls and "hey, little buddy" for Tommy. It occurred to me they probably didn't know the names of their brother's children.

"Hey, there, Elim," I called. "How is Eula and that sweet Jennie?" Eula gave birth to their fourth child just two days before Tom died. When Sis, Tom's youngest sibling at twenty-seven, had called from Tarboro to let me know they would not be able to make it to Tom's funeral, she also told me about Elim's newest daughter. And she'd reminded me Mama Jo, Tom's widowed mother, would have her seventy-first birthday just nine days after Tom's death. Mama Jo had lived with Sis and her husband Clyde since their wedding two years ago. I could never figure out how Sis (who was named Josephine after her mother, but always called Sis) and Tom had Otis and Elim for brothers. It seemed more likely they'd sprung from two different families.

"Otis, how are Sallie Mae and the children? Come on in and have breakfast and tell me all about them." I kept the screen door open for them to pass through as Martha clasped

Elim's hand and Tommy pulled on Otis's shirt sleeve to hurry him along. Irene caught my eye and glanced back at the empty truck beds. I nodded slightly to let her know I'd noticed. Inside, Celeste and Leah were trying to get their share of attention from their seldom-seen uncles, and the kitchen resounded with the scraping of chairs and young, high voices. Surprisingly, Baby Clarence didn't stir from his early morning nap.

While I scrambled more eggs, silently thanking my hens for their extra efforts the last few days, Irene went to the icebox on the back porch and brought back a small platter of sliced ham left over from the funeral three days before. I had kept as much food as could fit into the icebox and sent the rest home with my parents and sisters. Nothing would keep long in this heat. While I was glad to share, I couldn't help but wish we had two iceboxes. Tom had always said he was going to get us another one someday soon.

As Irene came back inside with the ham, I saw her eyes flare as she looked past me. I turned and saw Otis was sitting in Tom's chair at the head of the table, and Elim was in my chair at the other end. Being men, and, well, themselves, they must have thought the two important places should be theirs. Irene glanced at me, and I felt sure she saw the flash of surprise and irritation cross my face before I put my polite smile back on again.

"Elim, Otis, which one of you wants to say grace?" I asked as I pulled up a spare chair to the table. Celeste had already set two extra places, and Leah had poured the milk for the children. I got up again and quickly poured three cups of coffee. Noticing the two men seem to be looking for something on the table, I remembered they both liked sugar, a lot of sugar, in their coffee. I took the sugar bowl from the high shelf in the cupboard (a wasted precaution, as no shelf was too high for young Tommy) and put it on the table. At last, I sat down.

Otis cleared his throat as everyone bowed their head and began in what I privately always thought of as "church talk," a stilted, pious attempt to sound as if whatever the speaker was saying was coming straight out of the Bible.

I once had a Sunday school teacher, the elegant and college-educated Miss Scott, who had explained the reason our Bible said "King James Version" on the first page was that all the original languages used to write the Bible were translated into English when King James was the king of England, back in the early 1600s. The way things were said in the Bible was the way educated people talked back then in England, but not way, way back when Moses was living. Not even when Jesus was living. That had stuck in my young head, especially when Miss Scott had added, "So, it's perfectly all right for you to just talk to God in your normal, everyday way of speaking. After all, he knows what you really sound like." That had made me smile, and so I always spoke to God in the same natural and respectful way I would speak to my parents. I wasn't sure he really listened, but praying usually cleared my mind and made me feel more peaceful.

Listening to Otis was not having that effect on me, however. If he said "poor little homeless orphan children" just once more, I felt it likely his next cup of coffee was going to accidentally splash in his lap. If he asked once more that his brother Tom's many, many sins be forgiven so he could enter the Kingdom of Heaven, the entire pot of coffee was going to land there.

Finally, he droned to a theatrical, "Amen."

I looked up to see five children who seemed stunned. Martha had tears in her eyes. Leah whispered, "Mama, are we homeless? Are we orphans? Is Daddy in the bad place? Isn't he in Heaven?" Even Tommy looked stricken.

Otis began to stammer a reply, but I cut him off. "No, darlings. Uncle Otis was being dramatic, so God would pay attention to him." I cut an icy glance at Otis, and he had the grace to blush. "Of course you aren't homeless or orphans. I'm right here. And I'm sure, very sure, your daddy was no more sinful than, say, Uncle Otis, for instance. All humans make mistakes. But your daddy was a good man, and if anyone is in Heaven, I'm sure he is. Isn't that what you meant, Otis?"

Otis tried to speak, thought better of it, and just nodded. I smiled coldly at him. "Let's eat while the food has a little heat left to it. Children, show your uncles what good manners you have." I bet Otis was not quite sure if I'd put an emphasis on "you" or not, but he let it go. He'd told Tom more than once over the years he always thought I was a little too feisty for a woman. Tom would always laugh as he told me Otis's latest comment about me and then conclude with, "If he only knew the half of it."

Deciding Otis understood I wouldn't tolerate him upsetting my children and telling myself I had to remember both these men were Tom's brothers, I turned my head to the other end of the table and asked, "Elim, tell us about your new baby. And how she and Eula are doing now."

Elim blinked, no doubt surprised by my handling of Otis and then my quick return to the expected role of female politeness. "They both doin' real good. And I sure hope you understand why we wasn't there for Tom's funeral, Mary. I'm right sorry about that. Today was the first day I felt like I could leave Eula with the baby and the other children. Her sister is with her, and I just wanted to make sure she knowed how to work the stove, take care of the young'uns and the animals, and such. Just in case we don't get back 'till tomorrow."

I had been wondering what Otis's excuse would be, but saw it was my turn to be surprised. Did they think they would be staying here? I could only hope they'd enjoy sleeping in a rocking chair on the porch. Maybe the mosquitos would take them off.

"Why might that be?" I asked. "Are you going somewhere else after you finish your breakfast here?"

Elim shifted uncomfortably in his chair and took a large bite of biscuit and muscadine preserves. He chewed slowly with his mouth open and stared down the table at his brother. Otis slurped his coffee from his saucer, where he'd poured it to cool. I thought about slapping the saucer right out of his hands. Tom never drank from a saucer or made noise when he ate. Again, I pondered how hard it was to believe all three men had the same mother. Mama Jo had such lovely manners and taught them to her three daughters, Tom, and two other sons, but Elim and Otis both seemed to have emerged from childhood unburdened by any social graces. Or even an appreciation for basic hygiene.

I waited. Finally, Otis muttered, "We don't know how long it'll be taking us to load up."

Now I was genuinely confused. I raised my eyebrows. "Oh? Are you going into town to pick something up?" It seemed odd, as they would have had to go through town to get out to our place. It was hard to believe they'd go to the trouble of a condolence visit, having missed their own brother's funeral.

Elim and Otis exchanged glances. Elim said, "No, Mary. We come here to help you get rid of Tom's farm equipment. And as many of the animals as we can get in one of the trucks. We figure we'll have to make more 'n one trip to get everything. Not like you need it, right? We're doing you a favor."

"That's right for sure," echoed Otis, nodding his head and reaching for another slice of ham. "Best thing we can do to help out our brother. Well, that and one more thing." He looked around at the children, all watching the adults with large eyes. "You gotta find homes for Tom's children, and I reckon we can help you out there, too."

A few minutes later, I led the way down the crushed oyster-shell drive that went from the road to the Sound, where our pier used to be before the last big hurricane. Elim and Otis followed, each carrying a slop pail for the two hogs, whose pen was far enough away from the house so the smells wouldn't reach there. The younger children slumped on the back porch, watching us. I had to be very firm they wait there while I had a word with their uncles.

Finally, we reached the pen, and the men tipped the pails over the fence into the feed trough. The hogs scuttled over and began the noisy process of eating. Now we wouldn't have Tom to fish for us anymore, the hogs would be our family's only source of meat other than our chickens. I motioned for the men to continue down the drive.

"I wasn't going to talk about this in front of the children," I began, still walking and looking straight ahead at the water's edge, "but you both have made a trip for nothing, I am real sorry to say. I appreciate your kind offer, but I am not looking for you to help me out by taking the animals and the farm equipment. And I sure do not plan to let go of my children." I tried to keep my voice polite. I paused, afraid I was either going to scream at them or burst into tears.

For a moment, there was only the sound of the oyster shells crunching under our feet and the squeaking of the tin pails swinging from their metal handles. I hoped they couldn't hear that my breathing was so uneven. I stopped and turned to face them. "Well, I am sorry you made this trip for nothing, but at least you can get back home well before sunset and get some of your work done." I forced a smile.

Elim took his cap off and wiped his face with a well-used handkerchief. Otis looked off into the distance and frowned. The two brothers glanced at each other and then back at me.

Otis began, "Well, Mary, I am real sorry you see it that way. We was just trying to help out our brother's widow and his orphans."

I felt my face flush furiously as my eyes snapped to his. "Otis, my children are not orphans. They still have me, their mother. I am still alive. They are fatherless now, I grant you, but not orphans. I will thank you kindly not to refer to them as orphans again, especially in front of them." I dug my nails into my skin as I clenched my fists, which were shoved into the pockets of my apron.

With great effort, I kept my voice calm. "I do not know exactly what I am going to do, but I do know what I am not going to do. I am not giving away farm equipment and animals. I cannot do that. My daddy is going to come soon for everything we can keep and move it to his farm. He's got plenty of room. What equipment I do not keep, I will have to have auctioned off. I need as much cash as I can get to support these children, so I cannot just give it away or let it go cheap. If you want to come bid for it, I will let you know when that's going to happen. I do not know where we will wind up living, but I will surely let you know when I figure it out."

Elim started to say something, but I brushed past him and headed back to the house. "Thank you kindly for coming to pay us a visit and helping me slop the hogs. And eating breakfast with us. I'd have cooked more if I had known you were coming." I bit off the comment I wanted to make about how much of my children's food they shoveled into their ungrateful mouths. I felt ashamed of myself for being so ungracious. My mother raised me better.

In a brighter tone, I said, "I know you both got so much to do back home, and Eula will be so glad you're back early today, Elim. I know you want to get back to your baby. You give Jennie and Eula kisses from me. Otis, you give Sallie Mae a big hug around the neck from me, too. I sure hope we can get all these cousins together sometime soon. Maybe you can come for a picnic when we get settled. Probably won't be until next spring, what with the colder weather sure to be here soon. I certainly hope it will be, don't you?"

I continued my wall of chatter until we were once again back by the two trucks. The younger children ran out to meet us, while Irene sat in a rocker holding the baby, who was fussing. I wished them a safe trip back home and climbed the porch steps to take Clarence in my arms. Otis looked at Elim, shrugged, climbed up into his truck, and began heading out to the main road. Elim stared at the house for a moment, ruffled Tommy's hair, and told the children to get away from the trucks so they wouldn't get hurt. He finally climbed into his truck, smacked the steering wheel with the flat of his hand, and followed Otis out, black smoke belching as he gunned the engine. As Elim pulled out of the backyard, I turned back, gave a final wave of my hand, and went into the house. Irene called goodbye and followed me inside.

We walked to the front window to watch them go. As the last of the black smoke disappeared and the roar of the two trucks faded, I looked at my eldest child and smiled grimly, "Kind of your uncles to visit, but I don't think we'll be seeing those two for quite a while."

Irene nodded. "I thought they were nice when Daddy was with us, but now…" She trailed off. "Why did they want to take our things, Mama? What did they mean about helping you find us homes?"

I shook my head. "Don't you worry about that now. Those two thought they'd just have themselves a big time helping themselves to Tom's belongings. And try to make me think they were doing me a favor at the same time."

"Weren't they?" Irene asked, watching my face carefully.

Tom and I raised our children to respect their elders, so I knew Irene was unsure how I would react to outright criticism of the uncles.

"What do you think, Irene? You're getting to be old enough to understand why people act like they do. It's important you learn how to figure that out. If only I had learned sooner myself." Raising an eyebrow at her, I sat down to nurse Clarence.

"I think they were mostly going to do themselves a favor, Mama. At least, it seemed to me that way," Irene said cautiously.

"You're a smart girl, Irene. A very smart girl." I nodded and smiled at her.

CHAPTER 4

Auction & a Haircut

Saturday, October 20, 1928

The previous week, the three older girls went back to school, even though they wanted to stay home and help me get ready for the move. But I didn't want them missing any more schooling. As it was, they'd have to change schools next month, and I didn't want them to start out behind the other children. Besides, they needed to say their goodbyes to their school friends and teachers. We would all be saying goodbye to our neighbors, who had been so good to us these last few weeks especially. I supposed we would even be leaving our church, as Mama and Daddy went to one closer to their farm.

Hopefully, I could get the children together with their friends every now and then after we moved, but I didn't want them holding on too tight, either. I wanted them to make new friends at the new school. If only I knew how long we'd have with Mama and Daddy. Sooner or later, I had to find a job so we could have our own house. Or apartment, more likely.

That meant moving into Wilmington and looking for work I could walk to from wherever we ended up living. My stomach tied into knots at the idea of trying to find a job. I had no idea how to go about it or even where to look. But it was a problem for another day. For now, I just had to do the next thing. That's how I was going to get through this. Doing the next thing that needed to be done.

We were almost ready to move out of our house. Our home. Daddy and Mr. Jones, the man who lived down the road from my parents, had already moved all the animals except the chickens. They'd be going soon to join Daddy's. I expected the children would make a game of catching them and putting them in the little cages he'd bring over. Heaven only knew when they'd lay again after all the excitement, and a new coop and new hens to get used to. Our young rooster, beautiful white even after all his scratching in our sandy soil each day, would have a larger harem to boss around; Mama made stewed chicken and pastry that day with their old one.

We decided it was time to retire old Molly, our mule. Bless her, she'd done her last day of heavy plowing. The worst she had to look forward to was children wanting to ride on her boney back around the paddock, which she seemed to enjoy, as they made such a fuss over her. Daddy promised she'd get to live her life out naturally; he wouldn't have the knackerman come for her until she took her last breath. The hogs, of course, would be headed to slaughter up in Burgaw in a few weeks. Until then, they'd be in with Daddy's two.

For the first time, I was almost glad our old dog, Laddie, died in June. Tom had been looking around for another little terrier for us, but they were hard to come by for some reason. Laddie loved all of us, but he was definitely Tom's dog, always in his shadow. I didn't think Tom would ever get over Laddie's passing—and I guess he never had time to—but I knew for sure Laddie would never have gotten over losing Tom.

Last week, Martha asked if I thought her daddy and Laddie were together in heaven. I said, "How could it be heaven if they weren't?" I didn't care what Reverend McGee, the pastor at our old church, might say. I believed that.

She and Tommy started a game of "what are Daddy and Laddie doing right now?" The older girls took turns answering, too. My favorites were "Daddy is reading the funny pages to Laddie," and "they're playing poker together—and Laddie's winning." We always smiled thinking about those silly answers, so I thought this little game helped all of us move on a little from losing both of them.

I was glad the children would have Toby, Daddy's little dog, to play with when we got there, although I'd have to make sure they weren't sneaking him too much of their own food.

The morning of the auction finally came. It nearly broke my heart to see so many of our things get sold, but it had to be done. We got pretty good prices for the farm equipment and tools we decided to sell.

I wasn't one little bit surprised Elim and Otis didn't show up for it.

Mama and Daddy stayed home, too; I think Daddy overdid it moving things last week. But my sisters who lived on farms came with their families. They helped watch the children and cook supper for all of us while the auction went on, with their husbands bidding for the things they could use. It felt better knowing at least some of our things would stay in the family.

The auctioneer did a special lot of goods, the contents of a tiny shed out past the hog pen. I'd noticed the men going in before the sale and coming out again smiling. Tom had told me it was a favorite place for snakes, so I kept myself and the children away, but now I realized he just wanted us, me especially, to stay out. I suspected the winner of the sale got himself a stock of canning jars full of what Reverend McGee preached against every Sunday, not to mention was against the law. I was glad those jars got taken away before any revenue officers came sniffing around.

After talking it over with my parents, I decided a good number of our household goods needed to be sold, too. I had no idea when or how I would be able to rent a place for all of us. Some things could be stored at Mama and Daddy's, but some just seemed too old and worn out to bother with moving. At least those old things added a little cash to what we had.

I grew up hearing "every penny counts," and I'd never believed the truth of that as much as I did then, when there was not a single penny coming in. Now I was the breadwinner, and I had no idea how I was going to "win" any. I never wondered before why it's called bread*winner*. Didn't bread*earner* make more sense? Tom always laughed when I'd puzzle over something like this, but I wished I had more education, so I'd know about things like that.

The one really nice thing I would have loved to keep was the hutch Tom built for the house. To me, at least, it was real nice. I didn't know how we would have got it out the door, it was so big and heavy, but how proud I'd always been, seeing our dishes set out on the shelves, cups hanging from little white hooks along the edges of the top shelf, and being able to store all our table linens, candles, and such in the cabinets below. Tom added a little hook on one side for me to hang my apron and painted the whole piece a pretty blue he said matched my eyes. That man was always trying to make me blush.

The hutch wasn't put up for auction. When he heard about the upcoming sale, Mr. Garner came over a few days early and bought it to stay with the house, along with the old cookstove. He paid more than he needed to for them, too. A lot more, but he insisted. I reckoned it was because he felt guilty for having us leave, but I couldn't blame him none. He needed the house for his next manager, a Mr. Brown, who was all ready to get his family moved in there November 1. I hoped they'd appreciate the work Tom put into that piece of furniture. And the love.

The children finally settled down for the night, even Baby Clarence, who'd been fussy all day, and Tommy, who got too wound up with all the hustle and bustle of the last few days. That little boy had been having himself a big time, what with all the people coming and going. I think it helped him take his mind off missing his daddy. I guess it helped all of us to be busy again.

After such a long day, I was ready to go to bed, but walked out to make sure the chicken coop gate was latched tight. I stopped on my way back to the house and looked east towards the Sound. Just a sliver of the moon was visible in the sky, but it seemed to put out extra light, glinting on the water. I'd taken this view for granted for fifteen years, and now I realized how much I was going to miss it. Mama and Daddy's farm was farther inland; I didn't know when I'd see the moon shining on the ocean after we moved.

As I stood there, it hit me. It was my birthday. My thirtieth birthday. In all the hurry and rush of getting ready for the auction and then talking with all the neighbors and family today, I hadn't thought of it. Even my sisters didn't remember. Thirty years old.

I turned on my heel and marched inside to the kitchen pantry, where years ago, I'd hung an old mirror on the back of the door so I could check my face and hair when someone came calling or Tom was due to get home. I lit a kerosene lamp to make it brighter in the small room and gazed at myself. No wrinkles yet, except maybe a few hinting to come around my eyes.

My hair was pulled back in a bun that I always tried to keep tidy but rarely succeeded at. Tom had not wanted me to bob my hair in the new fashion. Now I took out the pins and let it fall down my back and over my shoulders. A little wave to it and still dark and thick.

My figure was fuller, of course, but I still had a definite waistline, unlike some of my older sisters. But with my hair down, I looked more like a young girl than a matron with six children. A widow. A sob caught in my throat, and suddenly, I was furious with Tom. He had up and died and left me all alone to deal with this. He let me think this house was ours. He left us, all of us, with no warning and no help for the future. He let me think we were safe.

Before I could think too much about it, I grabbed my scissors from my sewing basket on the shelf, picked up a strand of hair, and cut. When I was done, there was a pile of my hair I'd set by the basket and a new woman with a lopsided bob looking with amazement at me in the mirror. She had no idea who I was or what I'd just done. I gathered up the cut hair, tossed it in the trashcan, and blew out the lamp—and remembered something from years ago.

My younger sister, Etta, had had a long-time beau. He'd courted her for almost two years when he came by one day to tell her he'd met a new girl and he intended to marry her. Etta was broken-hearted the first day, then mad as blazes the next. She'd bobbed her hair in a rage, and I had not understood how she could mutilate herself like that—as I saw it then—but now I completely understood. Sometimes you needed proof something had ended and you were done with that part of your life. Physical proof you could see, to mark the changes inside you no one else could see.

Shaking a little, I walked back out onto the back porch. So, I was a thirty-year-old widow with six children, no home, no job, and no money to speak of. I looked up at the crescent moon and said, "You aren't the only one who gets to change, you know."

That old moon just grinned down at me.

CHAPTER 5

Porch Memories

Sunday, October 28, 1928

It was another full moon, like it was the night before Tom died. A lot of packing happened in the past week, and our home hardly seemed like itself anymore. But I let all that go, as I sat in my front porch rocker, and remembered sitting out here last month at the last full moon. We'd stayed here later than our usual bedtime because it was too beautiful to miss—almost magical. It was so bright I could see his face clearly as he sat in his rocker. Tom wasn't used to sitting and doing nothing, so it was rare for him to just sit and quietly rock. I could tell he was tired from the long day, but he had still been his usual self with the children earlier, laughing and telling them stories as they got ready for bed.

Tom usually let me take care of getting the children to bed, but that night, he gave each one of them a kiss as he tucked them in. He needed to get an unusually early start the next morning to run some errands, so that was the last time the children saw their daddy. I hoped they could hold on to that memory, although I knew the younger ones wouldn't be able to.

I'd often wondered if people could sense when they were about to leave this earth. We'd had several family members who paid unexpected visits just days before they would pass. It's not that I thought they actually had that in their minds, but maybe something moved them to go out of their way to make what would be final goodbyes before their final leave-taking.

My Uncle Bernie did that when I was eight or nine. He mostly was a homebody, but he'd shown up at our house one cold day a week before Christmas, just to say hello. Mama, his sister, gave him a slice of fruitcake and some coffee. She and Daddy sat with him around the kitchen table and talked for a while. My sisters and I hung back, as we knew him the least well of all our uncles, and he didn't tease and joke with us the way the others did. He wasn't mean; he was just quiet. He only stayed a short while, and then left, after telling us girls we were sure growing up pretty. Two days later, he had a stroke, and he passed away the day after that. We went to his funeral a few days before Christmas.

I supposed that's why I'd always expected somebody in the family to die around Christmas. It didn't happen every year, but often enough I had a dread of it. Mama said maybe we just noticed it more when it's around Christmas because it seemed like that's the time of year that should be about joy and birth. I didn't know, but maybe Tom's passing would mean we were safe for this Christmas, at least. If so, it was a horrible price to pay.

As he and I sat out that last night, he finally turned to me. "Well, Mary Ellen, are you happy you married me all those years ago?"

I hardly knew what to say to him. He'd never asked me any such thing in the fifteen years we'd been married. I just looked at him for a moment. Finally, I said, "Tom, why are you asking me that? Have I done anything to make you think I'm not? I thought you knew very well I'm happy." Of course, now I was irked with him. Was he trying to say I should act happier?

Tom tipped his head back and laughed. He said, "Oh, Mary Ellen, don't get your dander up. I'm not saying that at all. I am not finding fault with you." He looked over at me and gave me such a sweet smile. "No, honey, I'm just wondering. I've been thinking how I married you so young, and maybe it was just selfish of me. I wanted to make sure you would be mine before some other fella came along and turned your head.

"Of course," he grinned, "they'd have to get past that temper of yours, wouldn't they? Not to mention your hooligan behavior."

"What? My what? What are you talking about?" I stopped rocking and sat up straight. I could tell he was teasing me, but I couldn't imagine what in the world he was talking about.

"Now, Mary, don't pretend you didn't once assault a Baptist preacher," he said in a serious tone, shaking his head. "That's what you were doing the first time I ever laid eyes on you. And at a church picnic, too." He sighed again, shaking his head sadly.

I huffed out my breath and went back to rocking. "That could have happened to anybody. It was completely accidental, and you know it, Mister."

Fifteen years ago, Tom had been visiting a cousin of his and had come with his family to our annual church picnic. I'd been sitting on a blanket in the churchyard with my sisters as we ate, when I bit into a fried chicken drumstick one of the other ladies had brought. Underneath the crispy golden crust, the chicken was almost raw. Blood red. Horrible.

Disgusted, I'd glanced around to make sure no one was looking in my direction. Then I quickly tossed it over my shoulder so it would land in the wooded area just a few feet behind me. Apparently, it was not my lucky day because I not only still had a mouthful of raw chicken, but I also didn't realize our minister was walking past behind me just then, and that bloody drumstick hit him upside of his head. It wasn't his lucky day either, I guess. I didn't realize my mistake until I heard him yelp. I froze and looked up to see this stranger across the yard watching me, his shoulders shaking as he tried not to laugh. Obviously, he'd seen the whole thing. I acted like I had no idea what had happened, and our minister never figured out who had assaulted him. Only Tom knew.

"I think maybe you married me, so I couldn't testify against you," Tom mused. "I should have known you'd have a temper to go along with your delinquent tendencies."

"Very funny, Tom. I've listened to you tease me about that for all these years, so I think I've been punished enough." I paused and then griped, "It's the woman who didn't know how to cook chicken all the way through who ought to have been arrested. I was an innocent victim of bad cooking!"

"Makes me almost wish there'd been a trial. It would have been an interesting defense." Tom chuckled.

After a moment, Tom became serious and looked off into the distance. "But lately, I've been thinking about how very young you were when we got married. I look at Irene, and I think I might have to shoot any boy who comes around in two or three years wanting to marry her. I just didn't see it that way when you were fourteen, though. You seemed so smart and growed up. You sure didn't let me get away with anything. Still don't."

He looked over at me and smiled. "You could handle yourself even back then and not let anybody take advantage of you. But you were still so sweet and so young. You seemed older, and at the same time younger, than you were. Confident, but also innocent. I just hope you're happy with the life we have now."

Looking back, I don't think it was a trick of the moonlight he suddenly looked sad, almost lost. Clouds were scuttling across the sky, and the wind was picking up. A storm was coming in from the sea.

"I'm nothing but happy we got married when we did, Tom," I whispered, and reached across the little table between us and covered his hand with mine.

His thumb stroked my fingers as he looked down at our hands. "You're sure? You'd tell me if you weren't?"

I sighed and laughed at the same time. "Tom, what is it? You know I was determined to marry you before some hussy tried to snag you. I still can't figure out how you escaped that Myrtle at church." I could still fume just thinking about how brazen that girl had been. Tom had started coming to our church on a regular basis to see me, before he asked my daddy if he could come calling.

"I think you mean how I escaped her mother," he laughed. Myrtle's mama had set her mind to have her daughter marry Tom. I'd once caught Tom's mama and my mama laughing about it years later, as they sat on the front porch rockers at Mama's house, shelling butterbeans in the big enamel pans on their laps.

"Tom, I'll tell you what would make me even happier than I already am." I hesitated because I hated ever asking for anything. But there were two things I really wanted, and I thought my birthday in a few weeks could serve as a good excuse. "I'd like two things for my birthday."

Tom raised his eyebrows and looked at me in surprise. "You mean I'm not going to have to guess and then go get you something you don't really want anyway?"

"Tom, you know I don't mean that," I said, cringing that he thought I hadn't liked the gifts he'd given me over the years. Although, to tell the truth, last year's gift of a new mop and pail had not been as thrilling as I might have let on, although I loved the stationery he gave me. "No, these are two things only you can give me, and I don't think you'd think they would be good enough. But they would be priceless to me."

"Sugar, if I can get them for you, I will. What do you want?"

The first one was easy. "I'd like you to do another drawing of the children, like you did when Leah was our youngest." Tom had a gift for drawing. He could draw animals, people, buildings, just anything, really. He hardly ever did it anymore, as his work took up more and more of his time, but I'd love to have one of all our children. Well, all our children so far. I didn't want to think about how many more babies might be in the future, although I dearly loved the ones we already had.

Tom smiled. "If that's what you want, that's what you'll get. What else?"

I was going to wait until November to ask if we could get a family portrait for Christmas, a photograph with all eight of us in it. But now I went on to the second thing I wanted from him for my birthday. "I'd like a letter from you."

Tom looked blank. "A letter from me?"

I took a deep breath and said, "Yes. A letter. A love letter."

Tom pulled back in surprise and looked away for a moment. "You want a *love* letter? Are you serious? Mary, our courting days are over."

I slid my eyes over at him. "Although I love you very much, of course," he added quickly.

"Yes, I love you too. But that is what I want, Tom. I want it for when I'm an old, old lady, and you're sitting there ignoring me. I can pull it out and read it. And remember how much you loved me when I was young." I let out my breath and watched him. I could tell my face was burning. He had no idea how hard it had been to ask. "And besides, I've never had a love letter, and I'd like to have one."

Tom couldn't read or write when we got married. He was the eldest son in his family, and he'd only had a few years of schooling before he'd been working in his family's fields full time. Any reading and writing he'd learned in that short period in school had all but vanished after years of laboring in the fields.

After we married, before the children started arriving, we would work in the evenings at our kitchen table. He'd been embarrassed to let me know he couldn't read or write, but he wanted to learn desperately. He knew his position as manager of Mr. Garner's farms would be more secure if he could provide written reports, as well as making him less dependent on others to manage his business affairs. And I think it hurt his pride I could do so easily what he found so difficult. We'd read the newspaper together, and he'd practice writing out sentences from stories that caught his attention. By the time Irene arrived almost three years after we married, he read well, although his handwriting was not quite as good. Still, he no longer had to have anyone's help to do either.

Tom looked at me and shook his head. "Mary, I think you should have asked me about a month ago if you want it in time for your birthday. It's probably going to take me that long to figure out what to say and how to say it."

He must have seen my disappointment. He sighed, "As long as you're not expecting anything like that Will Shakespeare fella could write, I suppose I could come up with something. But…" and here he looked sternly at me, "you sure better promise me you aren't going to show it to anyone. I mean it, Mary. My brothers would have a real big time with that, and I'd never live it down."

I leaned back in my chair and smiled. "I promise. And I don't want to hear what William Shakespeare would say. I want to hear what my Tom will say."

We smiled at each other and continued rocking for a while, the entire world lit up by the most beautiful full moon. I didn't think the storm was going to amount to much after all.

Looking back a month later, I was so glad we didn't know what would happen the next day.

And I wished I had that letter.

CHAPTER 6

Halloween Treat

Wednesday, October 31, 1928

I supposed it made sense the last day in our house should be on Halloween, even though I didn't believe in ghosts. Certainly not the kind that came covered in sheets and tried to scare you, but there seemed to be so many ghosts flitting about that day. I kept thinking I was seeing them out of the corner of my eye: Tom, walking into the pantry to get a jar of peaches; our baby Alice, sitting up on her blanket on the kitchen floor and trying to crawl; and even Laddie, who loved both of them as much as any of us did, racing out the screen door.

I felt them all around me as I swept and mopped the floors. I was pretty sure those ghosts would be heading over to Mama and Daddy's house with us. I wouldn't have wanted to leave them with strangers anyway. Those were ghosts I loved.

Dark, rainy, and chilly since early morning, it seemed the summer was finally, truly gone. I'd been alone all day with only Clarence for company as I did the final cleaning of this house I'd scrubbed and polished for so many years. I was not about to have Mrs. Brown saying I didn't keep a good house. And I didn't want her to have to start out having to clean, just as they'd be bringing in all her family's things tomorrow. With her children and all, she'd have enough to do.

The children and I moved in with Mama and Daddy yesterday, so poor Mama was riding herd on them while I was at the old house. Well, riding herd on Tommy, as I doubted the girls were any trouble for her. Irene and Celeste had begged to come back here with me to help, but I needed this time to say my own goodbyes to this place. Daddy brought me and Clarence over after breakfast, along with some ham biscuits and a slice of pound cake Mama packed for my dinner. He was due to come for me in late afternoon so we could get back before sunset—which was much earlier now.

I'd washed all the windows of the house in late September, so there had been no need to do that chore over. The pantry was the last part of the house I had yet to do. Now only a weak light came in through the pantry window, as the rain hit and slid down the glass. I was glad I'd left the kerosene lamp and matches there, and its light helped as I did the final wiping down of the shelves.

I'd completed the righthand side of the room and turned to the opposite wall that was partially covered by the open pantry door from the kitchen. Behind the door was that old mirror that had led to my new haircut.

As I paused to look at the mirror, I laughed, recalling how stunned the children had been when they woke the next morning and saw I'd cut off my long hair. I thought Tommy and Martha weren't quite sure it was really me. As they came into the kitchen, they both stopped, each mouth a perfect little "o" of shock, and Tommy reached over and grabbed Martha's hand.

Even Baby Clarence seemed startled, but he'd decided right quick his next meal was more important than that his mama seemed strangely changed. I guess the really important things about me, to him, were still the same. He was a bit of a piglet, that boy.

Irene, Celeste, and Leah got over their surprise quickly and clustered all around as I nursed Clarence, feeling the edges of the cut and admiring how my hair had natural wave. I'm sure Irene and Celeste noticed my new hairdo had a definite uneven slant to it, but they didn't say anything to me.

Later that day, Daddy and Mama brought over some boxes for us to use for packing. She took one look and asked for my scissors. She shook her head at my impulsiveness, but otherwise didn't say a word other than, "Let me help you even that up, honey." When she'd finished repairing my handiwork, she gave me a quick hug and went to check on the children for me, leaving me to gaze at the strange woman who at least had a good haircut now.

Of course, I'd noticed since Mama repaired my poor attempt, the three older girls want to get their hair cut, too. I gave them permission to cut off their braids as soon as we're settled and before they started their new school. They put up good arguments for getting bobs, including how much faster their hair would dry after being washed.

"And winter's going to be here soon, you know. We'll be less likely to get sick!" wheedled Celeste, who was always good at thinking of why she should get her way. And she did have a point, I had to admit.

I'd take a little braid from each one of them and keep it in my old tin candy box where I kept my treasures. I had a lock of Alice's hair in there. And one of Tom's, tied in a blue ribbon. I even kept a white curl from Laddie, our faithful, departed, four-legged family member.

The girls weren't asking me to do the actual cutting, which just went to show I had smart girls. Their grandmother was clearly the safer choice.

Martha said she wanted to keep her braids so she could let them grow really long. In case she ever got thrown into a high tower by an evil witch, she could toss them out a window so the handsome prince could climb up and rescue her. She's a girl who learned from fairytales.

"But what if a handsome prince doesn't happen to come by? What then?" I had asked after she announced why she didn't want her hair bobbed.

She had just taken a big bite of grits and fried egg, so she chewed and thought a moment. "I'll cut them off and tie them to the bedpost. Then I'll climb down and run away back home." She gave a big, yolky smile.

"It's always good to have a backup plan, Martha. Wipe your mouth, sweetie. No, with your napkin. All you girls, it's good to have a backup plan." I looked at Leah, Celeste, and Irene in turn. I thought Irene understood what I was really saying, but I intended to keep on sending that message to them.

I sure wish someone had taught me that lesson. But then, I'd been so sure, even when I was a young girl, that I knew exactly how my life was going to go, so I'd probably have ignored any warning and wound up here anyway. But I was going to do my best to make sure my girls were more prepared than I was. And my boys.

We don't know what's waiting for us. We might think we do, but we do not. It's so easy to get lulled into thinking everything is going to be all right, but life is not a fairytale.

Breaking myself out of those memories, I took the mirror off its nail hanger and placed it near the back door, where I was collecting the few things left to be taken away. The broom, mop, and a stack of dust rags, along with the one remaining kitchen chair that hadn't been taken over to Mama and Daddy's, were already there.

I put another stick of wood into the cookstove. I'd wanted to leave the stove all cleaned of ashes, but it was more important to keep the kitchen warm for Clarence, who dozed in his basket. He was wrapped in blankets, of course, but you didn't lose a baby to the cold and damp to ever risk letting another one get chilled. Not if you could help it. So I'd shut the doors leading to the rest of the house off the kitchen and the back door. The kitchen was warm, if not as cozy in its now-empty state.

Looking at the little watch pinned to my blouse under the bib of my apron, I realized I needed to hurry if I was to make sure I was done by the time Daddy came back. Only the lefthand side of the pantry shelves remained. Tom had added another shelf to the top to put things we rarely used, but didn't want to store in one of the outbuildings. But it turned out it was so close to the ceiling that pots and things we might have kept up there were too tall to fit. We wound up using the topmost righthand shelf instead for those seldom-needed things.

I had found another purpose, though, for that hard-to-reach shelf. From mid-October to Christmas, I used it to stash the little gifts I got or made for the children. We bought each child some kind of toy from Santa each year, but I also made gifts, of course: dolls, doll clothes, stuffed animals, aprons for the girls. I'd planned on making a little tool apron from a feed sack for Tommy this year. Tom had said he could find some small screwdrivers and a tape measure and such to attach to it, so Tommy could feel like a big boy and help his daddy do repairs.

Normally, I'd already be working on those gifts, doing the work after the children went to bed, but with Tom's passing, I had not even thought about Christmas. It was all I could do to get us through this month. So, I was sure the top shelf was empty, but then again, there would be dust, and quite possibly a dead bug or two. As I debated trying to reach that shelf, I had an image of Mrs. Brown finding dust and dead bugs up there.

I sighed and hoisted myself up onto the top of the lower cabinet shelf, which was wider than the shelves above it. Normally, I'd have a stepstool to reach the upper shelves, but it had been taken and stored in Daddy's barn. Really, though, I rarely used it; one advantage of being too tall was the ability to reach most shelves. I'd been five foot nine inches tall by the time I was twelve or thirteen, a little taller than even my mother, who was tall for a woman, and my sisters. I'd been embarrassed and teased by a couple of the girls at school who kept saying I should join the circus.

It was Tom who helped me be at peace with my height. "You look like a queen, Mary Ellen." I doubted the truth of that, but at least Mama had taught all of us girls to hold ourselves as tall as we could. If anyone looked like a queen, it was Mama, still slender and graceful after five children and all her hard work on the farm. She was my ideal of how a woman should carry herself.

It had also helped that Tom was a little over six foot two, so I still felt almost delicate next to him.

In fact, I'd rarely had to reach the topmost shelf; Tom would always put the Christmas gifts up there for me and then get them down late on Christmas Eve as we helped Santa with his deliveries.

Now I sat on the lower-cabinet top, pulled my legs under me, turned, and carefully stood up, holding for balance as I faced the shelves. I couldn't see the top shelf, but I took my dust rag and starting at the end by the window, swept it along over my head, pushing any clumps of dust or bugs off in front of where I stood. I was pleased no dead bugs—and especially no living bugs—seemed to be up there. Just as I was about to reach the end of the shelf, my rag hit something solid. I startled and had to clutch harder onto the lower shelf I'd been gripping as I moved down the cabinet top.

"I swanee, did I forget a present up here from last Christmas?" Now I was talking out loud, apparently to the pantry ghosts. I could certainly smell them or, at least, the lingering sweet-sour scent of the hogs' slop pail that had always been there, waiting for table scraps to be added. The pail was gone, but the aroma haunted the room.

No answer, except I could hear little Clarence making grizzling noises out in the kitchen.

"Well, Clarence," I called, "if you know, I guess you're not talking." Just more happy sounds from the kitchen. He was probably playing with his toes again.

I took a deep breath and reached up, nudging the object with the rag, slowly bringing it to the edge of the shelf. A corner of what looked like, and was, a cardboard cigar box came into view. I reached up and lifted it down. It felt almost empty. I set it on a lower shelf, finished dusting the corner, and carefully let myself down so I could hop off onto the floor. I decided to finish up the rest of the shelves and then I'd take a look inside. At least it wasn't a forgotten Christmas gift.

As I finished that last cleaning task, I went back to the kitchen and checked on Clarence. A quick diaper change and a cuddle, and he was happy to go back into his basket. I stowed everything that needed to leave when we did by the back door and looked around. One last time I walked through each room of the house and out onto the front porch, empty now of our rocking chairs. The rain was still coming down, and soon it would be sunset. I stood for a moment and listened to the patter on the tin roof.

Around the front stoop, two empty places reminded me Daddy had dug up my two pink rosebushes and taken them to his and Mama's house to replant. Tom had given them to me a few years ago, knowing how much I adored big pink cabbage roses. He loved coming home sometimes in the summer and finding I'd put a bloom in each of our girls' hair, as well as one back in my bun. That scent was of summer and of nights sitting on the front porch, with their sweet perfume coming in on the breeze. I could not bear leaving those roses here for the Browns. They got to have the hutch, but not my roses.

I stood there, the chilly rain misting onto the porch, and thought about the years spent and the memories made in the house. My baby Alice, dying here. Being told about Tom not coming home ever again. I blinked against the tears that wanted to come.

But mostly, good memories were here. My children, born here. The birthday celebrations, the Christmas trees—always some scrawny pine Tom cut down on the property and we thought was the most beautiful Christmas tree ever—and even the ordinary meals around the big kitchen table, getting another little face added about every other year.

I knew I was a lucky woman. A rich woman. I decided I would not pity myself one little bit ever again. I had been blessed more than most. Wiping my eyes, I forced myself to stand tall. I was my mother's daughter.

Finally, I went back to the warm kitchen and sat in the chair, waiting for Daddy. I'd forgotten about the cigar box until I saw it on the pile of used rags where I'd set it. I wiped it off and flipped the lid open to see a stub of a pencil and what looked like empty, used envelopes. Tom always saved envelopes from any mail we got. He'd use them to make lists or notes to himself, rather than paper we had to pay for. I couldn't think, though, why he'd store it on the top shelf.

I picked up the first envelope, a long one that had brought a bill, I supposed, and turned it over to see if he'd started a list. As I looked, for a moment, I was completely disoriented. In his awkward handwriting, it started with "Dearest Mary."

CHAPTER 7

Thankful for Sis

Friday, November 23, 1928

Mama and I baked and cooked for days and were up before dawn Thanksgiving morning with more baking and cooking. I felt like we had enough food to last us and an army another week. I was glad we'd brought our icebox with us instead of including it in the auction, so we now had two of them on the back porch, stuffed with food that might otherwise spoil. Of course, I'd be up early every day to cook breakfast all the same, but that was nothing. With our two combined flocks of chickens, there was no shortage of eggs for breakfast.

It was hard to think of Tom not being with us for this first holiday without him. I wore myself out trying not to think about last year's Thanksgiving, but to enjoy the one we were having this year.

In addition to the six children, myself, Mama and Daddy, Tom's mother and his youngest sister joined us for the big day and didn't plan on leaving until Saturday. I loved Mama Jo and

Sis and hadn't seen them since Tom's passing. Mama Jo's spell at learning of his heart attack in October became a cold that settled in her chest, and then became a serious infection she'd only recently recovered from. She still looked fragile, but her cough was nearly gone.

Mama Jo and Sis arrived around ten o'clock Thanksgiving morning, along with Teddy Bear, Mama Jo's black-and-white terrier. Teddy was twice Toby's size and several years older, but they both had the same long, square terrier faces and crinkly hair that made them look more like stuffed toys than real dogs. They seemed like old friends reuniting as the two of them chased each other around the yard.

I didn't know what Mama Jo would do without her Teddy Bear. We had a framed photograph of her sitting outside at a table set for tea in Sis's backyard. Mama Jo was in her hat and Sunday dress with her cup and saucer in front of her, and Teddy was sitting at the head of the table on his own chair, waiting for his teatime treat. I hoped he didn't give Toby any ideas.

Sis's motorcar was loaded with yet more food: apple pie, sweet potato pie, butterbeans cooked with fatback, and jars and jars of her pickles: chow chow, okra, green tomatoes, even pickled collard green stems, which I'd never had, and something called piccalilli, which I'd never so much as heard of. Clyde, her husband, worked as a bank teller in Tarboro, leaving Sis home all day, mostly to putter in her backyard garden. She always said she'd rather be gardening than cleaning house, although I was certain she didn't slack there, either. Sis was always full of energy.

She certainly made the most of her garden by putting up as much as she could for the winter. Although really, I thought she gave a lot of it away. She read the women's magazines, too, looking for recipes. I seemed to cook the same old things my mama taught me how to make when I was a girl.

Sis learned to drive after she got married, and Clyde had no objection to her taking off with Mama Jo, who lived with them, for Wilmington all the way from Tarboro. He was going to his parents' house in Tarboro for Thanksgiving dinner. Walking there, I imagined.

Sis didn't get married until she was twenty-five; Tom thought she'd be an old maid for life. But three years ago, she met Clyde, and that was that. They married the next year. I always thought she pretty much called the tune Clyde danced to, and he seemed to like it like that. He had no complaints when she said she wanted her mother to move in with them.

Mama Jo had been a widow for six years by that time and had been living with Sis in the family's farmhouse before Sis got married. When Sis moved out after her wedding and moved to Tarboro, her mother was left alone and getting frailer by the year. As much as they all loved their mother, it was a relief to Tom and the other brothers and sisters, each with their own large families, that Sis and Clyde were willing to take her in, and their mama was willing to go.

Sis was two years younger than me, but she had always seemed braver and more independent. I couldn't imagine taking that trip, about 150 miles, by myself. It reminded me I really needed to practice my driving, though.

While I helped her unload the food, I asked, "Sis, weren't you worried you might have a breakdown somewhere and be stranded?"

She pursed her lips and gave me the slightly naughty look that was often on her face. "Not really, Mary Ellen. I never thought for a moment Mama and I'd have to live out the rest of our lives on the side of the road if we had a flat tire or a breakdown. So, if that wasn't going to happen, it had to mean somebody would have to come by to help us." She tipped her head back and laughed. You never had the feeling Sis was laughing at you, only that she seemed able to find the humor in most situations that came her way.

Really, she had the face of a little pixie, her eyes and mouth usually crinkled up in merriment. Even her hair looked like it belonged on a pixie, a surprisingly short bob of light brown hair that fluffed all around her head like a dandelion.

I doubted she'd asked for Clyde's permission to cut it like that, either. Or to wear the dark red lipstick and the rouge that made her look so stylish. She didn't read ladies' magazines just for recipes.

It occurred to me if she were a few years younger, unmarried, and lived in a bigger town, she might have become a flapper. It was a startling thought.

Having Sis around was wonderful. She was always so lively and fun. I'd not had much of that in the last two months.

I thought it was good, too, for Mama Jo to have a woman closer to her own age to talk with. She and Mama sat in the front sitting room by the fireplace, visiting with each other all afternoon after our holiday dinner. They both seemed to be crocheting things they would set aside quickly when I'd pop in to see if they wanted some tea or anything. I noticed Martha curled up on the braided rug in front of the fireplace, arm around Teddy, as they both napped. She so rarely got to be with both of her grandmothers at the same time, but the big meal, the warmth of the fire, Teddy, and the lulling sound of their voices had defeated her best efforts to stay awake.

Sis and I sat in the warm kitchen with the baby and tatted while we talked. I finished a length of lace edging I planned on using on a dress for Martha, and then Sis showed me how to make tatted snowflakes. Irene, Celeste, and Leah wandered in after a while and wanted to learn, too, so we had a pleasant afternoon around the kitchen table. Now we had new snowflakes, some with shapes probably not to be found coming out of the sky, we could hang on our Christmas tree next month after we starched them. Snowy Christmases didn't happen here very often, but we'd have snow on our tree. We were all delighted with that notion.

Daddy made himself scarce, probably out in the barn puttering around, keeping Tommy and Toby with him most of the time. That certainly meant a calmer and quieter house.

We had a light supper of Thanksgiving leftovers and slices of the sweet potato pie Sis brought. Even Clarence liked the little taste of the filling I let him lick off my finger. I didn't think he'd ever stop smacking his lips. He'd just started being interested in solid food, so I was careful to let him have only a little. Sis was thrilled he liked it so. She always splurged and put lemon juice and finely grated lemon rind in her sweet potato pies. It made them tangy and sweet at the same time, with the grated cinnamon and nutmeg she added, too. Clarence wasn't the only one smacking his lips.

Before long, we were all yawning, even Tommy, and so it was an early night to bed for everyone. I was surprised to find myself more thankful—and with more things to be thankful for—than I had thought possible even a few days ago.

On Friday morning, I was up first for once. Waking before Mama and Daddy didn't happen very often. I put on my work jacket and headed out to feed the animals, thinking to let Daddy have a morning when he didn't have to do that. Teddy Bear and little Toby came out with me and watched as I fed Molly, our mule, the chickens, and finally, the four hogs. As I dumped the slop pail in their feed trough and pumped water for them, I thought about how they had no idea what was waiting for them next week when Daddy would take them to Burgaw to become hams, bacon, chops, pork roasts, and sausages. The heat of their bodies steamed in the cool, damp dawn air, and they seemed so happy guzzling their food. No idea at all.

Toby suddenly gave a small bark, and I turned to see Sis, bundled against the chill, walking out to meet me. She bent over to scoop Toby up into her arms, dodging his wet kisses and Teddy Bear's efforts to be held, and said, "Mary, you're up bright and early! Our mamas are getting breakfast started. Your daddy saw you were taking care of the animals, so he's sitting at the kitchen table waiting for the coffee to brew. Says he feels like he's having a vacation, like the rich folk do."

She gave me a quick hug, juggling Toby, who was still trying to land kisses, while Teddy danced around her. We turned back to the hog pen. "Healthy porkers there, Mary. Y'all have plenty of meat for this coming year."

"I was just thinking about that, sort of," I started. "They don't know what's waiting for them in Burgaw next week, Sis. 'Ignorance is bliss,' that's what they always say. They do look blissful." I turned away from the pen, and we started walking back to the house. Sis set Toby down, and he and Teddy raced ahead.

I took a deep breath. "Yesterday, I looked around the table at all the faces I love so much and wondered if we'd all still be together this time next year. It makes my heart ache to think we can't just assume that will happen. I wonder if I'll ever stop wondering about that at every special gathering. I wonder if I should even hope I stop wondering. Maybe it's better to never relax, to always be ready for something bad to happen. I have a feeling, though, it will never be the bad thing you are expecting to happen, but something you never saw coming."

This wasn't the usual conversation I had with Sis, but I needed to talk to someone about it. I didn't feel like I could do that with Mama and Daddy. Because they might be worried I thought one of them was going to die soon, given their age. I didn't want them thinking I was going to be looking at them all the time and wondering how soon they'd pass.

Sis, her face more serious than usual, looked over at me. "Mary, I understand how you might be feeling like that. You've had too many losses in these past few years, what with Baby Alice and now Tom. But I don't think that's how you want to live your life. I doubt you want to teach your children to always be expecting something horrible to happen."

I sighed. "I've already started telling the girls they need to always have another plan, Sis. I don't think I can feel right if I don't try to help them understand they need to think about what can go wrong and try to have some idea how to handle it. I felt so safe with Tom, and it never occurred to me he would die so young. Never entered my head. Never considered I would have to figure out how to find a job that will support six children and myself. Alice passing was, well, horrible, but babies do die. Thank goodness not as often as when our mothers were young, but it does still happen."

Sis waited for me to finish. "And I worried when the Spanish influenza came to Wilmington, ten years ago. They said every woman carrying a baby died if they got sick from it. I was so lucky I'd had Celeste in August, and the infection didn't get to Wilmington until October. None of us got sick, which seems like a miracle with all the people who did, and so many of them not surviving. I know we were all blessed to be living out of town, on our farms. And before that I was worried Tom might be called up for the Great War after they made him register, but that didn't happen, either. But it seems our luck ran out."

We had stopped halfway back to the house. I could see the lights in the kitchen, and the scent of bacon, coffee, and wood smoke was calling us to come inside. Toby and Teddy had run ahead and were waiting by the back door, eager for young fingers to drop food on the floor.

Sis took my hand and wrinkled up her forehead, "'As thy days, so shall thy strength be.'" Her face smoothed out, and she looked at me. "I'm pretty sure that's the right verse, from Deuteronomy something or the other. Mama will know exactly. I've heard her quote it often enough."

"I'm not sure I see." I was puzzling out the meaning.

"You'll have enough strength to face what comes your way, Mary. That's what it means. I don't think you have to spend your life trying to think of every awful thing that can happen. You just have to believe you will have the strength to deal with it, no matter what it is." Sis gave me a little smile. "As you said, it probably won't be something you think of anyway, so there's all that extra worry for nothing. And I think living like that would steal any happiness that might come your way, and a lot of happiness has come your way, Mary. I think more will come in the future, too."

"Of course," she continued, "it's still not a bad idea to teach your girls, especially, that they need to think how they could support themselves and their children if they had to do it on their own.

"I've always thought I'd try to get an office job at the railroad company if I had to," she surprised me by saying. "I'm good at numbers, and I'm going to learn how to type. Clyde said he'd get me a used typewriter for Christmas, if that's what I want. Poor Tom, being the oldest boy, he couldn't get much schooling. Daddy needed him in the fields. I'm the only one in our family who was able to stay in school and get my diploma. I know how fortunate I was to be the youngest."

I regarded Sis and realized I had underestimated her. To me, she'd always been Tom's baby sister, the one who always appeared as if she laughed her way through life. I'd never stopped to think about how she must have worried she'd never find anyone to love, never have a husband who loved her, and never have a home of her own. She and Clyde had been married for over two years now, and still no children. I wondered if she was worried about that. But she had a plan.

"Thanks, Sis. 'As thy days, so shall thy strength be.' Maybe that's what I need to learn. To believe. Maybe that's what I need to teach my children." I felt lighter.

We turned to the house and went into breakfast.

CHAPTER 8

A Death at Christmas

Monday, December 31, 1928

As it turned out, we didn't escape having a family death around Christmas after all, even though we lost Tom in October. Jim, my oldest sister Janie's husband, came down with influenza about a week after Thanksgiving. Then their four sons, ages two to eleven, got sick, too. Only Ella Mae, nine years old, didn't get it. She helped her mother tend to everyone, but just as Jim and the boys started getting better, Janie woke up with a fever and cough. She kept tending to her family, but finally had to take to her bed.

After a week or so of being ill, Jim was well enough to see to the boys and Janie, but while the boys continued to get better, she just kept getting sicker. The doctor came several times to check on everyone, and he told Jim on December 19 the boys were recovered enough to play outside if they bundled up. Jim said the doctor seemed a little concerned about Janie, given she was seven months along with her next baby. Ever since the Spanish influenza ten years ago, doctors were especially concerned about pregnant women during an outbreak, but he still thought Janie and the baby would be fine.

Janie kept trying to get up but would only last a few minutes before having to lie back down. Even so, she kept saying she was feeling much better.

There was a lot of influenza going around, and the doctor had many calls to make. Still, he promised to do his best to get back to check on Janie before Christmas. But on December 22, only twelve days before her forty-third birthday, Janie's heart stopped. Ella Mae, bringing her a hot cup of broth, knew her mother didn't look right, and she wouldn't wake up. Jim heard Ella Mae's cries and rushed in, but there was nothing to be done. Janie and her unborn baby were gone.

Janie wasn't the first child my parents had lost. Just two days before my fourth birthday, Mama gave birth for the last time. She had twins, Etta and Ethel. Poor little Ethel wasn't nearly as strong as Etta, and she died a month later. I was too young to remember much of that time, but Mama talked to me about losing Ethel when my own Alice passed. She understood my grief and my guilt. Mama kept telling me she knew—and deep down I knew—I'd done everything possible to keep Alice alive, just as she had for Ethel. She said many times to focus on the children still living, even though, of course, I'd never forget Alice. I thought she'd learned that lesson the hard way, herself.

Now, there was another loss for her and Daddy: their firstborn, the one who had always seemed so strong. Janie didn't get married to Jim until she was thirty years old. While I'd been only fourteen when I married Tom, my other sisters had married in their late teen years, and all but Etta were married years before our oldest sister. The house had emptied as we left with our new husbands, leaving our parents with Janie under their roof longer than any of the rest of us.

Being close to thirteen years older than me, Janie had almost seemed more like another mother or an aunt to me than a sister. In my memory, she'd always been an adult and always reminded me of Mama, and later, Irene. All three were beautiful, graceful, kind, and usually serious, although they all loved to laugh and see the humor in life, too. They all took their responsibilities seriously. Perhaps that was a better way of putting it. They always did their best. Not trying to get away with doing less or doing something in a slipshod way. I suppose I'd never really thought about how alike they all were. Janie and Irene were both first-borns, so maybe that explained some of it, but not all, as Mama was the fourth of six children in her family.

Mama and Daddy took Janie's passing hard. The last they'd heard, it seemed as if her whole family was going to come out of all the sickness and be well enough to enjoy Christmas, just three days away. We'd already been cooking and baking extra food to take over, so Janie wouldn't feel she needed to lift a finger while she recuperated.

My parents usually spent much of Christmas Day driving to visit as many of their children and grandchildren as they could and continuing on paying visits for several days after until all the homes had been called on. Mama spent much of the year crocheting little gifts for her girls and grandchildren: scarves and hats, usually. Daddy gave his daughters' husbands cigars and, in the last few years since Prohibition became the law of the land, a mason jar or two of something that raised Mama's eyebrows at him.

He was very fond of his muscadine vine. I suspected more than preserves got made from those grapes.

So, to go from that holiday feeling, which seemed to be everywhere, to the devastation of losing Janie and her baby, well, it was even harder to bear than if Janie and the baby had passed in February or June. As Mama had told me long ago, it just didn't seem right such things should happen near Christmas, and it added even more to the tragedy. And now, every Christmas, we'd remember when we lost Janie.

Daddy had planned to take the children on Christmas Eve into the little woods near the house to choose and cut down a small tree to bring back and decorate with our tatted, starched snowflakes and the other little ornaments and strings of popcorn the children had been working on. Instead, a kind neighbor of theirs came by and took the children for the tree. Daddy and Mama went to Janie's house the day after her passing to help Jim out with the children. I was sure Mama picked out what Janie wore for the funeral so Jim or Ella Mae wouldn't have to do it.

Janie's funeral was on Christmas Eve, and then they stayed over for several days, through Christmas, to comfort Janie's family and try to help them learn to carry on without her. I thought it was better for both of them to be there, feeling useful, than sitting here mourning Janie and worrying about how her children were doing.

We decided I'd stay home with the children to keep them out of the cold and away from Janie's family, just in case they might catch the influenza. Clarence had had an earache and a little fever for several days before Christmas Eve, and I was worried about him. I just kept warming up sweet almond oil in the glass dropper and putting it in his ears. He'd cry while I did it, but once the cotton wool was in his ears and he could feel the warmth, he'd soon fall asleep. He was better by Christmas Eve, but I wasn't about to take any chances with him or any of my children, as much as I hated missing my sister's funeral. I certainly wasn't going to drive to the cemetery with the children in the back of Tom's truck, even if the weather was clear. I was still learning how to drive and was far from being competent or confident.

So, the children and I wound up being on our own at Christmas after all. They were all delighted with their gifts, small as they were. I think the big excitement was the orange, nuts, and peppermint candy stick they each got in their stocking. I'd put together little sewing baskets for the girls, even Martha, with colored embroidery thread, a pincushion, a packet of needles, and a plain handkerchief in each for them to practice sewing flowers or whatever they wanted on it. Celeste and Irene had said repeatedly they were too old for dolls, but they certainly made a fuss over the stuffed ones I'd sewed for Leah and Martha.

The three older girls liked their new barrettes to hold their short hair out of their faces, and Martha was delighted with her hair ribbons. They all had to try on the crocheted hats and scarves Mama had left for them. Tommy was especially thrilled with his new tool belt I'd made for him. He strutted around the house wearing it, refusing to take it off even for our meals. I had to keep an eye on him to stop him from fixing too many things that didn't need fixing.

Mama had made me a beautiful shawl out of bright blue wool. It was so large I could wrap it around me almost twice, and so tightly crocheted I knew I'd be able to wear it outdoors in place of a coat in all but the coldest weather. I was as thrilled as the children.

The children had as happy a Christmas as I had dared to hope, although we couldn't help but think often of Tom, Janie, and the baby. Next year would be better, I was sure.

On Christmas night, after the children were asleep, I gave myself a present. A present from Tom. I pulled out the partial letter I'd found from him in the pantry on Halloween and read it again. I tried to save it for special occasions, as a treat. He hadn't completed it, and it was clear he was struggling to find his words. Now I knew why he'd stayed up late that last night; he'd started writing right after I'd asked him for a love letter. It was on a used envelope, so there wasn't much space. I wondered what kind of paper he planned to use for the clean copy, but of course I'd never know.

He had unsealed the envelope so he could write inside. I opened it and read:

Dearest Mary,

You said I don't have to be a poet, which is just as well. I can only say what is in my heart. You are. You are in my heart, Mary. You have been since I first laid eyes on you. I never knew how much I could love until then. I wish I could give you real diamonds, but instead you've given them to me—our children. I will always love you and

That's all there was. Scrawled in pencil. Many words crossed out, then written again. I folded it back up.

"Thank you, Tom. Merry Christmas, darling," I whispered to the night.

✻

The next week flew by. The children helped me with the animals, but mostly, we stayed in the kitchen, where the cookstove could keep us warmer than anywhere else in the old farmhouse. Mama called every day to check on us and let us know how Jim and the children were doing. I think it helped Jim to have his father-in-law there as they worked doing the chores and mending things around the kitchen table late in the day.

Jim knew a woman he could get to come in and take care of the house, laundry, and the cooking. Mrs. Strickland had lost her husband a number of years before and lived just down the road with her son's family. He thought he could even take one of their bedrooms and fix it for her if she was interested in moving out of her son's house.

Mama told me later Jim had looked at my daddy and said, "I'm not too sure, but her daughter-in-law might be real happy about that too." She said she gave them both a look as they tried to hide their grins, but she'd been pleased to see Jim be able to find some reason to smile, even if it was at a woman's expense.

Before she and Daddy headed home, Jim had arranged with Mrs. Strickland, the widow, to move in with them just after New Year's. Turned out she was only in her early fifties and hated not having her own kitchen and house, but she knew her son's new wife should take the lead in her own home. Overseeing Jim's house would give her the responsibility and the free hand she longed for, and she knew it would be a relief to the young couple not to have her underfoot. She'd also still be close if and when her grandchildren started arriving. Jim and Janie's children were already fond of her, so it seemed to be an ideal solution for everyone.

Mama was so delighted, too. The night she and Daddy got back home, she said, "I'd been so worried Ella Mae would have to drop out of school to take care of everything, and her only nine years old."

I was astonished. "Do you think it would have come to that, Mama?"

She nodded. "Jim is left with boys only two, five, seven and eleven. Boys, Mary Ellen, boys. Even young girls of two and five need constant watching, but boys? Think of four Tommys running around."

I shuddered. "I see what you mean, but Ella Mae is only nine years old, Mama."

Mama shook her head and sipped her tea. "It's sad, but I've known many a girl that young or younger who had to drop out of school to take her mama's place. Sometimes even when her mama was still living. It's not right, but you do what you have to for the good of the whole family."

Something about that bothered me, but I couldn't think of another solution if the family couldn't afford to bring in a woman to help out. I was just grateful Ella Mae could stay in school, at least for now.

I wanted so much for my own girls to get a high school education. Then, if they ever had to provide for themselves, they could hope to get a job, maybe in an office, and not have to be a cleaning woman or go work in one of the textile mills new in town since the end of the Great War.

The girls had started at their new school as soon as we moved in with Mama and Daddy. It was a bad time to have them change schools, but it couldn't be helped. Even now, I had them work on their schoolwork almost every day of their Christmas break so they could catch up with their new classmates. I'd met with their teachers and found out what they needed to do. And I had Irene working with Martha, and even Tommy, to teach them their alphabet and how to write their name. Martha learned so quick and loved being a little schoolgirl. Tommy hated sitting still, but he amazed us with how well he could add and subtract already.

Celeste struggled with her studies and wasn't really interested in getting better. I think she enjoyed looking more at the fashion magazines Sis had left on her Thanksgiving visit. Irene liked them too, but she was more likely to pick up a book or her Bible. Celeste wanted to study the clothes and the hairstyles, and she and Leah had a running game of describing the wardrobes they'd have when they were grown ladies. A lot of fur was involved. A lot.

And so, 1928 came to an end. Daddy said the money men on Wall Street in New York City said 1929 was going to be even more prosperous than anything we'd seen in ten years. I didn't know what stock was or what went on at Wall Street, despite Daddy's attempt to explain it. I wasn't sure Daddy exactly understood it either. Anyway, as long as those folks were making money, and apparently they were, it was supposed to keep on making things good for the rest of us. Farm prices were up, and downtown Wilmington was always bustling with businessmen going about town making money and ladies spending it in the shops. At least, that's what the newspaper said. It certainly seemed busy, especially with all the trolleys that crisscrossed town the few times I visited the bank right after Tom passed.

In the summers, people lined up on Front Street downtown to take the beach trolley all the way out to Wrightsville Beach. They just lay on the sand there or swam in the ocean, and some of them had boats to sail in Banks Channel or even out to sea. At night, people got all dressed up to take the trolley to the end of the line at Wrightsville to dance at the huge, beautiful

Lumina pavilion. It was so lit up at night with electric lights that sailors used it like a lighthouse to guide their way. They even had an enormous movie screen out in the surf where they showed movies at night. I only went there once, but I saw a Charlie Chaplin movie. It was amazing with the waves coming in all around it.

Anyway, with business going so well, Daddy said I should be able to find a job downtown, and an apartment nearby for the children and myself as soon as Clarence got a little older. I wasn't sure how it was going to work. I certainly wouldn't be able to bring him to a job with me. Maybe I'd be able to make enough to hire a woman to mind the children while I was working. I'd have to wait and see. Until then, they said we should just stay.

At least there was the hope 1929 would be a much better year. I was sure it would be.

CHAPTER 9

Measles & Irene

Saturday, April 27, 1929

I was too optimistic about 1929 being a much better year. It had not had any of the losses of 1928 so far, but winter was harder and longer than usual. The only spots of color outside were the four camellia bushes that almost reached to the roof on the north side of the house, red flowers blooming all winter. A little vase of them on the table brightened the kitchen from Christmas to March.

The weather took its toll on the children. Leah came home from the new school with a cold that went into her lungs and became bronchitis. Celeste came down with it in mid-January and Irene a week later. It was all I could do to keep Martha and Tommy away from them.

One neighbor, a mother of two girls a little older than Martha, heard about my girls being sick and offered to have Martha stay at their house for a few days. I was grateful to get her out of our sick house, and Martha was excited about a visit with those older girls. I should have realized something was wrong when the neighbor lady brought Martha back a day sooner than planned, giving the vague excuse she had a lot to do at home.

What she had to do was take care of her girls, who had come down with the measles.

I figured that out within a few days, when Martha broke out in red, itchy bumps all over her body. Irene and Celeste had had the measles when they were young, as had Mama, Daddy, and I, so at least we were safe from a second infection, but Leah, who was just getting back to normal from bronchitis, was down with measles a few days after Martha. Tommy followed.

The real worry was for Clarence, who was so young still, not even a year old. Mama insisted Clarence and I stay away from the sick children. Irene and Celeste, themselves recovering from bronchitis, tried their best to help Mama with Tommy, Martha, and Leah. Clarence and I stayed in Mama and Daddy's bedroom most of the time, and my parents slept in my bed, where they could be near Tommy. Irene slept with Leah and Celeste with Martha, so they could get their grandmother if there was a crisis in the night.

Dr. Webb came every few days and gave what care and comfort he could. I sometimes thought the medicine was to make the parents and grandparents feel like something was being done, more than it did any real good. Still, I did think the cough medicine helped, if only to let the children sleep. The calamine lotion didn't seem to do anything for the itching, though, and it was hard to get Martha and Tommy to understand they could not scratch the bumps.

Leah's new teacher came by with valentines her classmates had made for her. She wouldn't come into the house and risk taking any disease to her other students, of course, but stood outside on the stoop and chatted for a few minutes. Mama and I huddled in our shawls on the front porch as she told us how well-liked Leah was and how well she was doing in her studies. She'd also brought over some of the classwork for Leah to work on when she felt up to it, as well as schoolwork for Irene and Celeste, who were unable to attend school as long as we had measles in the house, even if they were immune.

The end of February came before the coughs and red bumps and fevers completely left the children. Clarence stayed well, which was a mercy. Poor Leah took the longest to recover. She'd been so weakened by bronchitis and then to have the measles, too; it was a real blow to her young body. But she began to regain her strength and talked about wanting to go back to school.

✥

March arrived, but the damp, wintry weather stayed with us.

Easter came on the fifth Sunday in March that year, but we woke to a heavy, icy rain, so we had to miss Easter Sunday service, as there was no way to get to church without most of us getting soaked to the skin. I wouldn't have taken the children in rain on any Sunday, and especially not after the sickness we'd had during the cold months.

Easter dinner was ham, deviled eggs, rice, red-eye gravy, baked sweet potatoes, and cabbage cooked with bacon. Usually by that time of year we'd be having tender salad greens, but the growing season didn't want to get started, it seemed.

I was worried Mama's Formosa azaleas weren't going to bloom, but they finally came out in mid-April. Drifts of pink clustered under the shade of the trees and along the front of the house. Breathtaking, even if a couple of weeks later than usual.

Mrs. Webb, Dr. Webb's wife from Illinois originally, said they had azaleas there, but they didn't get to even half the size of ours. Mrs. Webb came with her husband to get out of the house, she said, and Mama and I had a pleasant chat over tea with her while Dr. Webb checked on the children and visited with Daddy.

At one point, Mrs. Webb looked around to make sure none of the children were close by, and whispered, "We have a plant in Illinois that I don't think I've seen here. Each bulb puts out a stem about two to three feet high, no leaves on the stem, but has pale pink or red flowers at the top. You'll never guess what they are called."

Mama and I shook our heads. "No leaves, just a stem?" Mama asked.

"Yes. Well, they have leaves when they first come up, but then they die down before the flowers bloom. Odd-looking plants and I don't like them much, but people do love to grow them. Frankly, I think it might be because of their name."

She stopped and looked around again to make sure she wouldn't be overheard. "They're called… please forgive me… they are called *naked ladies*!" Mrs. Webb's cheeks were bright red.

Later, Mama and I made the mistake of telling Daddy about them. He immediately thought we needed some in our front yard and laughed so hard he set off a coughing fit, but he seemed cheerier the rest of the day.

Along with the azaleas, there were the dogwood trees, of course. Mama loved her dogwood trees, and Daddy planted one a year for her. With the pink azaleas and the white dogwoods, it looked like a fairytale house for two weeks each spring. Tommy kept asking why it didn't look like this all the time.

I was relieved to see my two pink rosebushes putting out new leaves, too; I wasn't sure they would survive being transplanted, but they did.

Now, if only the children would thrive here, too.

Just as it looked as if we were free of sickness, Daddy started coughing. He held up while the children were so ill, but the grief of Janie's passing, along with the stress of all the sick children, finally caught up with him. His cough got deeper, and his lungs were wheezing before he let us call Dr. Webb for him.

Like so many men, Daddy thought doctors were fine for children and women, but unnecessary for men, especially himself. He took to making quacking sounds under his breath whenever Mama said he needed to see the doctor again or that it was time to take his medicine.

"Why are you quacking, Granddaddy?" Tommy finally asked him.

Daddy's bright blue eyes crinkled up. "Oh, because of Dr. Webb. Do you think he might have that name because his feet are like a duck's? I can't think of any other reason I'd want to quack when your grandmama mentions him." Daddy seemed serious as he asked Tommy. He avoided looking over at Mama or me.

Tommy was astonished. Never in his young life had he thought that a man could have webbed feet like a duck. Not to mention that could account for his last name. "Does he really have webbed feet, Granddaddy? Can we ask to see them next time he comes here?" Tommy was lit up with excitement.

Mama cleared her throat and set down Daddy's hot tea in front of him with more vigor than usual. He gave a weak cough. Apparently the "quack" had helped him after all, as it certainly was a forced cough, and said, "No, no, no. I don't think we should do that, boy. It might embarrass him. Not to mention your mama and grandmama would have more to say than either of us wants to listen to if you do."

"Oh, you'll be hearing more about that later anyway, Bob. You can bet on that." Mama frowned at Daddy, who looked up and winked at her.

She gave a short laugh and tweaked his nose. "Tommy, I'm not sure your granddaddy is a good influence on you sometimes. But I'll tell you two this: I better not hear quacking or anything about webbed feet when the doctor is here. I mean that now."

Tommy murmured, "Yes, ma'am."

Daddy, all innocence now, said, "Yes, ma'am. Tommy and I will be on our best behavior. Maybe we'll just talk to him about getting some naked ladies for the front yard."

"Naked ladies, Granddaddy?" Tommy goggled. "Eww! Do we have to?"

Mama and I both sighed.

Leah had her ninth birthday on April 24. We made a fuss over her all day. Mama made Leah's favorite dinner of fried chicken, rice and gravy, and cornbread. Leah got to have first pick of the chicken pieces. Of course, she chose the pulley bone. She gnawed off all the sweet white meat and held up the bone. We all started clapping, and Tommy was as excited as she was. "Make a wish, Leah, make a wish!"

Leah got up and walked over to her granddaddy. He took the other end of the wishbone, and I know he made sure she got the larger piece when they snapped it in two, just as he did when my sisters and I were coming up. I still couldn't figure out how he could make his end break off short every time. Naturally, Leah refused to say what she'd wished for, but I just hoped it wasn't for her daddy to come back from heaven. Whatever it was, she was delighted to have won, so it was a happy day for her. I thought her new basketball had a lot to do with that.

Three days later was Irene's thirteenth birthday. Thirteen, of course, was a special birthday, and she wasn't a little child anymore. This time it was chicken and pastry, and then her favorite chocolate layer cake. Irene asked to decorate the chocolate icing; pulling the tines of a fork in one direction all over the cake, then again at right angles, she made a neat plaid design. We all marveled at how steady her hand was to make it look so perfect. It seemed a shame to cut into it, but we certainly did.

My special present to Irene was her own copy of *Little Women*. I had loved it when I was her age. Irene reminded me of Meg, the oldest sister in the story. Irene unwrapped it and held it to her heart. Then she leaped up from her chair and came to hug me again.

"Maybe you can read it to your sisters in the evenings before bed," I suggested. The other girls squealed in excitement, and Irene smiled and nodded.

Tommy looked at me in outrage. "Why don't I get to hear it?"

"Well, sweetie, I'm sure you can if you want to. It's about four sisters, just like your four sisters. They are poor but love each other very much. And some of them go to a ball!" I smiled sweetly at him.

"*Go* to a ball? You mean a ball game?" His little forehead could really crinkle up when he was confused. I wondered if he'd be a wrinkly old man.

"No, dear. A ball is a very fancy dance. All the ladies get really dressed up in ball gowns—extra fancy dresses—and long gloves, and the gentlemen are dressed up special, too. The story talks about what a time the two older girls have finding the right clothes to wear to the ball."

Tommy huffed. "Don't sound like a very good story to me. Now, if they went to a ball game, that would be interesting."

"Well, you can listen to as much of it as you want. It's not all about dances." I had a feeling he'd find other things to do.

CHAPTER 10

Mamie

Sunday, May 19, 1929

My cousin Mamie came to visit in May, a few days before Martha's sixth birthday on May 19. I certainly saw why Mama kept her guest room ready all the time. Mamie sent a letter saying when she was coming, and she should get to our home midday, about dinner time, but the letter arrived only a few hours earlier on the same day she did.

She's something like a second cousin to me, or maybe it's a first cousin once removed. One of those connections Mama was so good at keeping up with. I usually just let it wash over me when she tried to explain our complicated family connections. I'd noticed, though, Irene followed along and asked for even more detail. She always loved knowing about our family, and that kept Mama happy. The two of them sat at the kitchen table sometimes while Mama drew family trees for her. It was more like a forest, frankly, with most everyone coming from a family of seven or more and then each one having that many children themselves and so on and so forth. Unmarried and childless, Mamie probably didn't realize she was making at least one little part of our future family tree a welcome glen, with no new sprouts coming along.

Mamie was five years older than me. Thin as a beanstalk, no claim to beauty other than her thick dark hair, and, as we found out shortly after her arrival, she had picked up the habit of dipping snuff. Her teeth were terribly stained, poor thing, and most folks who dipped snuff lost their teeth sooner than they would have otherwise, so stained teeth were probably as good as it was going to get for her. I didn't think marriage would be in her future.

Shortly before she arrived, Mama read her letter and hurried off to the guest room to make sure it was ready. I followed with Clarence on my hip. "Mama, what is it?" In her hurry, she hadn't told us what the letter said.

"Your second-cousin Mamie is coming to stay for a few days. One of her brothers, Archie Junior, I think, has to go into Wilmington, and he's going to drop her off here today on his way in. In three days, her other brother, Ben, is going to come carry her home," Mama huffed as she pounded the feather pillows and then slid them into fresh pillowcases.

I went and put Clarence down for his nap in the crib Daddy had set up a few months ago and came back to help Mama dust the already-clean room. Lovely warm air blew the white starched curtains, and I could see Tommy and Martha playing "Simon Says" with their granddaddy, who was always the Simon of the game. He had probably figured out it was the only way to hold Tommy still for a while. Martha beamed, knowing she was going to win again; Tommy simply couldn't listen long or well enough before doing whatever "Simon" said, and so he kept getting sent back. I was amazed that he didn't get upset, but would just laugh, go to the start line, and begin all over again with not listening well enough to advance very far.

All the while, little Toby danced around them, yelping with excitement, happy to be with the three people who seemed to be his favorites, until Mama or I had some food for him, of course.

Mama tried once again to explain Mamie's relation to us. "Your granddaddy, that's your daddy's daddy, don't you know, and Mamie's granddaddy were brothers. It was her granddaddy who was captured at Gettysburg," she said. Her voice was muffled as she knelt by the bed to run the dustmop under it.

"Mama, do you think Mamie will check under the bed for dust?" I couldn't help but tease her a little.

Her head popped up, and she eyed me across the bed, where I was dusting the framed photos on top of the chest of drawers. "Well, missy, if she slides her suitcase under here, I sure don't want it coming out looking like a snowball."

I turned back around and kept dusting, biting my lip to hide my smile. She was a little worked up with the short notice of Mamie's arrival.

"I feel right sorry for that girl, Mary. She hasn't had an easy life. She was the eldest child, and her mama died, leaving her to take care of her two little brothers and two little sisters and the house, and her only fifteen years old. You'd think it was a good thing when her daddy got married again less than a year later, but come to find out, his brand-new wife, Mary

#2, because Mamie's mama was also named Mary, wasn't but fourteen. Can you imagine?"

I stopped dusting and looked over my shoulder at her. "Well, I was fourteen when Tom and I married." I might have sounded a little snippy.

"Well, of course I know that, honey. My point, though, is Mamie was going on sixteen, and her new step-mama is over a year younger than she is. And you know her daddy would insist Mary #2 be in charge of everything now. Where did that leave poor Mamie? Well, I'll tell you where. They had her move next door to her old aunt and uncle's house and start keeping house for them. Come to think of it, they were really her Great-Aunt Edith and Great-Uncle Robert Henry, because Robert Henry was another brother of your and Mamie's grandfathers, don't you see?"

I could see enough to know to just nod my head. No wonder she and Irene always drew these things out to understand them. I really didn't care enough to worry too much about it, and I doubted I'd have to spout all this out again.

"So," Mama went on, "Mamie stayed there for several years, all the while her new step-mama started having babies of her own. Great-Aunt Edith passed and Great-Uncle Robert Henry moved in with her family, so back she came, too. I guess Mary #2 needed the help, is what I think.

"Anyway, that's where she's lived her whole life, out on the farm where she isn't even the woman in charge of the house. Her sisters—by that I mean her full sisters—have married and moved out, of course, long ago, and her two brothers have farms of their own now and their own families. All seven of her half-brothers and half-sisters are still young enough to be home, last I heard, but maybe some have moved out by now. One's just a baby, but the oldest girl must be seventeen or so. And there's Mamie, thirty-five years old, and more or less a maid in her own home." Mama stopped and glared at the pillows as if they needed some extra whacking. I was sure only the thought of putting creases into their ironed perfection stopped her.

Turning to me, she said, "I heard you sigh when I said Mamie was coming to visit. I expect you will have some compassion, Mary Ellen. I'm sure she feels for you in your situation. At least you have had your own home, and you will again, and your own husband and your own children to care for, but I don't think Mamie ever will. And she isn't able to get away very often, so let's think of that and behave accordingly."

Mama took a deep breath and said in a softer voice. "You know, just being somewhere where she's truly wanted and treated like she's a little special, well, what a gift that is to give her, at no real trouble to ourselves. She'll even have a room all to herself. Do you have any idea how this must feel like heaven to her?"

By now, I was staring at the tips of my shoes. Mama was right to think I'd not thought about it like that at all. She looked around the room and nodded. "You take care of anything you think needs doing. Maybe make sure the top three drawers in the chest of drawers are dusted out and no old silverfish around in them. I'm going to go make sure we have enough dinner to give her and her brother. I'll make a fresh pan of biscuits, too, so they'll be warm for them. If they want something sweet after, it'll have to be biscuits and molasses. They should be here soon.

I'll tell Tommy and Martha their Aunt Mamie is coming here. I know the older girls will be excited when they get home from school and have that surprise."

I stood there feeling like I did when Mama put me in my place when I was a little girl. I felt ashamed I'd let her see I wasn't too happy about Mamie's visit.

What Mama didn't seem to remember was we visited Mamie's family a few years after her father had remarried. I'd heard about them sending her to the old relatives' home to care for them and then having her back when the great-aunt passed away—just in time to help with all the little children the new stepmother was having and the great-uncle who also lived with them. It wasn't that she was expected to help out that I saw as a problem; no, it was only right to help out your family.

It was the way she was treated. The way she was spoken to when she was present and the way she was referred to when she wasn't. I remember how horrified I'd been by how scornful her stepmother and even her own father had been. It was as if she didn't count for anything because she was *just an old maid.* That's how they referred to her when she wasn't around: an old maid. I had never heard the phrase "second-class citizen" at that point, but that really described how they treated her. Being unmarried and dependent on her family made her an object of ridicule and disdain. She was next to worthless in their eyes.

Even Mary #2, the younger stepmother, looked smug every time she mentioned Mamie. She never had any soft feelings or compassion for her stepdaughter. Instead of seeing her as a potential friend, even as a sister, Mary #2 somehow felt the need to rub

Mamie's nose in her low status and did everything she could to make her feel like a poor relation right there in her own home. That Mamie was older probably made her even more vigilant in making sure she was seen as a lesser member of the household.

As I finished dusting the guest room, remembering how I'd felt all those years ago, I suddenly had a thought: what if Mamie was partly the reason I'd been so determined to marry and start a family of my own when I was so young? Something about her life as a spinster—another word used to describe Mamie, and I wasn't so sure it was better than *old maid*—had truly horrified me. Terrified me, in fact. I'd sworn I would be *not Mamie*, as I thought of it: Not Mamie, not ever. To be Mamie was to be nothing. A living death of drudgery without the consolations of being a wife and mother. A regretted burden who would come to be despised.

I found myself sitting on the floor, still holding the dust rag, leaning against the foot of the bed. My heart was pounding. How had I never thought about that before? And was that why I dreaded seeing Mamie each time I knew we'd meet, which had only been a few times in my life, because her life scared me?

Well, I'd certainly married young and would never be Mamie. I would always have my children with me. I might be a widow now, but I had been married. I could never be called a spinster or an old maid. Everyone respected a widow. And I had my children. I would always be treated with respect. Always. I'd never be looked down on like Mamie. Never sneered at.

Why was I dreading her visit? It was never Mamie herself who bothered me. I hadn't seen Mamie for years, so I didn't really know what she was like. She was five years older than me anyway, so of course as a child I'd not been close to her. I decided I'd mend my ways and welcome her just as Mama and Daddy had welcomed me and the children. After what Mama had told me about Mamie, I felt ashamed I'd been almost as unfair to her as her father and stepmother had been all these years.

I went out and clipped off some rosebuds just coming out on my transplanted bushes. Without warning, my throat closed, and my eyes filled. Had anyone ever cut flowers for Mamie?

The pink rosebuds looked nice in one of Mama's cut-glass vases on Mamie's bedside table. Special. For Mamie.

The children loved their Aunt Mamie. Naturally, she made a fuss over each one, and her delight in them was genuine. There could be no doubt. Tommy was certain she wanted to see the tricks he'd taught Toby or, at least, *thought* he'd taught Toby. I was quite certain that little dog had begging and sitting mastered before we arrived. Martha was sure she'd come to help celebrate her sixth birthday; Leah, to admire her improved cooking skills; Celeste, to rhapsodize over hairstyles in Aunt Sis's old magazines; and Irene, to tell her more family stories. Only Clarence, soon to have his first birthday in June, didn't seem to have expectations other than Aunt Mamie join his group of devout worshippers. And, of course, she did exactly that, kissing the soles of his little chubby feet enough to satisfy even his cheerful, if nearly bottomless, appetite for adoration. She was an avid audience for the other children as well, so cries of "Aunt Mamie, watch me do *this*!" were a constant refrain around the house.

Sunday, May 19, arrived and the celebrating of Martha's birthday began. Mama made Martha's favorite breakfast of sausage, bacon, and pancakes topped with last summer's peach preserves. I hurried the younger children along so we could all pile into Daddy's truck to get to the church service on time. We were lucky to have such a beautiful spring day for the trip. Mamie sat in the cab between Mama, who held Clarence, and Daddy. I sat with the other children in the truck bed, on an old quilt we put there to keep our clothes nice. The girls and I had to hang onto our hats the entire ride.

I saw Mama have a word with Mr. Prince, the minister, before the church service started, and much to our delight, Martha's birthday was announced from the pulpit. The entire congregation of about a hundred souls turned and called out, "Happy birthday!" to her, as he had her stand. Martha blushed, but it was clear she was thrilled. She sat back down, and I felt she glowed all through the sermon. I reached over and squeezed Mama's hand, and she looked as happy as Martha.

It occurred to me this was the second time in her short life Martha had been the center of attention of an entire congregation. One hot summer Sunday years ago at our old church, we'd had a visiting preacher for the service. I guess he was unusually impressed with the sound of his own voice, and he kept on preaching and pounding the podium and calling on the congregation to give up the ways of the devil. These evil ways included dancing, and most especially, dancing with the wives of other men, something he said he'd seen with his very own eyes. I wondered just how often he went to Lumina or some other dance hall to have made such a study of it. He had taken careful note of just where men were likely to rest their hands on their descended-from-Jezebel dance partners. He did not approve.

He sidetracked to the sins of jazz music (it was evil even when not accompanied by dancing, apparently) and lost the rapt attention of the congregation he'd won by detailing the misbehavior of dancing couples. The sermon continued on and on for over twenty minutes past our usual time to head home for Sunday dinner. The crowded sanctuary was so airless and stifling that I, almost seven months along with Tommy, thought I might faint. I'm sure I wasn't the only woman wondering if her pork roast or stewed chicken would be cinders by the time we got back home.

He reached the end of a particularly long, loud rant and stopped to take a breath. Martha, hungry, tired, and at only three showing a wonderful understanding of both time and timing, leapt up onto the pew and, at the top of her lungs, demanded, "Let's go *home*!"

Tom and I froze for a moment. But then from all over the sanctuary, men, and maybe a few women, called out "Amen" so firmly that the preacher wrapped it up right quick. Martha got plenty of smiles and waves as we left, but not from the visiting preacher, who acted like he didn't see us as we walked past him at the church door.

Tom and I laughed every time we thought of sweet Martha doing that. She never did like to be overheated.

Now, more than three years after that happy memory, the congregation members of this different church came up after the service to shake Martha's hand and wish her happy birthday yet again. As we rode home, our hats in our hands on this return trip, Martha put her head in my lap and napped, worn out from the excitement. Tommy was far from tired and kept trying to lean his blond head outside of the truck bed to catch even more of the breeze. Irene reached over and pulled him back just as I was becoming alarmed he was going to tip right out onto his head. He sat back on the quilt with an irritated eye roll for his sister, then turned to me and asked, "Mama, why didn't the preacher wish Leah and Irene a happy birthday last month?"

I saw Leah look over and realized she'd been wondering, too. "Because their birthdays didn't fall on a Sunday this year, honey. Mr. Prince usually just does that for someone having a birthday that very day, or maybe someone who is having a special birthday that week."

Tommy thought for a minute. "Why would some birthdays be more special than others?"

"Well, a few weeks ago, Mr. Jones turned eighty. That's a big birthday. And a month or so ago, Mrs. Lewis turned 100 years old. That is very rare. Not too many people make it to that age. So, Mr. Prince wished them happy birthday from the pulpit, to mark how special those birthdays were."

Tommy turned his head back to the wind. "I bet he doesn't think he'll have to do that for Mrs. Lewis again next year."

It took me a moment to get his meaning, and then my eyes must have nearly popped out of my head. Where was my baby boy, and who was this little smart aleck that seemed to be taking his place? Irene, Celeste, and Leah looked as shocked as I did, and then fell against each other laughing. I just pressed my lips together; no need to set a bad example or encourage that boy, who already had a little smile on his face thanks to his sisters' reaction. But I had to admit, silently, he had a point.

Back home, we had Martha's birthday dinner. Mamie made an entire pan of baby biscuits, as we called them, small biscuits no bigger than a quarter. Mama did that for me and my sisters as we grew up, and I still remembered how wonderful such tiny things had seemed. They were only for children, and no grownups could have any, which made them even more special. They were just large enough for a dot of butter and a smidgen of preserves, and then the whole crusty thing could go into your mouth. Mamie, who surely had a lifetime of practice, knew exactly how long to bake them so they weren't too dry. She'd added some mashed baked sweet potatoes from yesterday's dinner to the mix, so each biscuit was a beautiful orange color all the way through. I thought I could taste a little nutmeg in there, too, for she'd made a pan of normal-sized biscuits for the adults from the same mixture. I knew Leah and Irene, my girls most interested in cooking, were going to remember them for the future. So was I.

Mamie was very discreet about her snuff dipping. She excused herself every now and then, no doubt to spit out tobacco juice in her bedroom. In bringing some towels to her room for the washstand, I noticed a dark blue mug tucked behind one of the framed photos on the chest of drawers. I assumed it was used as a spittoon, although it seemed doubtful she spat from a distance, as I'd seen years ago in cowboy picture shows. I just hoped she wouldn't forget to take the mug with her when she went. What if she forgot? Would we have to clean it and mail it to her? I decided I could help her out by giving her room a final check to make sure she had all her belongings when her brother arrived. It was only what a good hostess would do for a guest.

I spotted Tommy watching her mouth once. His little forehead wrinkled up in concentration. I caught his eye and gave a stern headshake.

Daddy must have seen that exchange. "Tommy, son, why don't you come help me feed Molly? You know she likes to see you." Diverted, Tommy raced out to see our old mule. I think Daddy had a word with him, and although Tommy always paid rapt attention when his Aunt Mamie spoke, he never asked any embarrassing questions.

Like Tommy, I was fascinated by this most unfeminine of habits. I noticed she didn't have the small telltale lump in her cheek or bottom lip all the time. It seemed she was content to dip snuff about three times a day, and only have it in her mouth for thirty minutes or so each time. And I couldn't help but notice she went outside several times a day to admire the blooming flowers and shrubs in the yard, and she liked to take the blue mug with her. I hoped the plants benefited from tobacco juice, as I was sure they were getting baptized with it on a regular basis. At least the mug wasn't sitting out in her room full of the smelly stuff. I shuddered to think what Tommy would do if he'd ever found it.

Apart from that, I hardly noticed her habit at all.

Mamie's brother was due to come for her by midafternoon on Monday after Martha's birthday, so we agreed the children could stay up late for her last night. Martha, of course, saw it as yet another way to celebrate her birthday, and we didn't tell her otherwise.

The moon, although several nights away from being full, was so bright we could see each other clearly as we sat on the front porch. Mamie started by asking the girls if they wanted to know how to find out who they were going to marry. Even six-year-old Martha was keen to learn.

"Well, darlin's, I know of two ways. First one's the easiest. You have to sit alone in front of a mirror at midnight, with only one candle lit in the room, and brush your hair until sparks crackle from it. Keep your eyes on the mirror, and your future husband's face will appear there. I do think this might work best for girls who haven't bobbed their hair, though."

Martha preened a little and patted her long braids as her bobbed-haired sisters groaned.

"Fashion has its price," said Mamie, too complacently, in my opinion.

"The second way will work, too, but it's harder. You have to do this with a sister or a close friend. With only one candle lit in the room, you both have to cook a supper, all of it, doing everything together, even both holding the same serving spoon at the same time. You set the kitchen table for two people. Oh, I almost forgot—you have to hang a horseshoe over the door frame that leads into the kitchen. And you have to fix this supper so it's ready right at the stroke of midnight. Did I say you two girls cannot speak a word all the while you're doing all this? And you cannot laugh! If you do all that, right on the stroke of midnight, two men will open the back door into your kitchen, pass under the horseshoe, sit down, eat the supper, then go back out the way they came. They won't say a word. Those are your future husbands."

Leah wrinkled her forehead. "But how will you know which one is yours?"

Mamie shook her head. "Well, that's a problem with that method. But then, I've never heard of two girls who could do all that without laughing, so I suppose it's not the biggest problem. At least you'll narrow it down if you can follow all the rules."

Tommy just looked annoyed. "Why d'ya even care? And who would ever want to marry my sisters?"

The three older girls fell to discussing which method they wanted to try first, as Martha and her two brothers started nodding off and soon got tucked into their beds.

Mamie was quite a storyteller and had entertained us each evening during her visit. Tonight, though, she started sharing her grandmother's stories about the Civil War.

"Grandmama said those Yankee soldiers was just as mean as they could be when they come to the farmhouse. All the men was gone off to soldier, don't you know. Some of the neighbor women'd come running to her house when they heard the Yankees was coming down the road, and they was all huddled together like, with the children crying and all."

I saw my mother look over at my father, and he shifted his weight on the porch swing, looking like he was about to say something, but Mamie kept on.

"And do you know what they did when they got there, those Yankees? They went inside to Grandmama's pantry, and they took every single thing they could carry. Every single bit of food Grandmama needed to feed her children. Yes, sir. She said some of them throwed down glass jars of preserves and such and made a big old mess in her kitchen."

Irene, Celeste, and Leah sat there, each one with eyes big as saucers. I hoped Mamie stopped with these stories, and soon. I tried to divert her.

"Mamie, tell us how Emmy's wedding went. What did she wear?" I could hardly remember when this distant relation had gotten married, but it was the only thing I could come up with that might get Mamie's mind off the Yankees and her grandmother's stories.

"I'll be tickled pink to tell y'all 'bout it, but first let me finish telling about what happened next. You see, there was this officer—he was on a horse, don't you know—rode his horse right into the house! You'll never guess what he did next. No, you won't. I'll tell you, though. He rode his horse right up the stairs to the second floor, if'n you can believe it. And what did he do then?"

I hoped the girls wouldn't have dreams about this, but Mamie seemed to be oblivious to their horrified expressions.

"I'll tell you what he did. He took the mattress off'n Grandmama's bed, dragged it down the stairs behind his horse, into the front yard. And then he rode his horse back and forth over that mattress and those feathers flew. He done that to every mattress they had in the house. Every single one! Up and down and up and down those stairs. Dragging those mattresses to the front yard and running them over. She said it looked like snow in the front yard, and all the soldiers stood around, pointing their guns at the women and children, and laughing their fool heads off."

She stopped for a breath.

"Aunt Mamie, how horrible!" Irene was truly shocked. Celeste and Leah seemed unable to do anything except nod their heads.

"Well, Mamie, I suppose they were right lucky if that's all that happened," my mother said.

"Aunt Ella, I sure do wish I could say that were all they done." Mamie shook her head sadly.

I had a feeling she didn't wish that at all. Not one little bit.

We waited while she took a sip of her iced tea and cleared her throat. She sure knew how to keep her audience hanging on.

"I think these girls need to be heading to bed now," I tried to interrupt, but Mamie was not to be stopped until her story was done.

"No, the last thing that officer did as they was all leaving the yard was trot his horse by one of the neighbor women, lift his sword up…" My mother gasped and gripped Daddy's arm. He stood up from the swing just as Mamie finished her tale, "and he sliced off her," she tapped her left breast, "and stuck it with his sword and put it on the gatepost as he left." She finished with a dramatic flourish.

My first thought, when I was finally able to have one, was how glad I was little Martha and Tommy were in bed asleep. I looked at my three older girls and saw nothing but horror and shock on their young faces. Even Mama and Daddy couldn't speak.

Mamie took in our reactions and nodded. "Yes, it was plum horrible. That's what they was like. I could tell you more besides…"

My own civil war between my lifelong training to always be polite, especially to a guest, and my duty to protect my children was over. I found my voice, and it was on the sharp side. "No, Mamie, I think we've had enough, thank you. I certainly hope we don't all have nightmares."

I attempted to put some sugar in my tone to counter the sharpness. "Your poor grandmama, left with no food and all the mattresses spoiled." I tried to turn the girls' attention to the less awful part of Mamie's story. "I'm sure all kinds of horrible things go on in war, especially when it happens right around you. We need to be grateful we don't have to live through anything like that, don't we? Thank you for reminding us of that, Mamie."

Mamie seemed put out at first, but then pleased with my final comments. I could feel my temper coming off the boil.

Before she could say anything more, Daddy spoke. "Well, ladies, I think I've stayed up past my bedtime. Those critters are going to want to be fed and watered early tomorrow no matter how little sleep I get, so I'm heading to bed. Toby, you already done everything you need to do for tonight, so let me put you in with Tommy. Ella, you coming?" The little dog and Mama both jumped up to follow Daddy inside.

I don't think Mamie had heard him speak as many words in her entire visit, and she looked a little surprised. The three girls were still rigid in their rockers, and I touched Leah on the shoulder. "Girls, let's get you ready for bed. We'll have to hear about Cousin Emmy's wedding tomorrow morning at breakfast."

All three stood, clutching each other's hands, and followed me inside, Mamie trailing behind us. As she went to her own room, I followed the girls into theirs. Speaking softly so I didn't wake Martha, I said, "Girls, your Aunt Mamie might have exaggerated that story, or maybe her mother or her grandmother did. People like to tell stories like that, just like they enjoy hearing ghost stories. It's not something you need to dwell on. All right?" They nodded. "And I know you know not to tell any little bit of those stories to Martha and Tommy, right?"

There was a soft chorus of "Yes, ma'am." They followed with a more enthusiastic, "Yes, Mama," agreeing not to tell the stories to the little ones.

I kissed each of them and said what I always say at bedtime. "Night-night, sweethearts. Say your prayers and have sweet dreams. Your mama loves you." I closed the bedroom door behind me. I hoped we'd all have sweet dreams, but it seemed doubtful.

CHAPTER 11

Honeymoon &
a Nightmare

Friday, May 31, 1929

The first year after someone's death was full of small, unofficial anniversaries, such as, "this time last year we were having Christmas, and Tom was handing out the presents." Or "this time last year we were wondering when Clarence would decide to be born." But today was an official anniversary. Sixteen years ago, Tom and I got married.

I remembered how starry-eyed and innocent I'd been. Growing up on a farm, I knew how animals mated to produce their offspring, but I was confident it must be quite different for humans. Probably an all-night cuddle in our marriage bed would result in God sending a little baby to be born a few months later. Something like that. Even when my mother tried to prepare me for my wedding night, I was too excited to pay much attention to her hesitant and vague explanations. Of all that she said, it was her final comment as she hugged my shoulders before leaving the room that made it through my romantic haze. "You'll get used to it."

I'd had a feeling then I should have listened more closely or, even better, asked one of my married sisters. But I was certain I knew all I needed to know: Tom loved me, and I loved him.

Much to my parents' surprise, Tom had arranged for us to have a short honeymoon. After cutting our wedding cake back at my parents' house, one of his brothers drove us to Front Street in Wilmington, where we caught the beach trolley to Wrightsville Beach.

I'd only ridden the trolley once in my life, when my father took our family to the beach for the day. The trolley was the only way to get to Wrightsville, an island, except by boat. Idella was already married, but the rest of us had a wonderful excursion to the seaside. That was in 1910, and I'd been eleven years old. It was the first time I saw the ocean. I remember being disappointed. Somehow, I had thought it would be bigger. I'm not sure how that would have been possible, though. Maybe I thought I'd be able to see all of it at once somehow. I also remembered all the sand in my delicate parts on the endless trip back home.

My second trolley ride to the beach was as a married lady, only four months from turning fifteen.

I kept thinking that in a few days when we took the return trip, I'd know all there was to know about being married and whatever it was my mother had been trying to tell me. I alternated touching my hat and tugging on my white crocheted gloves until Tom reached over and took my hands, icy despite the heat of the day, in his warm ones.

As we neared the coast, the trolley tracks rose over channels of water snaking through tall green grasses. I asked Tom, "What is that smell?"

Before he could answer, a young man wearing a flat straw hat I later learned was called a "boater," turned around in his seat in front of us and answered, "That's the smell of the wetlands, miss. My daddy always says it stinks so good." He laughed and went on, "It's the smell of all sorts of water critters dying and new ones being born, is what he says. Fecund, that's the word he uses. I guess it's a twenty-five-cent word for fertile." We thanked him, and he turned back to the young lady sitting next to him.

I turned to Tom and mouthed, "Fecund."

"Guess we learned a new word today, Mrs. Heath." His eyes were as warm as his hands.

Below us, we saw a small boat with two men fishing; they waved, and everyone on that side of the trolley waved back. Every single person on the trolley seemed to be happy. I supposed it might be impossible to be on your way to the beach and not be happy.

When we arrived at the last stop, there was the Lumina Pavilion in all its splendor. Still daylight, it seemed magnificent even without the added glory of its tens of thousands of electric lights that would later illuminate the night. People were strolling all around. On the Sound side, sailboats glided by on Banks Channel, and children screamed in joy on the large swings set up in the shallow water off the Sound-side pier.

As we climbed the steps to our seafront hotel next to the Lumina, I could see a vast crowd of people lounging on the warm sand of the beach in front of the three-story pavilion and wading into the cold Atlantic. A ticket on the beach trolley also paid for a bathing costume rental from Lumina, and they weren't going to let that go to waste. It was early summer yet, and even I knew the water would still be frigid. I shivered.

We approached the hotel's front door, and the uniformed fellow standing there opened it for us, saying, "Welcome to the Tides Hotel, madam, sir." I was now "madam," much to my delight, as well as relief he had not thought I was Tom's daughter. I hadn't realized I was worried about that.

Tom walked up to the front desk to check us in. When the clerk handed him the pen to sign in, Tom hesitated. We hadn't started working on his reading and writing lessons yet, and I knew he was caught off-guard by the need to write both of our names and where we were from. I smiled and said, "Tom, dear, why don't you let me practice signing my new name?"

The hotel clerk beamed at us both. "Newlyweds? Oh my, yes, I see!" He took in Tom's boutonniere and my pink rose corsage. Also, no doubt, my pink face. "How wonderful! Congratulations, Mr. Heath and very best wishes, Mrs. Heath!" He put extra emphasis on the "Mrs. Heath," for here was a man who knew a new bride couldn't hear her new title and new name often enough. Of course, I blushed even more, and the two men, apparently now the best of friends, shook hands.

"I believe we can make your stay here even more special. The Honeymoon Suite is available, and I shall simply put you in there." At Tom's slight hesitation, he continued, "At no additional cost, of course, sir."

We thanked him and turned to go to our room, Tom refusing the assistance of the bellhop, much to that person's affronted dignity. As we neared the stairs to our floor, the clerk leaned out over the desk and called, "Enjoy your stay!" I had been wrong in thinking my face couldn't be any redder.

We had supper in the dining room there. I was astonished at how expensive everything seemed, but then I couldn't remember eating in a restaurant before. Tom took the menu from the waiter, and then, after he left, said, "I'll have whatever you're getting. Tell me and I'll tell the waiter when he comes back."

I had no idea what some of the food was that was listed on the menu. To make sure we knew what we'd be getting, we ordered fried fish and shrimp, and it came with coleslaw and cornbread. There was even half a lemon on each of the two plates, in cheesecloth tied with a red ribbon. I'd never seen anything so fancy on a dinner plate. After studying how other people were eating, I figured out we weren't to unwrap the lemon. Just squeeze it on the fish and let the seeds go into the cheesecloth. Maybe people who went to hotels didn't expect to have to pick out lemon seeds from their food. Not at those prices.

I worried Tom was spending too much money on our honeymoon.

We could hear the waves hitting the sand and what seemed to be a separate, strange sort of roar coming from the ocean outside the windows of the dining room. The curtains kept billowing out into the room with the breeze coming off the water, and even with the heat of the day still lingering, it felt refreshing and without the mugginess we'd have at home. That "fecund" smell had disappeared once we were on the island. Here I seemed to smell the scent of water and hot sand in the breeze.

Tom said we wouldn't like the drinking water—"beach water," he called it—so we got sweet tea, and that came with a lemon slice on the side of each tall glass and lots of chipped ice. I didn't see any seeds in the lemon slices; I guess someone in the kitchen had the job of picking them out. I wondered if that was all they did, or if maybe the same person chipped the ice. I had three glasses of sweet tea. I couldn't believe how thirsty I was and how delicious it seemed. Tom said it was the salty air that did that.

I started to think about needing an outhouse or a chamber pot eventually, and how I'd manage with Tom around. Being married had some difficulties I'd not thought of before.

As we ate, I watched the other diners. They were all very well dressed and seemed comfortable talking to the waiters and asking for things that weren't already on the table. Tom and I both would rather have had hot-pepper vinegar to put on our fish instead of lemon, but neither one of us felt we should ask for it since it wasn't offered.

I wondered how many of them would be headed over to Lumina for the dancing. Tom had told me to bring a dress for that, so I knew we'd be going tonight. That suited me fine. No need to go to bed too early, I thought. Dancing was good exercise, I was sure. Maybe a walk on the beach at some point. I told myself no doubt the moonlight on the water would be beautiful. I wondered if they'd be showing a movie on the big screen I'd spotted from our room's window. Right in the surf, it was! We could watch some of that when we weren't dancing. It would probably be very late when we came back to the hotel. So late we'd probably go right to sleep with the sound of the waves out our window.

We danced at the Lumina to a band playing in a shell-shaped alcove, a mirrored ball twirling over the dance floor, dazzling with the reflected lights. Several men tried to cut in as we danced, but Tom told each one we'd been married that very day, and he wasn't inclined to share. Each man had to shake his hand and wish us happy. It was lovely. So lovely that I didn't care my dress wasn't as nice as most of the other ladies. I didn't see anyone who looked like they might be a farmer or a farmer's wife. No, most of these folk were from Wilmington or other cities and probably worked in banks or owned their own businesses. Some of them looked very wealthy, so wealthy I doubted they worked at all. Some even sounded like they were from up North. Another time I would have felt out of place, but this night, Tom and I danced in a bubble of happiness, and I didn't care about anyone else.

At the intermission, we went downstairs, and Tom got us lemonades. I asked for a second one. I couldn't seem to drink enough. Then we took off our shoes and walked out onto the sand.

"Look, Mary!" Tom said. "That's Charlie Chaplin up there." We stood watching the enormous screen out in the surf, playing a silent picture show now it was dark. Or, it would be, if all those lights on Lumina weren't so bright.

After a few minutes, we walked down the beach and turned back to take it all in. I gasped. On top of the three-story building, the word "Lumina" was lit up in huge letters. Now I understood how sailors could see it from miles out in the ocean. It wasn't only the sign that was covered in light bulbs; the entire building was edged with strings of lights on each level. I'd never seen anything like that magic palace by the sea.

At midnight, we returned to the hotel with the half-moon beginning its rise out of the ocean. Back in our room, I went to the window; a moonlit path rippled from the horizon to the lacy edges of the waves not far from where I was standing. The sea was falling asleep, the lulling laps of water whispering to the stranded shells on the shoreline. I exhaled and felt my shoulders and belly relax, only then realizing how tense they'd become. I licked my lips and tasted the sea salt. Tom came up behind me and put his arms around my waist.

As kind and loving as Tom was, it still came as a shock that although we females were expected to permit no more than a quick kiss before being married, on the night of our wedding, we were expected to allow intimacies we didn't even knew existed until then. I couldn't believe every married woman I'd ever met was party to that kind of behavior. My own *mother*? Needless to say, I tried very hard not to imagine such things.

I was a bit put out Mama hadn't tried harder to make me listen to her.

The next morning, I sat up in bed and watched Tom shaving with the hot water the maid brought. He asked her to bring up more so I could bathe.

"I'll be downstairs out on the porch waiting for you," he said as he bent to kiss me. "I don't mind sitting there a spell and watching the waves. Then we'll get us some breakfast."

The maid came, giving me a saucy wink I didn't appreciate. I was sure she bit back a grin when I didn't smile back at her. She hurried out after she emptied the water into the hip bath behind a screen in the corner, and I gingerly settled in to soak. A small bar of soap in the shape of a heart was there; it smelled of lavender. I looked down at myself and wondered if a baby was already on the way. I wasn't sure if I wanted that yet or not. I wasn't sure of anything that morning.

Marriage was turning out a lot like my first time seeing the ocean; I thought there would be more to it. But maybe you couldn't expect to see all of it when you were only beginning to wade in. I hoped Mama was right and that I'd get used to it, all of it. Including having to pee when Tom was in the room.

Sixteen years later, I had to smile at that younger version of myself. As Tom had said that last night on the porch, I was innocent. Now, at more than double my age as a bride, I felt even older. Seven births, the loss of a baby, the loss of my husband, and now the overwhelming problem of finding a way to support myself and the children.

I realized I was marking time: focusing on the day-to-day tasks of laundry, especially the daily need to wash diapers and feeding everyone, as well as trying to take on more of the housework and our vegetable garden so my parents wouldn't be overburdened. Even though he started renting out most of his land several years earlier, Daddy continued to plant a garden big enough for his and Mama's needs through the year. I was sure he had expanded that space to provide for the additional mouths it had to feed, which meant a larger area to plant and hoe throughout the hot months. I helped as much as I could, but six children, three of them so young, took a lot of attention. I feared Daddy was going to overdo it.

Although Mama still had beautiful posture, it was clear her knees were bothering her more than ever. She had taken in the last few months to needing a cane by the end of the day and had to sit down several times while cooking a meal or ironing. Her days of helping Daddy in the garden, walking on the uneven sandy furrows between the plants, were over.

Still, the children had been sick throughout the winter, even after the measles outbreak cleared up: the usual colds and coughs, but those also came with the worry they could go into the chest and be much more serious or even deadly, as with my Alice. I didn't know how I could hope to keep a job, assuming I was fortunate enough to ever find one, when my children would surely get ill and need nursing in the years to come. Or how many times I could not go to my job before I'd be fired.

With Clarence still nursing, I didn't know how I could take on a job anyway. The doctors warned weaning a baby too soon was dangerous for the child's health, but I had five other children I had to think about, too. And a shrinking bank balance, along with two parents who seemed to be declining in front of my very eyes. I'd been lucky I could come to them. I couldn't imagine what I would have done without their offering refuge to me and my children. All my sisters had houses full of children, with more always arriving, and now Jim, Janie's bereaved husband, had five he was trying to manage while working his farm. I knew Mama wished she could help him more.

There always seemed to be something that needed my attention, and, I had to admit, I was using that as an excuse to myself for not thinking about the future. For every urgent reason to get a job, there seemed to be an equally urgent reason why I could not. At least, not now.

I was not about to even think of asking Tom's brothers for help. Never. Never.

I needed to plan, to act, and I couldn't hide from it anymore, but equally, I felt unable to do anything yet. I was caught in limbo.

The night of my sixteenth wedding anniversary, I dreamed of harvesting corn with Tom. The rows were so long I could barely see down to the end of them by the edge of the woods. Tom was ahead of me, a feed sack with rope handles slung over one shoulder, dropping ears of corn from the row on the left into it as he moved along. He kept turning to smile at me, a cool summer morning making our work pleasant for once.

I followed, a long leather strap connecting my belt with a light woven basket on the ground, allowing me to pull the basket without having to bend over and lift it. It slid behind me in the sandy furrow easily at first, then got heavier as I worked down the row to my right. I usually dropped the ears into the basket behind me without looking, but I noticed the increased heaviness and turned to see if I needed to empty it. To my surprise, now another basket was tied to the first one. Both were empty.

I kept pulling off ears of corn and tossing them into the baskets, which filled up finally.

Tom called something to me, but he was far ahead of me now, and I couldn't make out what he was saying. Again, the baskets I pulled seemed heavier, yet they were empty when I looked back. Then I saw a third basket had appeared. Alarmed, I tried to get Tom's attention, but he was beyond hearing me, his figure now small in the distance. I kept working, looking back more often, only to find baskets kept appearing in the chain of baskets until there were six. Heavier and heavier and harder and harder to pull along, and still they would be empty when I looked back at them. Finally, turning my head the other way, I realized I could no longer see anything of Tom.

"Tom! Where are you? I need you!" I felt panic beginning to rise in my throat. I couldn't understand what was happening. Then, as was the way in dreams, it all changed. Instead of a summer morning and a field full of tender Early Queen white corn with soft, green husks, it was late on a fall afternoon, and the stalks were a shriveled yellow brown. This was dried corn we'd use for animal feed, with crackling husks that chafed and cut into my hands. The sky darkened; the wind picked up. I needed to get the corn in before the storm hit. It was vital, but I could barely get the baskets to budge. I needed Tom to help me, but he was nowhere to be seen. I looked back yet again; the baskets were no longer thin, woven lath, but the large cast-iron cauldrons used during hog butchering. All empty.

I was screaming "Tom!" in my dream as I woke sitting up in my bed, panting, my hair and nightgown soaked with sweat.

Gradually, my heart stopped racing as I realized it had been a dream. But the question and the despair remained. I whimpered into the night air, "Tom, you left us, but I need you."

Then icy fingers seemed to squeeze my heart as I remembered the cauldrons. I could understand now why there were six of them. And why they were so heavy.

But I couldn't understand why they were all empty.

CHAPTER 12

Mr. Meyer

Saturday, June 29, 1929

I'd started trying to wean Clarence around his first birthday in early June, but he knew what he wanted, and it wasn't pap. When I managed to get some solid food down him, he cried with cramping. I wanted to cry too each time I changed his diaper and saw what it was doing to his insides, not to mention what I was going to have to scrub away. Dr. Webb said Clarence would need more time nursing to let his system develop, and to begin again in a few weeks.

I had dark thoughts about Dr. Webb having never nursed a teething baby. Looking for a job and a place to live would have to wait a while longer.

Meanwhile, my mother came back from church one Sunday, humming with excitement. I'd stayed home with an unhappy Clarence, who'd continued letting me know weaning wasn't in the near future. Mama waited until the girls and Tommy had gone to change out of their church clothes. Then she joined me in the kitchen. I'd just put Clarence down for a nap and was warming up our Sunday dinner. Mama started setting the table.

"Mary, it's too bad you had to miss church today."

I turned to her, thinking she was criticizing. "Mama, you know I couldn't take Clarence out."

"Honey, I know. What I meant was you didn't get to meet a new church member." She set a plate down and looked over at me. I knew there must be something special about this person to get her eyebrow in that position.

"I just mean," she went on, "everybody wanted to meet him. He certainly is a fine-looking man, probably about Tom's age, come to think of it. Well, maybe a few years older. Anyway, he's inherited his bachelor uncle's farm only about five miles from here. You remember old Mr. Brewer? This is his sister's son."

I thought a moment if I'd met Mr. Brewer and conjured up a picture of a frail, elderly man. I'd only seen him a few times. Probably it was just too much for him to hitch up his mule to his cart to get there, although his neighbors sometimes brought him to services. He had seemed nice enough, but somewhat vague with old age. "Yes, I believe I do. Did he pass?" I was busy dishing up field peas and fatback in the serving bowl.

"Yes. In April, I believe, poor man." Mama paused respectfully for a moment, then hurried on with the more exciting news. "His nephew, a Mr. Meyer, is a widower." She said this in an off-hand manner, and added, "Mr. Brewer owned a big farm. He had to rent out the land to be farmed. The same as us when he got too old to handle it. It's a lot of land."

I set the bowl on the table and gave her a look. "Mama, I hope you aren't thinking what I think you're thinking. Tom hasn't been gone even a year." I suddenly felt exhausted.

"Mary, how could you think I'd forget?" Mama was all innocence. She rounded the table and finished setting the plates down. "I'm just letting you know about our very handsome new church member who happens to be single. That's all." She gave a little huff.

I laughed and pulled the large platter of fried chicken out of the warming oven. Mama had done most of the cooking before they left for church, so I could tend to Clarence.

"And does this eligible widower, who now owns a lot of land, have any children?"

Mama started setting out the silverware. Before she could answer, I realized those girls were dawdling. I called to them to hurry up and help us set out our dinner. Choruses of "Yes, ma'am," "Yes, Mama," and "Yes, Mother"—that last was Celeste, of course—came from down the hall.

Mama examined a fork she was holding, wiping an imaginary smudge off with her apron. "Well, his children, all girls, mind you, are older than yours, but not too much older. Two of them are married and have two babies each already back in South Carolina, of course, where Mr. Meyer and his younger daughters just moved from. He hardly looks old enough to be a granddaddy! I think he said the oldest married daughter is nineteen. His youngest two girls are twins, a year older than Irene, so fourteen or thereabouts. The oldest one at home is almost sixteen. I reckon they'll all be getting married not too long from now, a few years at the most. He'll be on his big farm all alone, don't you know."

I nodded to myself. "Mama, how did you learn all that so soon?" I had a clear picture of all the mothers with girls needing a husband, and, no doubt, many of the girls themselves, ambushing this man after the service ended.

Daddy walked into the kitchen from the backyard, carrying a handful of tomatoes and cucumbers he'd just picked for our dinner. Toby, having escorted him safely from the garden, raced off to find Tommy. Daddy had heard what we were talking about.

"Mary Ellen, your mama and those other mamas all but beat the details out of the poor man. He didn't have a moment to breathe hardly. Us men could just squeeze in long enough to shake his hand before we got edged out by another mama working herself into the group. I skedaddled out of there fast." Daddy laughed as he went over to the sink and washed the vegetables. "Now, there's a man who won't be without a wife for very long."

He pulled out a bowl and started slicing the cucumbers into it. "Ella, were you ever on the little pier Mary and Tom had by the Sound when they were crabbing?"

Mama just looked at him. The change of topic didn't fool her. She knew he wasn't ready to stop teasing her yet.

"Well, see, they'd tie a chicken bone to a piece of string for bait and let it go into the water for a while. One time I was out there with Tom, and when he pulled up the string, I'll be if there weren't a whole line of crabs, each clamped onto the other, fighting over one little drumstick bone." He splashed white vinegar into the bowl over the cucumbers. "And poor Mr.

Meyer don't know it, but he's a right meaty chicken bone, just dangling there. Yes, sir." He kept laughing to himself.

Mama glared at his back. In an injured tone, she said, "We were just being friendly and letting him know we were interested."

Daddy managed to laugh and snort at the same time. "Oh, I'm pretty sure he got that idea, Ella. Don't you worry none. He knows you are all very interested." He shook his head, still laughing.

Irene, walking in with Martha, said, "Those twins told me their mama was real sick for years and couldn't even get out of bed for the last year or so she was alive. She hasn't been gone but a few months. They both had tears in their eyes, and I felt right sorry for them. Their family just moved here in May, and they don't know anybody at all."

She put her arms around my waist. All my children clung to me more now that Tom was gone, and I was sure meeting girls who'd recently lost their mother had deepened her fear of losing me. I kissed her forehead and realized suddenly she was only a couple of inches shorter than me. When had that happened? I looked at her as she pulled away to go help her grandmother and saw that her old dress was pulling across the bust and hips. My girl was growing up too fast, too fast. And she needed new clothes. And shoes, no doubt.

As I turned to Martha, I noticed the sound of a ball hitting the packed dirt out back. Leah had gotten her heart's desire for her birthday back in April—a basketball. Daddy had rigged up an old bottomless basket to the side of the barn for her to practice her throwing, and Tommy was always willing to run after it for her when it bounced away. That girl and her brother must have slipped out the front door and gone around to the back to play. I looked out the back screen door. Sure enough, there they were.

"Leah! Didn't I say you girls were to help set out our dinner? Put that down, wash your hands there at the pump, and get on in here, young lady. Tommy, same goes for you." Honestly, if it wasn't one thing, it was another. And where was Celeste? Mooning over Aunt Sis's magazines, no doubt. She'd mailed some new ones and Celeste couldn't look at them enough.

"Irene, go get Celeste. Tell her if I have to come get her, she won't have any magazines to look at for a month." I sighed.

I knew I was taking my irritation with Mama out on my children. I just wished she could understand I still felt married to Tom.

✾

The next Sunday, Mama couldn't wait for us to get to church. Mr. Meyer was easy to spot in the dozen or so clusters of people talking outside before the service began; his dark head rose from the center of an excited crowd of women and girls, although his face was blocked by the ladies' hats.

I stayed back, holding Clarence. He was having a good day with his tummy, and I'd decided to take a chance going to church for the first time in several weeks. Mama gave me a meaningful look and tilted her head towards the group, but I turned to Daddy. "Let's get a pew near the back so I can leave easily if Clarence fusses too much."

"Of course, baby girl, I understand. It's a little early in the day for chicken, even a tasty drumstick." He grinned as I shook my head at him. All week, Daddy kept teasing Mama about her hopes of a romance between Mr. Meyer and me. Not that she admitted she had such hopes, of course.

We got settled in the pew and were joined by the rest of the children and Mama, who had a satisfied smile on her face. I soon found out why. As most of the congregation worked their way into the church, three teenage girls walked down the aisle with the dark-haired man I'd seen at the center of the female crowd outside. This time I could only see the back of his head, but he seemed as tall as Tom, if broader in the shoulders.

I thought I'd have to wait until after the service to see if Mama was right about him being good-looking, but as they walked past, he turned his head and scanned our row. He smiled and nodded, his gaze passing over Mama, at the end of the pew, the children, and came to rest on me. He stopped and smiled more broadly, dipping his head in greeting. I smiled in return, breathing a sigh of relief when he turned to join his daughters a few pews in front of us.

Well, it seemed Mama knew a fine-looking man when she saw one. In fact, I wasn't sure I'd ever seen a more handsome man. Or one his age, at least, with whiter teeth, and they looked to be his real teeth, too. He'd be attracting the ladies with that smile and those teeth alone, never mind the dark wavy hair and the rest of it.

Although I thought he needed to trim his mustache. It was a wonder I'd even been able to see those teeth. I hoped he didn't take cream in his coffee. I certainly didn't want to think about watching him eating soup. Or eating grits.

I might have shuddered at that thought. Daddy put his arm around me for a moment and gave me a quick hug. Really, I didn't see any reason for that little smirk on his face. We were in a place of worship.

I returned to my thoughts. Yes, the mustache was quite a drawback, and I decided he wasn't as attractive as I'd first thought. After that, naturally, I only thought about the service, although I couldn't help but notice Mr. Meyer's daughters kept peeking back at our pew. And Mr. Meyer had very good posture, even sitting. Also, his wavy hair was very close to being curly.

Myself, I preferred men to have straight hair, wavy at the most, and leave the curls to us ladies.

After the service, we led the exit, being near the rear of the sanctuary. We'd stopped outside to speak to some neighbors, the Blakes, when the conversation tapered off. Mama and the rest of them gazed past my shoulder toward the church door behind me. I turned to see what drew their attention, and there was Mr. Meyer striding toward our little group. Even my children seemed struck silent. I feared Celeste would be openly staring. Irene, standing beside me, made a little sound in her throat and reached for my hand. Apparently, his looks affected even young girls. Fortunately, Tommy was off chasing some of the other little boys, so I didn't have to worry about what he might pipe up with.

"Mr. and Mrs. Evans, Mr. and Mrs. Blake, children, greetings again," he said, nodding at them, then to me, "and you must be Mrs. Heath. I'm Mitch Meyer."

I used Clarence, sitting on my hip, as my unspoken excuse for not extending my hand, but gave a small smile and nodded as well. "Mr. Meyer, happy to make your acquaintance."

"My pleasure entirely, and I want to congratulate you on your fine brood. You must be proud to have so many strong, healthy children." He beamed while I fought down the urge to cluck.

"You are too kind, Mr. Meyer. Likewise, you must be proud of your girls. And I hear you have two others in South Carolina and four grandchildren already. You must be delighted, but sorry to be so far away from them." I was only too aware of the Blakes and my parents, along with my children, watching this exchange. I shifted Clarence to my other hip. He was squirming to get down and crawl in the dirt.

"Yes, my little granddaughters are a joy to me. I just hope my daughters will be able to have sons for their husbands as well. You have such strong boys yourself. That little Tommy is quite the pistol, isn't he? And it looks like this one in your arms is going to be just as full of beans. You really do have your hands full."

At that point, I realized our audience had increased as several ladies stood around us, waiting for their chance to engage his attention. I was happy to make their wishes come true.

"Yes, and my arms. Mr. Meyer, you'll have to excuse me, but I'm going to round up Tommy so we can head on back home. I'm sure you don't want your Sunday dinner to be overcooked either. So nice to meet you."

"Let me go snag up that boy, Mrs. Heath. He's having a big time over there, but I bet I can round him up for you right fast. You and your folks go ahead, and I'll bring him over." He said goodbye to our little group and strode over to where Tommy and his friends were playing catch.

As I turned to head to our truck, I saw Mr. Meyer's three daughters off by themselves to the side of the church, staring in our direction. I gave a little smile and inclined my head, but they didn't appear to see me.

Mama caught up with me and took Clarence from my arms. "Honey, you know I can hold Clarence for you if your arms are tired. We didn't need to rush off." Although her tone was slightly admonishing, she had a small smile that suggested she was pleased about something.

"Now, you thank Mr. Meyer when he brings Tommy over. You know you'd have had to chase that boy down. He's done you a nice favor." Her smile broadened. "Even though those other ladies were waiting to talk to him."

Daddy caught up with us and said, very innocently, "Yes, Mary Ellen. Our dinner isn't going to burn if you take a few minutes to be kind to a grieving man who's new here. You just take your time."

Mama beamed at his helpfulness, but I cut my eyes at him. He saw my expression and chuckled. Grabbing Martha and Leah's hands in his own, he said, "Well, girls, let's mosey on and let the ladies work their magic on Mr. Meyer."

Leah smiled, but Martha took him at his word. "Mama and Grandmama are going to do magic? I never knew they could do that!"

Daddy laughed and said, "Oh, you'll be working magic real soon now yourself. You'll see. But first it will be Irene, then

Celeste and then," he turned to Leah, "our very own Leah Grace will be working magic. And then it will be your turn, Martha Marie. What kind of magic do you suppose you'll do, girls?"

Leah laughed. "My magic is going to be for being the best girl at school in basketball. Maybe even better than the boys!"

As I sped up my steps, I heard Martha's high voice, "Granddaddy, I'm going to spin straw into gold, so Mama don't have to worry about us having enough money. And then she can get me a pony."

A few minutes later, as the children got settled on the old quilt in the back of the truck, Mr. Meyer came around the side of the church building with Tommy on his shoulders. Tommy was smiling and wearing Mr. Meyer's hat. He set Tommy down as they approached the truck.

"That was fun, Mr. Meyer." Tommy was hanging on to the man's hand as if he'd known him all his life, looking up with a happy grin. For a moment, I wondered if Tommy could remember his father carrying him like that. At only four years old, those eight months since Tom's death must have seemed so long ago that his father might have been only an idea rather than a memory to him by now.

Mr. Meyer smiled at Tommy, took his hat back, and lifted him up into the truck bed. After thanking Mr. Meyer, I started to get into the truck with my parents and Clarence.

Mr. Meyer walked up to where Daddy and I stood by the truck door. "Mrs. Heath, maybe our families can get together for a picnic soon. With school out, my girls don't have any friends to visit with, and I thought it might be nice to go to the big lake I've heard about that's near here." He stood there, holding his hat in his hands.

"Well, I… I suppose that would be nice." How I hated when I was caught off-guard like that. I could never think of what to say, but my Mama hadn't drilled manners into me all those years for nothing. I tried to look pleased. "The children would enjoy it so much."

"How about this Saturday? Mr. Evans, may I get your phone number? I'll call tomorrow, and we'll figure out how to do this. Of course, you and Mrs. Evans will have to join us."

My father walked over, and Mr. Meyer took a little notebook and pencil stub out of his jacket pocket. As he jotted down the number Daddy gave him, I looked past them to the church and saw our conversation was entertaining half the congregation, although some of the female faces didn't exactly look as if they appreciated the show.

Finally, we were on the way home. Daddy whistled some annoying tune, and Mama looked smug. I wanted to pinch the both of them.

<hr>

We met Mr. Meyer and his girls in the church parking lot the following Saturday. Daddy and Mr. Meyer had decided it was the best meeting place, as it was in between our farms and on the way to the lake. Mr. Meyer had been quite correct that my parents had to join the outing; I certainly didn't think the truck bed filled with food hampers and nine children, or even eight with Clarence up front with me, sounded like a very comfortable trip on a hot July day.

After he introduced his daughters, I started to do the same with mine, but to my astonishment, he knew each of their names. Mama suggested his three girls and Irene ride in their truck and Tommy, Martha, Leah, and Celeste ride in his.

"And Mary, you ride with Mr. Meyer, and I'll take Clarence in our truck. That way, everyone has room to move some." Mama smiled sweetly at me.

Short of being rude, I couldn't think of any excuse for not riding with Mr. Meyer, and my mother ignored my protests about her taking Clarence. The children were clambering around, switching truck beds, and chattering. I was glad to see Celeste didn't seem put out about not being allowed to ride with Irene and the Meyer girls. The novelty of riding in Mr. Meyer's truck was a sufficient reward, I supposed.

In a few moments, we were on our way, Daddy in the lead, as he knew the route better. Mr. Meyer got his truck, a much newer model than Daddy's or Tom's old ones, into a gear he seemed to like, and he looked over at me and smiled. Well, look at that. He'd realized his mustache needed a trim. Probably his daughters told him so.

"So, Mrs. Heath, I should have said when we first met I was sorry to hear of your husband's passing last fall. I know his loss must have been hard on you and your family."

"Thank you, and of course I feel the same way about your loss, Mr. Meyer, and it so much more recent than my own.

You and your poor girls must be devastated." I was glad I had prepared for this inevitable exchange.

"And thank you, but our situation was quite different from your own. I understand Mr. Heath's passing was completely unexpected and very sudden. My wife's, on the other hand, was a long time coming, years, in fact. We had time to get used to the idea of losing her, although it was still a shock when it finally happened, of course. The girls were very close to her, as you might imagine. I'm hoping moving away from our home there will help the three younger girls get over it soon. I keep telling them their mother would want us to be happy. She's in a better place and no longer in any pain, and we need to move on with our lives now."

I gazed out my window at the passing scenery, mostly live oaks dripping in Spanish moss, and thought about that.

"Don't you agree, Mrs. Heath?" There seemed to be a note of concern in his voice.

"I'm sure you're right. It's just that people do grieve in their own time, Mr. Meyer. Your girls are young, and I'm sure they will get past their mother's passing, but I'm also sure they must miss her very much. Even if she had been ill for a long time. They still had her there with them, and now they don't. You know how different these things are for children than for adults, of course. They will come around. Especially once school starts back up, they'll have lots to think about with new friends and new teachers."

He nodded his head, and our conversation turned to the local community and the nearby town of Wilmington.

"I had to run some errands a few Saturdays ago, so I took the girls with me to have a look around," he said. "We lived near a real small town, if you could even call it that, in South Carolina, and the girls were amazed by all the buildings and people in Wilmington. We were all impressed at some of those big homes there. Mansions, really. Then, for some reason, they wanted to go into the Atlantic Coast Line terminal there and see the trains come and go. You watch, they'll be trying to figure out how to take a train trip next. I think they've got a taste for a bigger life now. Well, I hope they find husbands who can give that to them."

"Do they know about the beach trolley?" I asked, smiling.

"Do what? What's a *beach* trolley?"

"I'm sure you saw the trolleys running downtown. Well, there's one that takes you right to Wrightsville Beach. It's still the only way to get on the island. At the end of the trolley line is the Lumina Pavilion. You sure you haven't heard about all that?" I didn't want to bore him with what he already knew.

"No. I really only know about my new farm, our church, of course, some of the local stores and then a little about Wilmington, but even that is more about farm supply stores there. Tell me."

The next forty minutes flew by as I told him about the area. I hadn't been to the beach in many a year, but I knew others at my old church who loved to go, so I had an idea of how things were there still.

Before I knew it, we were pulling up by Daddy's truck at the lake.

We made quick work of spreading our old quilts near the lake's edge, with our packed food set out on the truck gate. Mr. Meyer's family also had brought old quilts as well as bowls and platters of food, so there was no danger anyone would go home hungry or be crowded while they ate.

We were all hungry after the drive, so we dove into the fried chicken (my father winked at me when Mr. Meyer took a drumstick), sliced ham, biscuits, potato salad, tomatoes, deviled eggs, and sweet pickles, followed by lemon pound cake. We had large glass containers of sweet tea and lemonade. Mr. Meyer had even brought a block of ice, which he chipped for our drinks; the beads of condensation running down our enamelware mugs were the most refreshing part of the meal, I thought.

After we had stuffed ourselves, we all walked over in our bare feet to the lakeshore, where the deliciously cool water lapped at our ankles. My entire body seemed to cool off as I walked out a few steps more, and I wished I had a bathing costume on so I could go all the way in. Not that I would wear such a thing in front of Mr. Meyer, of course.

Daddy held Tommy's hand as they walked along, Tommy pointing out all the sights for him. Mama stayed with Clarence, letting him splash diaper-less in the shallow edge of the water, making sure he didn't put anything in his mouth. Leah held onto Martha, and the five older girls stood in the water up to their knees, holding up their dresses and chattering away.

"We were lucky to find such a nice spot that we could have all to ourselves, weren't we?" Mr. Meyer was at my elbow, his pants legs rolled up to just under his knees. I couldn't help but notice.

He was right, although I remembered Daddy taking us to this same spot when I was young, and it always seemed to be empty and waiting for us.

"I think it's because we made an early start. So many people seem to like to come later when it's even hotter in the afternoon. I like it best in the morning, I think. Of course, you come too early, and I imagine the mosquitoes would eat you alive." I laughed awkwardly. I hoped Mr. Meyer hadn't looked at my legs the way I'd looked at his. Not that I could help it, of course.

Mama always said I talked too much when I got nervous. Looking over my shoulder, I saw her watching us. I wondered what Clarence would find to eat while she kept her eyes on us. I raised my eyebrows at her, and she looked down at Clarence and started talking to him.

As we were turning to head back in, I glanced over at Irene, Celeste, and Mr. Meyer's daughters (Bertha and the twins, Louise and Lily, I reminded myself) and smiled to see my quiet Irene laughing as she was telling them about one of Tommy's misadventures. She threw her hands out as she finished the little story and stepped back—and the lake simply swallowed her. Everything froze for a moment, and there was only the sound of Clarence humming to himself as he splashed. Just as I was taking the first step to where Irene had been standing, Mr. Meyer surged past me, racing farther out into the lake towards the girls. He suddenly faltered and went down, too, but almost immediately reappeared, pulling Irene up and out of the water. She was choking, falling to her knees as soon as he got her to the grass.

Everyone tried to talk to her all at once as they clustered around, my mother holding Clarence and Daddy pulling Tommy back. Mr. Meyer was speaking softly to her and thumping her back. He moved back when I arrived, and I held her shoulders as she got the last of the water out of her lungs. She finally leaned back into my arms and let me pull her sopping hair back from her face.

When she'd finally started breathing normally, I asked, "Baby, what happened? You seemed to just disappear."

"I just took one step back, Mama, and it was like I fell off a cliff. I couldn't get my balance, and I went under. I was so shocked I took a big breath and sucked in lake water. Then I don't even know, but Mr. Meyer was pulling me out by then. It seemed to last forever, but I think it couldn't have been very long, really." She turned her head into my shoulder and started crying.

"No, honey, it wasn't, but it sure felt like eternity to me, too. Thank goodness Mr. Meyer was able to move so fast and pull you out." I hugged her and let her cry out her scare. I didn't want her to have nightmares about this.

"Mama, I'm sorry I spoiled our picnic." She looked up at me, her blue eyes filled with tears, and noticed Mr. Meyer beside me, still crouching down. "Mr. Meyer, thank you so much, and I'm so sorry you got all wet. I don't know what happened that I fell like that."

He reached over and squeezed her shoulder. "Miss Irene, don't you worry none. I'm right glad I had an excuse to cool off. You and me are the only ones here not sweating. 'Course, we are dripping a bit."

Irene smiled, and we all laughed, so relieved you could feel it in the air.

"I know why you fell, by the way. I'm not sure if it's a hole in the lake bottom there or if the whole edge drops off. It's deep. Are you sure you didn't hurt yourself? Are your legs all right?" Mr. Meyer held out his hand and helped her to stand.

"I'm fine, thank you." Irene took a few steps. "Just my pride is hurt."

We all laughed again, and the girls, including Mr. Meyer's, hugged her. I took Clarence and got him rinsed off and diapered, while Mama finally got her arms around Irene and held her to her breast.

"What are we going to do about you being so wet?" Mama asked.

"Mama, look in the truck bed. See that bag? Each child has a change of clothes. I thought they might splash each other too much, and it would be a good idea just in case." I couldn't help but feel a little smug. Mama had thought I was bringing too many things in our truck when we packed up this morning. "And of course, the old towels are there by the blue quilt. I knew we'd need those."

Mr. Meyer looked over and said, "I sure wish I'd thought about a change of clothes. I'm just going to have to drip dry, I suppose."

And he did, all the way home.

CHAPTER 13

A Friend from the Past

Wednesday, July 24, 1929

I came into the kitchen carrying the basket of eggs Martha and Leah had just collected. Mama was sitting at the table reading a letter while Irene and Celeste were dusting and sweeping the front room. Tommy and Toby were off with Daddy, who was running an errand to the feed store. I was about to wipe off the eggs when Mama looked up.

"Honey, I think you're going to want to read this letter. You'll never guess who it's from." She had a curious tone, and I couldn't figure out if she was happy to have received her letter or not.

"Mama, is it bad news?" I quickly washed and dried my hands and walked over to the table.

"Sit down, sweetie. There is some bad news in it, but I'm so happy to hear from her—and there is definitely good news here, too." She smiled. "Don't you want to guess who sent it?"

I couldn't imagine who would have such an effect on her, so I shook my head. She handed over the letter. As soon as I saw the handwriting, I knew who it was from. I think I gasped and started reading as fast as I could.

Dear Mrs. Evans,

It has been so long since we've been in touch, but I hope you know I think of you and Mr. Evans—and of course, dear Mary—so often and with true affection. I have decided I should stop being embarrassed to have not written before this, and instead just say how sorry I am I've taken so long. Please forgive me.

I hope you are all well and happy.

As you probably know, Mary and I lost touch shortly after the birth of her Josephine Irene, which was the month before I graduated from high school. That fall, I went on to college in Virginia. It was such a time of change for both of us, so I suppose it's no wonder we were each caught up in our new lives. In my senior year in college, I met a very nice man, Robert Lundstrom, an attorney (yes, just like my father was) who had a practice in Richmond. We married shortly after my graduation. Mother insisted the wedding be held at Grandmother's estate in New Jersey, where she grew up, so none of my Wilmington or Virginia friends were able to attend, unfortunately. In a few years, we had a baby boy, Bertie, who is now almost seven years old.

That is all my happy news.

The very unhappy news concerns the loss of two most dear to me. First, my father died of a stroke the year after Bertie was born. I'm so glad he got to hold his grandson, but so sorry Bertie will never know his wonderful grandfather. The second is even more difficult to write. My husband was killed in a trolley accident when Bertie was only five. You may imagine how horrible the last two years have been.

Virginia no longer seemed like home after Robert died, so I finally decided in late May of this year to move back to Wilmington with Bertie, and I'm living with Mother again. You may recall how I always enjoyed art and painting. I studied art in college, and I am now giving drawing and painting lessons to young ladies at Mother's home. It helps to keep me occupied and feel useful. It also gives me an excuse to not spend all day in social calls, I must admit, although never to Mother!

This is turning out to be much longer than I planned, but I hope you don't mind. I recall so many happy days practically living in your home when I stayed those summer holidays with my grandmother, and Mary and I were inseparable.

As her nearest neighbor, you know Grandmama passed away only a few years after Mary married. She'd been renting out the farmland since Granddaddy passed when I was little, but she loved that farmhouse. They'd raised Daddy in it, and she wanted to live out her life there. After she passed, Daddy rented out the farmhouse along with the land. You probably met the family. Mother saw no reason to keep any of it once Daddy was gone and sold it all. I'm sad to think I'll never see my grandmother again and never walk through the rooms of her house one last time.

I can still see the two of you laughing and having tea at her kitchen table. I know she thought the world of you.

Although I could never forget your address, of course, I have no idea how to reach Mary. I sent a letter to her shortly after I arrived, using the only address I had for her, but it just came back with "Return to Sender—Forwarding Address Unknown" on it. I suppose she and Tom have moved to a larger farm by now. Could you possibly send me her address? Or just give her my information? I've written my telephone number at the bottom of this, along with Mother's address. Please ask her to forgive her old friend for losing touch, and to please get up with me.

I send both you and Mr. Evans my love. I hope to see both of you soon, and for you to meet my little boy, who is growing up much too quickly! I'm sure you understand very well. I look forward to hearing all your news, too.

With great fondness,
Your Lottie

I looked up at Mama, who was waiting for my reaction. I could hardly think what to say. There was so much to take in from Lottie's letter.

"Are you going to get up with her, Mary?" Mama knew how to cut to the chase.

I looked up at the wall clock. A little early, but Lottie had always been an early riser. Then again, I didn't want to offend Mrs. Vanderven, Lottie's mother, who was very strict about etiquette. At least, the etiquette of others.

I waited until ten o'clock and hoped I didn't have to speak with Mrs. Vanderven, although the chances of her answering her own telephone seemed unlikely. In her view, that would be for a servant to do, just as one would always answer her door for her.

At ten, I dialed the number Lottie had included in her letter. A servant answered, as I had expected. I gave my name and asked to speak to Lottie and in a few minutes heard her dear familiar voice. "Mary! Mary Ellen! Is that really you?"

"Lottie, Mama just received your letter and handed it to me to read, too. I can't believe you are really back here in Wilmington! And with a son! And, Lottie, I was so very sorry to hear about your father and your husband. You know how much I admired Mr. Vanderven. He was always so warm and friendly to me." I immediately felt guilty, as we both knew the same could not be said of her mother, and I didn't mean to make such a comparison. I hurried on, "And I wish I could have met your Robert. If he won your heart, he must have been a wonderful man."

"Oh, Mary, thank you. My father adored you and was so happy we were such good friends. He always said my summers with Grandmama and your family were the making of me. I think he knew … well, I needed space away from… home… to just be a young girl and have fun."

I laughed. "We did have fun, didn't we? Although, given how much work around our house and farm that you helped out with, it certainly wasn't what most girls would think of as fun."

"And you likewise helped me with jobs around my Grandmama's house. We kept ourselves busy, but it wasn't all work. Really, none of it seemed like work. Funny how it just seemed like one adventure after another. And remember all the books we read to each other?"

We went on like that for several minutes until one of the neighbors (I wasn't sure which one, but definitely an impatient man) interrupted on the line. "Ladies, I need to make an important call in the next few minutes. Would you mind ending your conversation soon?"

That was the problem with party lines. We had to share our telephone line with five or six other homes on our road, so calls needed to be short, and anyone might be listening in. Still, I had been surprised more than once by picking the earpiece off the hook to make a call and hearing a neighbor telling someone something highly indiscreet.

"I'm so sorry! We'll be off in just a few seconds, I promise!" I always tried to be considerate and was embarrassed when someone had to ask me to get off the line. Fortunately, that was a rare event.

Lottie and I quickly made plans for her to visit on Friday, when she didn't have any students to teach. I said I'd fill her in on my news when we were together. She promised to bring her son, and I was delighted we could meet without her mother being present. Mama was excited when I told her and immediately started trying to remember Lottie's favorite cake so she could bake it Friday morning.

I wondered how I ever got by with only one icebox. Having a second one on the back porch meant we could butcher a couple of the chickens on Thursday and wait to fry them the next day. It certainly made getting a nice dinner ready for Lottie's visit much easier. I never enjoyed having to kill our chickens, of course, but we didn't have the luxury of shopping in a butcher shop the way town folk did.

Daddy got the fire under the cauldron started early Thursday morning. I was grateful for the fine weather and for being able to do the smelly scalding and messy plucking of the chickens outdoors. Occasionally, in the winter all that had to be done indoors, and the reek seemed to last for days.

"Celeste, Leah, come help me," I called over my shoulder as I headed out to the chicken coop. I heard the grumbling from my reluctant daughters all the way from their bedroom.

"Mother, how come we have to help, and Irene doesn't?" said Celeste as she and Leah joined me.

"Irene has been in the kitchen scrubbing the floor while you two took your time getting into your work dresses," I said. "And she has volunteered to cook the chicken tomorrow morning and make the biscuits. I still haven't heard either of you talk about anything except what you plan to wear tomorrow." To be fair, that was mostly Celeste, while she had Leah trying to do something new with her hair. Leah had no ambitions to be Celeste's hairdresser, but gamely tried to keep her in good humor.

Now, at my scolding, Leah looked sorry, and Celeste mumbled, "Irene always jumps to take the fun jobs. Besides, she can cook better than we can."

"Fun jobs like scrubbing the kitchen floor? And she wasn't born knowing how to cook, Celeste. How did she learn, do you suppose?" I tried to be evenhanded with the girls, but sometimes it was difficult, especially when one of them always seemed to want to feel hard done by. And that "someone" usually was Celeste.

"Well, she's older, so of course she's had more practice." Celeste just was not going to give up on her grudge.

"That's enough now. Each one of you go get a hen for us. First, point to the one you plan to catch and let me see. We don't want to be frying up our best layers." I smoothed down the front of my oldest apron and walked over close to the chopping block and set the ax down I'd brought from the barn. Daddy was busy adding to the cauldron fire.

Leah chose a hen and, at my nod, brought it over to me. I took the poor squawking thing from her and held it a moment, trying to calm it down. Once the hen settled, I did as I'd been taught when I was younger than Celeste was now. I grabbed the hen by the neck with my fingers pointed toward her body, whipped her straight out in front of me, and spun her body around in a circle. Her neck broke immediately. I quickly put her on the chopping block and cut off her head. The body continued to walk around for a few seconds as the muscles got their last messages from the brain. At least, that was what Daddy had told me caused them to flop around like that.

"Celeste, it's past time you learn how to do this. You can do it. You've seen this done many times, and now it's time for you to do it." I felt sorry for her as she stood there holding the hen, patting the feathers. She hadn't seen this coming. Her eyes were filling with tears.

"All right, sweetie. We'll start out slow this first time. You have a choice. You can wring her neck and I'll chop off the head, or I'll wring it and you chop it off. That's just half the job of killing her. Which will it be?"

The tears started, and she didn't say anything.

I sighed. I remembered only too well how I'd felt the first time. "Celeste, how many chickens do you suppose I've killed so you could eat fried chicken? You've even watched Irene when she learned how to do this. Do you think any of us want to do this job? One day, you are going to have children who want to eat chicken, you know. We do what we have to do, baby girl. We don't have to like doing it. We just have to do whatever is necessary. Do you understand?" I tried to be gentle but firm.

Celeste gave a shuddering breath as Leah reached over and patted Celeste's arm. "Celeste, I'll cut off the head if you wring its neck," she said, her voice shaking as she tried to be brave.

"No, Leah, not this time. Celeste, I'm going to wring its neck. You pick up the ax. You be real sure you are careful and look where you are going to chop. Do not get your other hand in the way, you hear me? It will be over in a second."

And it was. She pulled herself together and was clear-eyed when she chopped. She looked down at her apron and saw the spot of blood splattered on the bib. I waited for the tears to start up again, but she bit her lip, picked up the hen by the feet, and walked over to the cauldron. Daddy took it from her and dipped it in the scalding water to loosen the feathers. He had watched silently, but now he looked at her and said, "I'm right proud of you, sweetheart. The first time is always the hardest, and you were very brave."

Celeste gave him a small smile and looked over at me.

"Your granddaddy is right, honey. I'd worry if it was easy for you to do. I'm proud of you."

At that, she turned away and wiped away fresh tears. "What do we do now, Mama?"

Daddy said, "I'm going to show you how to pluck these two hens, and then we'll clean them out. Toby is going to be in heaven if we let him have some of the fried-up liver and gizzards. 'Course, he'll have to share with me. And your grandmother is going to want the hearts. Still, I bet Toby talks her out of a bite or two. She spoils him rotten, you know."

Leah and Celeste were making noises to let him know he and Toby would get no argument from them. Daddy showed her what to do with one chicken and then watched as she followed suit on the other one. After they had given the chickens a final rinse, he showed her how to cut up the chicken, preserving the all-important wishbones. Later, Celeste walked into the kitchen as proud as she could be, holding a big white enamel pan with the two cleaned chickens to show her grandmother and Irene. They made a fuss over her, and what had seemed like a traumatic morning turned into a triumph for her.

As she washed her hands after the chicken was put into the icebox, I went over and put my arms around her shoulders. "I'm proud of you, too, Celeste. I know you'll always be able to do the difficult, necessary things. Now you know it, too."

She leaned over and put her head on my shoulder and sighed. "Thank you, Mama."

I smiled. For just a moment, I was "Mama" again.

CHAPTER 14

Lottie Visits

Friday, July 26, 1929

Lottie brought her little boy to visit us the next day. She was driving a sleek motorcar, the likes of which had probably never been seen on our country dirt road. I thought my heart would burst when I saw her. She was such a fine lady that I felt unnerved, but then she squealed my name, ran to hug me, and all the years we'd been apart simply disappeared. There was my dear friend Lottie, right there inside this beautiful, grown-up woman.

Mama gave us a moment, and then she had her turn hugging Lottie. All three of us had happy tears running down our faces.

I'd forgotten how striking Lottie's coppery hair was. No longer tamed into braids, it now curled around her head in a cropped style all her own. Turning, I saw her little boy had his mama's hair, too. He stood patiently while we women exclaimed and made a fuss over each other. He was dressed in navy-blue shorts, his white shirt neatly tucked in.

"Oh, Mary and Mrs. Evans, allow me to present my son, Albert. We call him Bertie. Bertie, this is Mrs. Evans, who is the mother of my dear friend, Mrs. Heath." Lottie smiled at her son.

"How do you do, Mrs. Evans and Mrs. Heath." Bertie sounded more like a young man than the small boy he was. I didn't know whether to be impressed or taken aback.

As I bent to shake his hand, I saw Lottie's freckles had also come his way. "You may call me Miss Mary, Bertie. Your mama and I used to play together when we were your size."

Bertie smiled, but the doubtful look on his face suggested he found it difficult to imagine his mother or me ever having been his size.

"Let's get in out of this sun and see about something cold to drink," Mama said, turning and taking Bertie's hand. "Bertie, do you like lemonade?"

"Yes, ma'am, I do! I like it a lot!" Bertie was suddenly the little boy he appeared to be.

"Girls, I know you two want to talk awhile. When we get our drinks, why don't I take Bertie and show him our animals? Tommy and the girls won't be back with their granddaddy for a while yet, so you'll have time to catch up some."

A few minutes later, as they walked out to see Molly, I heard Mama saying, "So Bertie, have you spent much time riding a mule?" Bertie gave a delighted gasp.

I started to lead Lottie to our front sitting room, but she said, "Mary, can't we sit at the kitchen table like we used to do? You know how I love this room. I can't go back to my grandmama's kitchen ever again, and this is the next best thing."

So, we sat and shared some of what had happened to each of us over the long years we'd been out of touch.

"Mary, I just can't believe you have six children! Of course, I'm not forgetting your little Alice, I want you to know. But six children to mind now! Just keeping up with Bertie can wear me out. I know they'll be adorable, just like little Clarence here."

Clarence was currently sitting on her lap, happy to suck on the finger she kept dipping into the lemonade for him. He wasn't entirely sure he liked the tanginess, but he was enthralled with the beautiful lady with the amazing hair. He kept smacking his lips and looking up at her. I wasn't sure if his lip smacking was due to the lemon or his early appreciation of feminine beauty. I hoped it was the lemon.

I heard about her happy marriage and then the return to her mother's home. At least I had two warm and welcoming parents to return to; Lottie had had a very different homecoming.

"Mama wanted me to come back to live with her. It's just that she seems to think I'm still fifteen years old and she should be able to control my daily schedule to her liking. She put up such a fuss when I decided to start offering art classes, but I think she finally realized it gave her something to crow about to her friends, especially as so many of them are the mothers and grandmothers of my students. I certainly appreciate that it allows me to use my small abilities. And to help those girls develop their talent as much as possible. I like that they will have something creative to do beyond running a household and raising children. Oh! Mary! I didn't mean that in any way to be denigrating! And you know what I mean; you always got so much happiness from your singing."

I smiled at my friend. "I know what you mean, Lottie. Men get to have all kinds of interests and skills, and no one thinks it stops them from being a good husband or father."

Lottie got the twinkly look I remember so well. "Unless, of course, their interests are too much alcohol or other women."

We both were laughing when Mama and Bertie came back inside. "Mama, I gave the chickens water from the pump! And you've gotta come see Molly. Mrs. Evans says I can ride on her after luncheon! I mean dinner." He was bouncing on his toes. "Oh. If it's all right with you," he added with a smile I was sure he knew his mother couldn't resist.

Lottie kissed his nose. "I think it will be fun. Mrs. Heath and I used to love riding on the mule they had way back when she and I were your size." She looked over at me. "Wasn't that Dolly?"

"Oh, yes, poor Dolly sure put up with a lot from us."

"I remember how sharp her spine was. Didn't make for a comfortable ride, but we didn't care. Was she what they call a razorback?" Lottie looked at Mama.

Mama laughed, "If she wasn't officially, they should have made her an honorary one."

"Bertie, you'll have to tell us what you think after you've had your first ride on Molly. She's old, so we're very gentle with her, especially in this heat," I said. "Do you want some more lemonade? Mama, I'll make some more for Daddy and the children, too."

We let Bertie have a turn with the glass lemon juicer. That boy was fascinated with everything, it seemed, and I had a feeling he wasn't allowed to do much in the kitchen at Mrs. Vanderven's mansion.

"Girls, Bob and the children will be back soon, so I'm going to get the food warming. You go on and chat. I'll put Clarence down for his nap, and then Bertie can help me in here. Isn't that right, Bertie?"

I'd never seen a little boy so happy to help out in the kitchen, so Lottie and I moved to the porch and left them to it. We both fanned ourselves with a couple of the paddle fans Mama kept on the little table between the rocking chairs.

"Mary?" Lottie hesitated. "Do you know yet what you're going to do? Do you plan to stay here with your parents? I hope I'm not being too nosy."

I sighed. "Not at all. I just wish I knew so I could tell you. I'm still nursing Clarence, and I think I've used that as an excuse to put off looking for a job. Although, really, I have no idea what kind of job I could find that would allow me to have him with me."

"Mary, I'm sorry. I didn't mean to distress you! Please forgive me."

"No, no, I need to start thinking about this instead of just worrying about it when I go to bed at night. I'm so busy during the day it's easy to ignore, but it sure bothers me at night." I looked over at her and smiled. "Maybe you can help me figure this out. I've gone round and round in my head so often over these months I can only think of the reasons this isn't going to work out. But it has to!"

Lottie reached over and took my hand. "I don't know that I'll have ideas any better than yours, but I'm always willing to listen and try to help you." She gave my hand a squeeze.

"Thank you. I think it's helping just talking about this. Clarence is finally beginning to tolerate pap, so maybe I can get him weaned soon. Mama and Daddy keep telling me we'll manage here, which is so wonderful of them, but I need to take care of my own children and myself, and not be a burden on them any longer than I have to be. It's not fair to Mama and Daddy, and we're all crammed in here. I need a job that will let me support the seven of us. I don't have a high school degree, much less a college degree like you do. I didn't even finish seventh grade, you know. What kind of job am I going to be able to get?" I stopped and blinked back the tears that wanted to come.

Lottie cleared her throat and gazed out to the backyard. After a moment, she said, "Mary, do you think you'll ever want to get married again?"

I hadn't expected that question at all. "I don't want to think of spending the rest of my life all alone, but do I want anyone now? No, I don't. At least, I don't think so. I still think of Tom too much. And, well," I wasn't sure if I should say this or not, but I'd been thinking a lot about it, "I just don't want to have more children, Lottie. I know until I'm well into my forties—maybe even older—a new marriage will mean more babies. I love each of mine, but I have all I want. So, I guess that's it, really. If another marriage means more babies, then no."

Lottie reached over again and patted my arm. "I understand completely. I've heard there are ways to prevent having a baby, but I don't know exactly what they are or how to find out, either. And I'd be surprised if it worked all the time, anyway."

"But what about you, Lottie? You only have Bertie. And you've been on your own for longer than I have. Do you want to get married again?"

"I think about it, Mary. I still love my Robert, but it's been over two years now. I'm restless. And I just cannot see myself still living with my mother ten years from now. Even five years, really. But the money Robert left me and the little I earn teaching art isn't enough to keep Bertie and me forever." Lottie seemed to hesitate. "I want to send him to college. Law school, if he wants it. I know Mama will help me—as long as I stay with her. Maybe even if I marry someone she approves of. I feel like I'm tied to her for Bertie's sake. Yes, I'd be happy to meet someone, fall in love, and have him be able to provide for us in that way. And yes, I'd like to have more children." She looked over at me. "Probably not as many as you have, I have to say. Plus, I'd be older having them, and that could be a problem. But anyway, I certainly don't want to marry someone just to get away from Mama or to have someone to support Bertie and me. If I marry again, there has to be love on both sides."

She glanced at me. "But I don't know anyone I'd even consider getting married to—or anyone who would want to marry me, for that matter. Every man I've met here is either married, or it's pretty obvious why he isn't." We both laughed.

"Well, Mary? Is there anyone you could see yourself getting married to?" Lottie looked at me closely.

I rocked for a moment and sipped my lemonade. I sighed. "Not really. No."

Maybe I didn't sound convincing. Lottie stopped rocking and turned to me, eyebrow raised. I suddenly remember telling her about a boy I thought was cute, back when we were eleven or twelve. Here we were again, age thirty, going on eleven.

"Don't get too excited. Mama just has her hopes up, is all. His name is Mitch Meyer, and he just moved here from South Carolina a few months ago—with three of his five daughters."

Lottie leaned toward me over the arm of her chair, her chin in her hand. "Yes, Mary? I gather he's a widower?"

"Yes, but his wife only died just before he moved here, Lottie. I can't say that he seems to be grieving much for her. Although she was sick for years, apparently, so maybe he had time to adjust to being without her. Still, it doesn't seem quite right."

"So? He's been courting you?" she whispered this, with a look back toward the open door.

"Not exactly. I mean, I'm not really sure. He seems attentive, but of course we always have our children with us, and usually my parents. We went on a lake picnic in June. He made ice cream for all of us on the Fourth of July over here. That's Daddy's birthday, you know, so we invited him and his girls for supper and birthday cake. He brought over this ice cream maker, and we made peach ice cream. He had to crank two batches for all of us.

"And he knows how to get things done. He's suggested improvements for our church building, and I'm sure he'll be organizing getting them done. Everyone seems to think the world of him." I finally stopped and took a deep breath. "And he might be the best-looking man I've ever seen, Lottie."

Lottie's eyes were huge; she sat back in her chair and started rocking. "Mary! But… are you two ever alone? Does he say anything to you about admiring you or anything like that?"

"Not really. I mean, we aren't alone very much. He says nice things, I suppose, but… well, it's hard to explain. I get the feeling he likes me. And the children, which is very important, of course. I'm just not sure what to think about it."

"You said he moved here with three of his five daughters. Where are the other two?"

"Back in South Carolina, both married and have two girls each. I think Mr. Meyer—Mitch—is Tom's age, or maybe five or six years older than he'd be now."

"So, forty-five or forty-six? And a grandfather. How about the three girls here? How old are they?"

"The twins are about a year older, so fourteen, and the middle girl is sixteen, I think. They seem quiet. I think Mr. Meyer believes that's best for females. Quiet and obedient."

That got both of Lottie's eyebrows up in the air. "Well now, Mary, I see a possible problem with you being the girl of Mr. Meyer's dreams." At that, we both reverted to our eleven-year-old selves completely and got what Mama always called the "silly giggles."

Holding her side, Lottie gasped out, "He would have to be the *world's* best-looking man, don't you think, for you to go silent and obedient?"

Daddy's truck pulled around the house and parked. Tommy and Toby climbed out of the cab while the girls scooted from the truck bed. Daddy came around the truck carrying two grocery sacks. Lottie gave Daddy a hug and kissed each of the children on their cheeks as they were introduced. Mama and Bertie came outside, and Tommy wasted no time saying hello to Bertie and introducing Toby. The two boys and Toby raced off to the barn, happy to escape all the female chatter.

"I best go keep an eye on 'em, ladies." Daddy was quick to follow their example.

"Let's go inside. Girls, you want to go wash your hands and straighten your hair? Then come on into the kitchen and we'll have dinner." Mama herded us inside.

Later, after we'd eaten chicken and dumplings, we all decided to wait before we had the lemon cake Mama had made. The boys and Toby went back outside with Daddy. I watched Lottie get to know each of my girls for a while, and then we decided we couldn't wait any longer for cake. As we ate, the girls started asking her questions about what she and I had gotten up to in summers when we were girls together.

That led to Lottie's retelling of the time she and I took a little ride on a horse down at a farm past her grandmother's house.

"We knew a girl our age who lived there, and she told us it would be fine for us to get up on the horse they kept in their large paddock. She told us we didn't need a bridle or saddle or anything. Oh no, she said, it would be just fine. Girls, if anyone ever tells you that, don't you believe them." Lottie drew up her eyebrows dramatically and wagged her finger at them.

"What happened, Miss Lottie?" Martha was bouncing up and down in her seat.

"Honey, it was a disaster. All three of us got on that horse. Your mama was in front, holding the horse's mane, then I was in the middle, and then that girl on its rump. I don't remember her name. Do you, Mary?"

"No, but I'm pretty sure her middle name was 'Trouble.' Or maybe it was just plain 'Liar.'" We all laughed.

"Well, anyway, at first it was all right. The horse was just walking around, and we were fine, but pretty soon it decided to go faster. Maybe it didn't like having three giggling girls on its back. That girl, Miss Trouble, bounced right off the back. We found out later she broke her arm."

The girls gasped. "What happened then, Miss Lottie?" asked Leah.

"The horse went a little faster. I tried holding on to your mama's waist, but I got bounced off, too. At least I didn't break anything, but I think I'm still picking out sandspurs all these years later."

Lottie stopped and sipped her lemonade and took a bite of cake. She reminded me of Mama; they both knew how to keep the attention of their audience.

"Miss Lottie, what happened then? What happened to Mama?" Even Irene couldn't stand to wait any longer.

"Let your mama tell you. I'm sure she remembers every moment." Lottie looked over at me.

I sighed. "When Lottie fell off, that horse celebrated. He just started going faster and faster, running in circles in the field.

I grabbed a handful of his mane, but my body was bouncing and slipping around to his left side with every step. I slid and I slid until I couldn't keep hold of the mane anymore. I tried hugging his neck, but of course I couldn't reach all the way around, so now my whole body started slipping. Next thing I knew, I was completely under the horse's belly, my arms and legs wrapped around him as tight as I could. That probably just made him go faster."

I looked around. Even my mother was frozen in horror. I'd never told her exactly what had happened that afternoon.

"So, there I was. I knew I couldn't hold on forever. All four feet were coming up near my head, my body, my legs, and I felt my legs and arms losing their grip. I remember so clearly thinking there was no way for me to let go without my head or my body being trampled by those hooves. I was certain I was going to die. Then I was completely calm, not panicked at all. I couldn't stop it from happening, but I could at least choose when it was going to happen. And then I just… let go."

Even Lottie was shocked silent. I realized I'd never told her that part. She probably thought I simply couldn't hold on anymore. I couldn't even look at my girls.

I took a deep breath. "Anyway, as you can see, I didn't get trampled. By some miracle, just as I let go of him, the horse swerved directly to the right and kept on running. That turn of his swung me off to the left instead of under him. Not one hoof touched me. Of course, I did land in sandspurs. And… my shoulders weren't right for the longest time. Weeks and weeks. I couldn't raise my arms up higher than my shoulders. And my right foot wasn't quite right. Maybe I broke some little bones, now that I think back."

My mother narrowed her eyes at me. "And wasn't that about the time I had to start hemming your dresses an inch higher on one side? Your hips weren't level all of a sudden. They still aren't. I never could understand that."

"That might have been about then, yes, ma'am." I looked at the toes of my shoes. I was really getting to relive being eleven. My girls were fascinated to watch my mama get upset with me. It was also coming back to me why I'd never told my mother about this little incident.

"And your hip started making that loud clicking sound when you turned over in bed at night, didn't it, young lady?" Mama was getting worked up.

"Well, that stopped eventually. When I was twenty or so." Even I could hear the whiny, little-girl tone in my voice. I looked over to Lottie, but there was no help coming from her. "Not a word of this to your brother, girls. Tommy doesn't need any more ideas on how to get into trouble."

Heads nodded all around the table. A moment later, Daddy, Toby, and the boys came in from the backyard. "We didn't miss the cake, did we?" Daddy asked, looking around at all of us.

Mama stood up. "No, Bob. We left cake for you men. And you might say Mary has a little story that takes the cake, too, but that's for another time." She huffed over to get dessert plates. I stood and poured lemonade and tried to look quiet. And obedient.

Friend & Beau

Sunday, August 4, 1929

There was no stopping Lottie from meeting Mr. Meyer. During her visit, Mama brought up what a wonderful man he was, and the older girls assured Lottie he was more handsome than she could imagine. Celeste couldn't understand why he didn't go to Hollywood and become a movie star. Irene smiled at that, although she agreed she didn't know any actor who was as good-looking as he was. Leah was more taken with what a good basketball player he must be, given his height. It was little Martha who pointed out that her daddy had been just as tall and just as handsome, which put a stop to any more discussion about Mr. Meyer.

Lottie called the next day to thank Mama for her hospitality. I knew a thank-you note would arrive the next day, too, for Lottie had impeccable manners. Mama finished talking with her and then called me to the telephone.

"Remember not to take too long, dear," she said. We tried to avoid being asked to end our calls by one of our party-line neighbors. We also tried to avoid supplying grist for the rumor mill.

"Lottie, thanks for calling. We all enjoyed having you and Bertie here so much," I started. I suddenly felt weepy; it was so good to have her back in my life again.

"Mary, we loved seeing y'all. What a wonderful time! Bertie can't stop talking about all he did—and ate—while we were there. I know he especially loved his time with your daddy, Tommy, and that rascal Toby." Her voice dropped to a whisper. "I think my mother has heard enough about our visit from him. It's so obvious being at your house is much more fun than being here." I heard a familiar giggle come over the line.

"I hope we can get together again soon," I said.

"I have an idea about that, Mary. What do you think about Bertie and me coming to church with you next Sunday? I mean on August 4. You mentioned your church is going to have a picnic after the service. Bertie and I could just meet you there before the service, and I'll bring a hamper of food, of course. I know Bertie would love to see all of you again, although he'll miss Toby, of course. And, um, you know that would give me the opportunity to meet, well, other members of your congregation. I'm sure you understand."

Oh, I understood perfectly well what that little nosy parker meant. She wanted to meet Mr. Meyer. Yes indeed, I could tell when I told her about him that she was burning up with curiosity. And I realized I wanted her to meet him. I wanted to see what she thought.

I laughed. "Yes, Lottie. I think that's a wonderful idea."

Across the line, I heard her let out a little squeal. "Oh, this is going to be the best church picnic ever!"

"Wait, Lottie. Is your mother going to be all right with you not attending St. James's with her? Or will she want to come with you? You know she'd be welcome." I held my breath.

More laughter on Lottie's end of the line. "Mary, you know my Episcopalian mother is not going to be interested in attending a Baptist church picnic out in the country. Oh my, no. I'm sure she will take the opportunity to have Sunday dinner with one of her friends. Oh!"

I heard the sudden concern in her voice.

"Please don't tell your mother I said that! I wouldn't want to offend her for the world."

"Don't worry, Lottie. My mother remembers your mother quite well. She wouldn't expect her to come with you. I just wanted to let you know your mother is always welcome." Welcome didn't mean joyfully wished for, however. Naturally, I didn't say that last thought out loud.

⚜

We met at the church. Lottie attended services there years ago with her grandmother over her summer visits and knew it well. I was sure many of the members would remember her and be glad to see her again. As for myself, I couldn't wait to hear what she'd think about Mr. Meyer.

August 4 finally arrived. It was a beautiful summer day, unusual only because it wasn't as humid as it often was that time of year.

"Coming down from Canada, I reckon," Daddy said as we placed the old quilts in the truck bed for the children to sit on.

Irene looked up from positioning her corner of the quilt. "Really, Granddaddy? Is that possible? Or are you joking?" Her head was cocked toward him. Even with her face scrunched up in a puzzled expression on her face, she was a beautiful young girl. I needed to remind her to be more faithful about wearing her hat when she was working in our vegetable garden; the light tan looked nice on her, but Mama had warned me when I was her age that tanning was how you made leather. I pulled my brim down around my face at the thought.

"Honey, I heard that from a completely reliable source: Mr. Barnes, who was giving me a real fine haircut down at his barber shop at the same time he was educating me about the weather." Daddy laughed.

Looking up, he saw Irene was more confused than ever. "Actually, I think Mr. Barnes is right. I read it in the newspaper. And I expect that's how Mr. Barnes learned about it, too. I sure wasn't going to question a man holding sharp scissors next to my ear. So I let him think it was news to me. It really is something to think about how the wind we have here came from someplace so far away, ain't it?"

"I wanna go see all those places, Granddaddy," Tommy piped up. "I wanna go all over the world."

Daddy ruffled Tommy's corn-silk hair and lifted him up to the truck bed. "Well, buddy, you best plan on joining the Navy when you grow up. They'll take you all over. 'Course, you'll have to go in a big ship and maybe puke your way around the world."

Tommy giggled, and I sighed. "Daddy, don't go putting ideas in his head. I need my boy right close by." Celeste lifted Martha up, and Leah and Irene got the two younger ones settled in.

Not too long later, we pulled in next to Lottie's motorcar. We all greeted each other, and I was pleased Bertie, even though he was a couple of years older than Tommy, seemed happy to see him again. I noticed Lottie was scanning the arrivals, and I had no doubt who she was looking for. Before the Meyer family arrived, however, she was kept busy greeting long-time congregation members who hadn't seen her since her grandmother's death, when her attendance there ended. Even after fifteen years, Lottie was easily recognizable, and it was no surprise to me she was remembered with such fondness by so many.

Finally, the Meyer truck arrived. The three daughters, Bertha, Louise, and Lily, emerged first, smoothing their Sunday dresses and putting on their gloves at the last minute. Mr. Meyer got down from the driver's side and reached inside for his coat and hat. He walked over to us carrying them, delaying putting them on until the last minute, just as my father and most of the other men were doing.

Mr. Meyer walked up to my mother and greeted her, shook Daddy's hand, then Tommy's, much to his delight, and smiled down at Bertie, who also received a handshake. At last he excused himself and walked over to where Lottie, my girls, and I stood in the shade of the live oak Daddy had parked under.

"Mr. Meyer, how nice to see you and your girls," I started. "Allow me to introduce my dear friend. Lottie, this is Mitch Meyer; Mr. Meyer, this is Lottie Lundstrom."

They both murmured polite greetings and shook hands. As Mr. Meyer stood back, he looked at my four girls standing there. "Miss Irene, aren't you a picture? Celeste, you need to teach my girls how to fix their hair like that. Leah, how about you let me play a little basketball with you? I hear tell you are a force with a basketball. And," here he squatted down, "Martha, I think you are going to be having gentlemen callers before your mama knows what's happening."

Martha looked pleased but uncertain. "What's a gentlemen caller, Mr. Meyer?"

"Oh, that will be some man who wants to court you. Then he'll want to marry you." Mr. Meyer smiled at her.

"Oh, then they don't need to come 'round. I'm going to marry my granddaddy. I was going to marry Daddy, but he's in heaven now, so I decided to marry Granddaddy." She smiled sweetly.

He smiled back at her. "That might be a surprise for your grandmama. Well, you've got a few years to think about it anyway." He took her little fingers in his large ones and gave them a kiss. She giggled and ran over to clutch my skirts.

I looked over at Lottie as Mr. Meyer straightened up and turned to answer a question from Celeste. Lottie leaned over and took my arm and whispered, "He's breathtaking."

We walked into the church building, trying to control our giggles.

After the church service ended, we women and girls returned to our vehicles (sometimes these were horse or mule-drawn carts) and retrieved the things we'd need for the picnic. Like most of the other families, we had enamelware or metal dishes and cups used especially for outdoor meals, along with old tablecloths, quilts, napkins, and jars for sweet tea. We set up our two quilts along with Lottie's in the shade of one of the many live oaks on the church grounds.

Meanwhile, the men got the sawhorses and boards from the shed behind the church and set up tables to hold all the food that had been brought. Many women had risen even earlier than usual to do the cooking and baking. No one wanted to bring less than their share, and of course, it was a chance to taste dishes someone else had cooked. Once covered with the tablecloths, we brought out the platters, bowls, and cake stands of delicious food. Before anyone started serving themselves, everyone bowed their heads for the blessing, which Mr. Prince kept mercifully brief.

Most of the food was covered with dish towels, mesh domes, or cake covers, but during the prayer, Martha and other young girls were waving their hands above the few uncovered dishes to keep the flies off, when I happened to peek at them just as Martha's hand skimmed slightly too low over my lemon meringue pie. She looked up in horror to see if anyone had noticed and saw me looking at her. I winked; she quickly licked the evidence off her fingers and gave me a relieved smile. I'd have to remember to ask her later if she wanted more lemon meringue.

I noticed when Mama, Lottie, and I were setting out our quilts that the Meyer girls placed theirs next to us, with Irene and Celeste helping them to spread them out. Once again, I was happy my girls were making them feel welcome.

"Lottie, I don't think you've met Mr. Meyer's daughters." I smiled at them as they walked over to us. "This is Bertha, and the twins Louise and Lily. Girls, this is my friend from when we were younger than you are now, Mrs. Lottie Lundstrom."

Lottie nodded and smiled at them. "I hear you girls just moved here a few months ago from South Carolina. Does anything seem different to you here from there? Do you have any favorite thing here yet?"

Watching Lottie, I realized I should have made more of an effort to get to know the Meyer girls. I really knew nothing about them as individuals. Those three girls became happy little chatterboxes as Lottie kept asking questions about what kinds of things they liked to do.

We quickly pulled their quilt over to join up with our three and eventually sat back down with plates of food and mugs of iced tea. Not surprisingly, Mr. Meyer had organized several other men to bring blocks of ice, and they had their own area where they were offering chipped ice. On such a hot summer day, it was such a treat to have an icy drink and even more special to watch the beads of condensation running down the metal cups and mugs. Even the most straight-backed lady there was holding her chilled cup to her cheeks and forehead from time to time.

After a short time, Mr. Meyer joined us with his own filled plate and settled down in between two of his daughters, who were more subdued in his presence. Bertie and Tommy, who had already finished eating, ran off to play with some of the other boys, knowing dessert was still a ways off.

"Well, Mrs. Evans, I take it Mrs. Lundstrom was a childhood friend of Mrs. Heath's. I bet you could tell us if they are just the same as they were back then. We wouldn't mind hearing about some of their adventures, you know." Only Mr. Meyer could pry so charmingly.

My mother glowed at being singled out and nodded her head. "Oh, I could tell a tale or two, but I sure wouldn't want to give these young girls any ideas." She laughed and then shook her head. "To tell the truth, they were such good girls. I always loved listening to them chatter. They are so different from each other and yet got along so well together."

"Different how, Mrs. Evans?" Mr. Meyer smiled at Lottie and me, and I was sure she was no more able to resent his nosiness than I was. My daughters and Mr. Meyer's were certainly finding this conversation interesting. I remember well enjoying hearing about the younger versions of grownups I knew. It always seemed impossible they had ever been my age.

"Well, my Mary has always been outgoing. Always seemed ready for anything life could hand her. She couldn't wait to start living her life. At least, I'm pretty sure that's how she thought of it." Mama reached over and squeezed my hand. "And Lottie seemed quieter, but she has a backbone of steel, this one. And she's so artistic. She was always pointing out things I hadn't noticed that were just beautiful once you really looked at them. Mary loved to cook, and Lottie would set the table in a way that made the food seem all the more delicious."

Mama wrinkled her forehead. "It's odd, but I would have guessed Mary would have been the one to go off and have adventures, and Lottie would have stayed in Wilmington, married very early, and lived the life her mother wanted for her with her society friends and all. But it was Lottie who went off to another state and lived away for so many years. And, of course, it was my Mary who married young and settled down with her family."

Mama shook her head. "I guess I'm not cut out to read fortunes, so I'll have to get that dream out of my head."

We all laughed and agreed she shouldn't save up for a crystal ball.

"So, you are an artist, Mrs. Lundstrom?" asked Bertha. I wasn't sure I'd ever heard the girl say anything before.

"Yes, well, I try to be," replied Lottie. "Do you enjoy art, Bertha?"

I could tell Bertha was pleased Lottie remembered her name. "I do, Mrs. Lundstrom, but I'm not very good at it. But I do like to try." Bertha was blushing now.

"Well, maybe your father will bring you and your sisters over to Mrs. Evans's house sometime when I'm visiting, if she doesn't mind. We could have a little drawing or painting class. I teach art to some young ladies in Wilmington, but we'd be doing it just for fun. Would you like that?" Lottie smiled around at the girls and then Mr. Meyer. Naturally, it really depended on him.

"Well, Mrs. Lundstrom, that is real nice of you to offer, but we couldn't take advantage of your time and talent. I'm afraid being a farmer doesn't lead to art lessons for my girls." Mr. Meyer seemed uncomfortable.

"Oh, heavens, no, Mr. Meyer," Lottie smiled. "I'm very serious that it would just be for fun. We girls could have a lovely afternoon if you'd be willing to chauffeur your girls to and from the Evans house."

Mr. Meyer hesitated. "Well, we'll just have to see. My girls have so much to do at home. I think they need to concentrate themselves on being able to run a household for their future husbands, and I doubt painting pretty pictures will be very important to those men. But maybe sometime we can take you up on your very generous offer."

The Meyer girls cast their eyes down, and I could see the color rise in Lottie's cheeks. My mother cleared her throat and started asking about how Mr. Meyer's crops were coming along. As they chatted, Lottie and I exchanged quick glances. Before we left for home, she and I gave each of the Meyer girls a hug. There was nothing else we could do for them.

CHAPTER 16

Unwelcome Visit

Monday, August 12, 1929

Dear Sis,

I hope you are enjoying our summer so far and not sweltering in Tarboro too much. We have a right long ways to go before we get any relief in the fall, don't we? And let's pray we don't get a hurricane come September and October. I won't breathe easy until November, I'm sure.

I also hope you'll forgive me for not writing in so long. It's just too easy to think, "I'll write tomorrow when I have more time," but of course "tomorrow" turns out to be every bit as busy. But Tommy and the girls are all in bed, except Irene, who is up reading for a while, and Clarence. I think he's trying to decide if he should demand more biscuit and molasses before he gives in to sleep. From the way his eyelids keep fluttering, and his head keeps nodding, I think sleep will win. You should see how much his hair has come in since you were here in the winter, so dark and wavy like Tom's. He'll be walking on his own any day now.

I told you over the telephone about my old friend Lottie reappearing in my life, and how wonderful that is. Now I'm wondering how I got along without her. I can't wait for the two of you to meet next time you and Mama Jo visit here, which I hope will be soon.

Today was trying. Martha and Irene both were down with heat headaches this afternoon. Mama made burnt toast for them. You know she swears by that old remedy, although I really think if it ever works, it's because it's so unpleasant to eat that awful bread it takes your mind off the headache. After they choked down a piece each, I put them to bed together, which delighted Martha, who usually sleeps with Celeste, drew the curtains closed, and put strips of brown paper bags soaked in vinegar on their foreheads. Now THAT is a headache remedy that actually works! And it's so cooling. I also kept wiping their faces and necks and arms with a wet washrag to help chill them down more. Celeste came in and helped, so both girls got as much relief from the heat as we could manage. It wasn't too long before they both fell asleep, poor babies. I told Celeste how much I appreciated her coming to help me and her sisters, and she looked so proud. After that, she made a point of getting Tommy and Leah playing a game quietly at the kitchen table. Mama and Daddy were happy to get a nap in until supper time, too. It's hard to want to do anything when you feel like you could wring out the air and make steam.

Fortunately, Martha and Irene woke from their naps feeling fine. It was too hot to get a fire going in the cookstove, not even to warm up the butterbeans, but they tasted right good cold, along with the tomatoes and cucumbers and leftover ham biscuits from breakfast. Celeste and Leah had all of us laughing while we ate. Celeste complained the mosquitos were eating her up every time she had to go outside to get the eggs or help feed the animals. While I strongly suspect she was hoping to be excused from those chores, I declare, those gnats and mosquitos do seem to love her. Horse flies, too. She is covered with so many swollen bites—bigger welts and more of them than the rest of us put together. Anyway, she said, "I think they must love me so much because I'm the sweetest one of all of us."

I saw Daddy hide his smile, which was more than Irene and Mama bothered to do. And Tommy rolled his eyes over at her just as Leah said, "Well, I guess we know that can't be the reason." Celeste looked right put out when we all laughed.

Daddy tried to make her feel better. "Honey, don't you mind them. I heard some of those skeeters talking the other day, and they said they come all the way from South Carolina to get a taste of you. Heard you was just that sweet." Well, that got her up from the table to run over and hug his neck, and we didn't have to have a pouting Celeste for the rest of the evening.

Sis, I have been fretting about my daddy. He tries to work on the garden in the early morning before it gets so hot. And as many of us as can help him with the weeding, of course, but I can tell it gets harder and harder on him. I just don't know what to do about it. I know he's taken on more since we're living here. At least that extra burden is almost done for the growing season, and I can't still be here next summer. I've got to find a job and get my own place for me and the children. But Mama and Daddy have always depended on their garden for so much of their food, and the chickens and hogs. Even without us living here, there will be so much work for Daddy, and I'm worried he won't be able to manage. I can't help but feel things are going to change, and not for the better. Not for them. As Mama is always saying about Daddy and herself, "We're not spring chicks anymore." I don't feel much like a spring chick either, and I'm only thirty. I can't imagine how they feel at sixty-seven and sixty-eight.

That reminds me. I hope Mama Jo is bearing up better than she was this winter. How I wish our spring and fall lasted longer than they do. It always seems to be too hot and humid or too cold and wet. I wonder if there is any place on earth that has "just right" weather all year. I sound like Goldilocks, don't I?

I need to get to bed soon now. Clarence is fast asleep, and Irene went off to bed some time ago while I've been writing this at the kitchen table. I'm the only one up now. It's odd when this old house is this quiet.

Sis, there is one other thing. I got a call today from a lawyer in town. He wants to come by tomorrow to meet with me. I'm not sure what it's about, but he says he has been trying to track me down since shortly after Tom's passing, and that he belongs to the same civic group Tom was a member of. He said he wants to talk to me about an opportunity I might need to know about. He wouldn't give me any more information, but we agreed he would come over tomorrow afternoon. He asked for my parents to be there, too, but wanted to know if we could talk without any of the children around. All I could think of was for Daddy to take them to the library in town. At least it will be cooler there for them, even though Daddy won't be able to hear what the man has to say. I'll keep Clarence here, of course.

So, I hope it isn't bad news, which he promised it wouldn't be, but you never know with lawyers, do you? I'll let you know what happens. Now I better try to get some sleep. I look forward to hearing your news soon. Give Mama Jo and Clyde my love.

And much love to you, too,
Mary Ellen

<hr>

I rose from my front porch rocking chair as the black motorcar pulled into our yard, clutching Toby in my arms to calm him. Mama sat holding Clarence, whose drooping eyelids let us know he would soon be ready for his afternoon nap. A tall man in a light gray suit got out of the car, removing his hat as he walked over to the porch steps. I noticed he carried a small pamphlet rather than any kind of satchel, and I was relieved legal papers didn't seem to be part of our meeting.

Mama and I greeted him and asked if he'd rather meet inside or out on the porch where we were getting a breeze. I set Toby down as the lawyer settled into one of the empty rockers. He rubbed Toby's grateful ears for a moment and then took a long sip from the icy glass of sweet tea I handed him. He wiped his forehead with his handkerchief.

Mama spoke up, "Mr. Adams, please make yourself more comfortable. That suit jacket must be a trial to wear in this heat."

His serious face broke into a relieved smile, and he followed her suggestion. "Mrs. Evans, I appreciate that. It's clear to me our ideas of proper clothing come from a much cooler climate than our own. I've heard England and much of Europe are considerably cooler than here, so I'm thinking we have them to blame."

After a few more pleasantries, Mama took Clarence in for his nap, but she returned a few minutes later with a slice of pound cake for Mr. Adams while I poured him another glass of tea. The cake disappeared as quickly as the first glass of sweet tea, and appearing much more comfortable, Mr. Adams began to explain his visit, lifting an ecstatic Toby onto his lap.

"Mrs. Heath, I mentioned I also belong to the Junior Order, same as your late husband, and I got to know him fairly well over the last few years."

I nodded. "I never really understood what the Junior Order did, but I know Tom looked forward to your meetings. He would just say you men were working on something that would mean the world to needy folks."

Mr. Adams seemed surprised Tom hadn't told me more. He took another little sip of his tea and started fanning his face with his hat as he gazed out towards the dusty road.

Finally, he cleared his throat and continued. "Well, ma'am, that's right. We've been working—our local chapter, that is, along with the regional chapters—to build a new orphanage over in Lexington. Do you ladies happen to know where that is?" He glanced at Mama and me. We shook our heads.

"I've never heard of Lexington, have you, Mary?" Mama looked at me.

"Only the one up north where there was the big battle in the Revolutionary War. Irene was just studying that in her history class this past year." I looked at Mr. Adams. "Is that the Lexington you mean?"

"Oh no, my apologies. I meant Lexington, North Carolina. It's about twenty miles south of Winston-Salem. About 200 miles by train from Wilmington. That's in the Piedmont part of the state."

Mama and I again shook our heads.

"Well, to continue, that is where we have just completed construction of the orphanage. Ladies, it is a sight to behold." His voice quickened with enthusiasm. "The architecture is based on the University of Virginia up there in Charlottesville. Thomas Jefferson designed that university, you know. Beautiful. Well, we wanted a place that would do us proud and not look as if no one cared for the children who would be raised there. It's a fine institution, and we've just started taking in children. We're planning for around 200. We think most of the children will be from North Carolina, but we already have a few from South Carolina, Virginia, Tennessee, and Kentucky." Here he paused and took another sip of tea, his other hand continuing to pet Toby.

Mama and I kept smiling and nodding. I'm sure she was also wondering why we were hearing about this, and then it hit me that maybe Mr. Adams was hoping we could make a donation. I was thinking about how to get out of that gracefully.

"So, Mrs. Heath, I think you probably have surmised why I'm here today. I just wanted to let you know about this possible course of action, should you need such an opportunity."

I stopped smiling and nodding. It seemed to me Mr. Adams had abruptly switched to some other language. I glanced at my mother, who seemed to be as confused as I was. "I'm afraid I don't follow you, Mr. Adams. What opportunity?" Could the man really think of donating money as an "opportunity" for a widow with six children to support?

Mr. Adams glanced from Mama back to me. He seemed unsure of how to proceed for a moment. Then he continued, "Why, the opportunity to care for your children, Mrs. Heath. I understand that with Tom's passing, you might have difficulty managing on your own to support your children, unless your parents are well placed to assist you, of course. If that is the case, I hope you will forgive my intrusion."

I was stunned. Put my children in an orphanage? I didn't care if it was designed by Thomas Jefferson. I didn't care if he built it with his very own hands. Not raise my own children? Put them 200 miles away? What was this man thinking?

Before I could get my thoughts together enough to even reply, Mr. Adams continued, "I just recalled Tom didn't make you aware of our civic project. I'm sure he felt there was no possibility, young as he was, you would ever need its services. But you see, Mrs. Heath, this is no ordinary orphanage. We raised the funds for it and built it specifically as a haven for our own children—that is, the children of the Junior Order's members, should either or both of the parents pass away. It is not an orphanage open to the public, as it were. A decade ago, we had the Great War, and then we saw what the Spanish Influenza did. So many parents were taken, while their elderly parents and young children survived. It was the strange thing about that illness that the healthiest young adults were most likely to be taken off, as I'm sure you remember."

Mama said, "I recall reading how so many grandparents simply couldn't raise their young grandchildren. They were too old or frail or too impoverished to do so. Or they passed away from old age before the children were grown up."

Mr. Adams nodded. "Exactly. We never know when we could face another war or disease on a large scale. We decided to take measures to provide for our own children should a disaster strike this nation or our families again."

I was beginning to get over the shock of realizing what the lawyer was talking about, and I could see the sense in what the Junior Order had done. Still, it seemed strange to me that all these months later I was hearing about this.

"So, Mr. Adams, you're saying you just wanted to make sure I didn't need such help? Is that why you waited to talk with me?"

"I wanted to make sure you were aware of this option, Mrs. Heath. I have to apologize for taking so long to contact you, though. I did write to you when I learned of Tom's passing, but the letter was returned with 'not at this address' written on it. I didn't know your maiden name, so tracking down your parents was not easy. In fact, it was only by chance I mentioned to a Junior Order friend last week at lunch my disappointment in not being able to find you. He finally recalled meeting your father at Tom's funeral and, eventually, he was able to remember your father's last name. A little bit of footwork, and I finally located you."

"I see, Mr. Adams. And I'm grateful to you for trying to find me, though I can't imagine letting someone else take care of my children and being parted from them. I am just now, with my youngest finally being old enough to eat regular food, about to look for employment. My parents have been so kind to keep us here this past year, but of course I need to take on a job and get the children into our own home. I expect we'll be moving into an apartment in Wilmington, as that's where I'm most likely to find work. Now, should you hear of anything you think I might be suitable for, I'd greatly appreciate you passing that on to me." I nodded my head and took a deep breath. I hated to even ask that favor, but I knew I'd better take advantage of any possible assistance with finding a job.

And I didn't want to offend the man, but I didn't need to hear any more about this so-called opportunity. I could certainly see why Tom didn't bother telling me about what in particular they were working on because he would have known I'd never give up my children, no matter what. Such nonsense. As if I were some kind of bad mother. I could feel my face getting hotter the more I thought about it. Give up my children to make it easier on myself? Never!

"Mr. Adams," my mother soothed, shooting me a look, "it was so kind of you to drive out on these dusty dirt roads all the way from Wilmington—and in this heat—to talk to Mary. I know Tom is looking down and grateful his friends are doing what they can to let Mary see she isn't all alone in this, and that there is help if she needs it."

Mr. Adams looked from her to me, set a disappointed Toby down, and picked up his hat and jacket. "Well, Mrs. Heath. Mrs. Evans. Thank you very much for your time and hospitality, and for hearing me out. Here is my card—if you ever need to ask any questions or think of some way I can help you out. And I will indeed keep my ear out for job opportunities for you. I know Tom would have done the same for my family."

We shook his hand, and as he turned to go, he seemed to remember the pamphlet he'd brought. "Ladies, this little brochure shows some photos of the orphanage and gives some information. At least you can see what Tom had been helping with." Mama reached out for it; he nodded and walked over to his car. He pulled out of the driveway slowly, no doubt to spare us the cloud of dust that got kicked up, and drove off.

Mama took the man's card and the brochure and slipped them into her dress pocket. "Don't worry, Mary. You're going to be able to find a job. I know you're ready to start looking, and I guess you're right." She gave me a quick hug and went inside. I stood a moment longer, watching the distant dust cloud that followed Mr. Adams's car. I wasn't sure why I felt I might burst into tears.

CHAPTER 17

A Bolt from the Blue

Thursday, August 22, 1929

Every year in late summer, we started worrying about a hurricane hitting our area. In previous years, of course, this was even more of a concern, as we lived within sight of the Sound and the ocean. Everyone in this area was aware of the damage that could be done by the winds and the storm surge. Although my parents' home was farther inland by some thirty miles, we would still be greatly affected by any storm that came up the coast. September and October were the months we most closely watched the weather, but we all knew hurricanes could come earlier in the summer and even after Halloween, although those were rare. Mama always said worrying about it wouldn't change anything, and we just needed to be prepared. She was right, as always.

It doesn't take a hurricane to cause damage, of course. On August 22, two weeks after we'd celebrated Celeste turning eleven, the skies darkened suddenly in the late morning. The wind picked up, and I raced outside to pull in the diapers I'd washed and hung out earlier, when it had looked like any other sultry summer day. By the time I'd unpegged a day's worth of Clarence's diapers, the wind was blowing so hard it was like swimming against a strong current to make it back to the house. Leah had to chase her basketball down a long row of corn, while Irene and Celeste went to shut the chickens up in their coop.

When Daddy, Tommy, and Toby returned from the barn, having made sure Molly had food and water and was secure in her stall, we all gathered around the kitchen table. It was so dark Mama lit the kerosene lamp and suggested we go ahead and eat our dinner, although most of us were too concerned with the howling wind and the pelting rain to have much appetite. Except little Clarence, of course, who was by now happy to chew on and drool out a biscuit with molasses.

We were just finishing the dishes when the thunder and lightning started. It was Celeste's turn to do the dishes, and she was about to empty the dishpan water when there was a loud boom of thunder, instantly followed by a bright flash out the kitchen window. Celeste hurled herself back from the sink, gripping her right hand with her left.

"Celeste, what is it, honey? Did you cut yourself?" Mama cried, as I reached Celeste and turned her to me, looking for the blood that must be on her hand.

"Mama, Grandmama, no! I… I think I just got a little shock from that lightning! My hand is sort of burning and tingling all at the same time!" Poor Celeste was clearly frightened.

I took her hand and looked at it carefully, then at her arm. Seeing no damage, I pulled her to me and hugged her fiercely.

"Baby, I'm so sorry I let you do those dishes. I should have gotten you away from the window the moment that first lightning flashed. I'm so sorry. Are you all right now?" I pushed her thick hair back and looked at her teary blue-gray eyes.

She shuddered and put her head on my shoulder. "I think I'm all right, but it really scared me. I think it struck outside, and I just got a little bit of it."

Mama came over and took her out of my arms; then her sisters came to hug her. Even Tommy, standing beside Daddy's chair, looked horrified. Daddy put his arm around Tommy and told him Celeste was going to be just fine.

After that, we all sat back down at the table and waited for the storm to pass. Irene got Martha's book of fairytales and read several to us. Martha sat on Celeste's lap, arms wrapped around her big sister. In the lamp's glow, I glanced around the table at all my loved ones and almost wept to think how close we'd come to a tragedy.

The next day, we found we were not the only ones to have a run-in with the storm. Lightning had struck our church steeple. Fortunately, the rain had almost immediately extinguished the fire that followed, but the steeple was left in ruins and appeared to be in danger of falling to the ground soon.

That Sunday, our minister decided we should have a short outdoor service of thanksgiving for the church's survival through the storm, and afterward, we discussed what needed to be done to repair the steeple. Having a congregation of so many farmers meant we had a host of capable men with the skills needed to rebuild the simple structure. Mr. Prince asked for a volunteer to lead the repairs and coordinate getting materials donated and a work crew organized. I was not one bit surprised when Mr. Meyer raised his hand and was greeted with a general round of applause. After all, he'd led the effort earlier in the summer on work on the church building. In such a short time of being with us, it seemed everyone sensed he was the natural leader needed for this endeavor, too.

Two weeks later, September 8, our church held another Sunday thanksgiving service, followed by an outdoor picnic. We were celebrating the completion of our new steeple, which received its final coat of white paint just the day before. Mr. Meyer had supervised its construction brilliantly, and everyone was amazed at how well he had led and completed the effort. Our steeple was even two feet taller than it had been. Fortunately, the original bell was intact and undamaged, so it had also been reinstalled. Mr. Prince had invited Mr. Meyer to have the honor of pulling the bell cord to bring us all into the sanctuary for the service.

Many of the men had donated their labor to the demolition and reconstruction effort, along with numerous material and cash donations from shop owners and the more well-to-do of the church members, as well as the food supplied by the many church ladies for the working men. All had contributed as they could while making sure their own children, homes, animals, and ripening crops were being seen to as needed.

Coordinating who could do what and when had been a feat few could have pulled off with such effectiveness, and Mr. Meyer had the gratitude and admiration of all. Even his three daughters basked in the overflow of affection that came to their family. Before this, it had seemed to me they were often over-looked, as their father shone so brightly, they were in his shadow. But now, they also had their share of our congregation's love and attention, and I think their regard for their new community warmed considerably in return. They lost the withdrawn, sullen expressions they had so often displayed and exuded the warmth and friendliness that attracted friendship. I saw the three of them now, in their own admiring circle, which included Celeste and Irene. The group of about ten girls were all laughing and talking.

I walked over to them. "Girls, you must be so proud of your father for doing such a fine job for our church. I'm sure he's depended on you three to run the house on your own these last two weeks. He's been so busy, but I'm certain he's proud of you, too." It was important to make sure they knew their extra efforts were also noticed in case Mr. Meyer hadn't thought to tell them.

They blushed and beamed. Soft "Thank you, Mrs. Heath" replies were murmured, and I could tell they appreciated being acknowledged, along with their father. At that moment, he joined the group and stood between Irene and me.

"I think I just heard Mrs. Heath complimenting you girls, and she is so right. Guess our farm would have fallen apart these last weeks without my girls stepping up. Of course, they do most of the work anyway," he laughed and nodded at the girls, who were clearly even more delighted by his praise.

I thought it was good for him to be reminded what he took for granted—for I would have bet good money it had not occurred to him to notice, much less acknowledge, the additional burden placed on the shoulders of these young girls. Perhaps it was unfair of me. I'd been told more than once I could leap to conclusions about people. But I suspected Mr. Meyer was used to being catered to and having his way—simply expecting those closest to him should go out of their way for him. It was also likely they'd been running the household for the years Mrs. Meyer was ill.

Later, Mr. Meyer took my arm and led me away from the noisy crowd. "There's something I have been wanting to talk to you about, Mrs. Heath."

I tried to mask my surprise and sudden worry. He seemed quite serious, more serious than I'd ever seen him. I looked back over my shoulder and saw Mama watching us walk away. She was clutching her hands together and smiling. I wished I hadn't just eaten so much at the picnic.

We walked away from the churchyard, along the empty road. The cicadas were still making a racket, and I could hear the harsh call of crows in the distance. We came to a little path, which led to the creek, and stood next to it under an old live oak. Its largest branch stretched out at least fifteen feet, almost resting on the ground, and the gray Spanish moss gave the scene a mournful air.

"Mrs. Heath, do you mind if I call you Mary? I wish you'd call me Mitch. I think we've known each other long enough to be less formal, don't you?" I wondered if I imagined he was nervous. He didn't seem to be his usual confident and take-charge self.

"No, Mr.—I mean, not at all, Mitch." I smiled, but felt more uneasy by the moment. I was glad I'd brought along one of the paddle fans we used in the church; it gave me something to do with my nervous energy.

"You probably have noticed how attentive I've been, and I suspect you have guessed the reason. I know you might think it's too soon, but I believe I should make my intentions clearly known. I wouldn't want you to think later that I was hiding my…well, my deep affection. I just hope I have been proving to you the kind of man I am, and that I take my responsibilities very seriously. I don't trifle with the affections of any lady. I know I'm older, but I think that can be a good thing in a husband, don't you? After all, your Tom was ten years older than you were."

Now my stomach clenched. I really did not want him to go on, but I couldn't think of any way to stop him. I tried to keep any expression other than mild interest off my face.

"I'm a man of property, and I'm in fine fiddle, Mary. I'm healthy as a horse; I think I can say without bragging that I'm really in my prime. I'm a good provider. I think my five girls would tell you I'm a good father, too. Maybe sterner than they'd like sometimes, but I think the good Lord means for the man to be the head of the household, and hold everyone in it to the highest personal and moral standards." Here, he stopped a moment and took a deep breath. I just kept on fanning myself at top speed while I mulled over that last statement. I didn't like the sound of it very much.

Meanwhile, Mr. Meyer got his second wind. "I hope I don't sound boastful, Mary, but I can't rely on the fact that you had years to get to know me because we've only known each other since late June. And I don't have any old friends here to speak on my behalf. So, I'm in the uncomfortable position of having to toot my own horn, as it were."

He finally stopped and took another deep breath. So did I. I hardly knew where to look. I could not form a coherent thought in my head other than "Mama was right!" I was stunned to find myself in this position. And I just wasn't sure what I thought of Mr. Meyer—Mitch—as a potential husband. I knew he'd been interested, given how often we saw him, but at some level I just didn't feel he really wanted me, the real me. That he even knew me. I could believe he wanted a wife, but a thirty-year-old woman with six children?

And I was not at all sure I liked some of the things I'd learned about how he viewed women. His opinions were hardly so different from most men from what I could tell, but I'd never had the feeling from my father, or my Tom, that they saw women in such a narrow way as was so common. I couldn't imagine being married to someone who saw me as a lesser being.

I stood there, watching the water in the creek flow by as the cicadas seemed to get louder and louder. I could think of nothing to say. That was fortunate, as it turned out.

"Mary, I know you've noticed how attentive I've been to your family. I've come to love them all. Your parents are wonderful people, and you are a marvel as a mother. You've done a great job with your brood. You should be very proud. Before I get my hopes up, I want to go ahead and ask you, Mary…"

I squared my shoulders and forced myself to look at him. His handsome face looked at me earnestly as he twisted his hat round and round by the brim.

"Mary, may I have your permission to court Irene?"

I was still in a daze when I rejoined my family. Mr. Meyer had said he understood by my reaction that I needed time to think about his request, and we'd walked back to the church. Mama was watching for us, and her eyes kept jumping from my face to Mr. Meyer—never to be "Mitch" to me again—with her hopes clear as day in her expression. I gave her a stiff smile and nodded to Mr. Meyer as he took his leave and went to find his daughters.

"Mary?" Mama hissed. She gripped my elbow and, nodding to the various ladies standing in groups chatting, walked me over to our truck. She pretended to look for something on the floorboard while watching me. "Well? What did he say?"

I gazed over her head, feeling my stunned response melting away as a new feeling took over: outrage. I still didn't know if I was truly sorry he wasn't interested in me. My pride was hurt; I had to admit. But that was nothing compared to the outrage I felt on Irene's behalf. It apparently had never crossed his mind that I, at least fifteen years younger than him, was a more suitable potential mate than my beautiful daughter, who was thirty-five years younger! No, this pig felt he deserved a thirteen-year-old virgin, a girl he thought he could intimidate and control. Not to mention make her bear him baby after baby. Sons, of course.

"Well, Mama," I choked out, "he does indeed want to come courting."

Mama smiled and was about to say something when I added, "Irene."

"What? What about Irene, honey?" Mama poked her head up and looked towards the church, apparently thinking I'd just been distracted by something Irene was doing in the churchyard.

"Mr. Meyer wants to court Irene, not me." I moved so I was facing the church crowd, and Mama, in looking at me, turned away from them. I didn't want anyone to see her shocked expression I knew was coming. I hoped I was doing a good job at looking as if I was just having a casual chat with my mother.

Mama leaned in the open door against the truck seat as if her legs would no longer support her. She blinked several times and struggled for words. Finally, she said, "But Mary, he's been courting you! He's said such nice things to you and has been so attentive and…" She shook her head and reached out for my hand. "Baby, are you all right?"

I smiled and turned to stand by her, facing away from any onlookers, desperate to hide the sheen of tears that appeared at my mother's concern for me. "I was as shocked as you, Mama. I never felt sure he was interested in me, and now I know why, but it never occurred to me he had his sights on Irene. Never! It makes me furious he has been trying to ingratiate himself with our entire family so he would stand a better chance at getting approval to… to… STEAL my baby!"

Mama shushed me gently and thought a moment. "Well, most smart men would do exactly that, Mary. If Irene and he were much closer in age, and she was a few years older, of course, you would expect him to get to know the entire family, not just Irene. But I understand how you feel, and I agree. I think he went too far in making us think it was you he was interested in." Here, she wrinkled her forehead and paused. I could tell she was trying to puzzle it out. "But the more I think of it, the less I think he did it deliberately. He probably assumed we understood he had his eye on Irene."

I huffed. "What am I? Chopped liver?" Now I was torn between being angry about my hurt pride and being angry about the nerve of that old man thinking he should have my Irene. But I was very, very sure I was angry.

Mama smiled and squeezed my hand. "Now, Mary, I think we both know you are a very attractive woman. A young woman still, although you probably don't see it that way, but you will when you're my age. I'm afraid Mr. Meyer is like most men, though. I had hoped he was different." Her head snapped up. "But, Mary, what did you say to him?"

"I was so taken aback I think my mind just froze. I sure hope he took it for surprise for Irene's sake. He probably thought I was overwhelmed with her good fortune. I pray it never occurs to him I thought he might be asking to court me. That would be truly mortifying. Mama. Nobody can know that's what we thought, and what you hoped for." I gave her an accusing glare, but then leaned over and kissed her cheek as she started to look guilty. She only wanted a happy ending for me and the children. I knew that.

I tried to think of his exact words leading up to saying he wanted to court Irene. As I repeated them to Mama, I realized everything he said had been about convincing me he was a good match for Irene, not me. Especially how I understood marrying an older man could be just fine. I now saw everything he'd said today and in our other meetings was really referring to his interest in *her*, but I'd taken all of it the wrong way.

Later that night, I remembered Mama's comment that most smart men would get the family to like him, and I thought of all those years ago with Tom. He talked to my parents after church every time he came. And later, he got to know each one of my sisters. I had thought he was interested in me, and he was, but I couldn't be sure at first that he wasn't just being nice to us. I even worried he was really interested in one of my older sisters, especially Janie, who was closer to his age.

But Tom was only ten years older than me. Mr. Meyer was more than thirty-five years older than Irene, for Pete's sake! And she was only thirteen. Here I had to pause. I'd only been fourteen. But… I searched for something to justify my anger. Times changed. Yes, times changed, and it was now far less common for girls to marry so young. Not that it was exactly common, at least, not in my family, fifteen years back when I was such a young bride. Besides, I'd had no business getting married that young, and my parents should have stopped me. What had they been thinking to let me do that? I punched my pillow. The real question was what had *I* been thinking? Tom and I should have waited at least a couple of years.

Sleep didn't come for many hours that night. I wasn't looking forward to talking with Irene the next day, but I felt I had to tell her about Mr. Meyer's interest. I just prayed she wouldn't have her head turned. Even if it was, Mr. Meyer would not be courting her until she graduated from high school. Somehow, I didn't think he'd be waiting five years.

That pillow really took a beating that night.

CHAPTER 18

Friends & Family

Wednesday, September 25, 1929

Walking up the steep steps to the front porch of Mrs. Vanderven's house was not what I wanted to be doing, but I needed to talk with Lottie without the children around. First, though, I had to get past the dragon, her mother.

I'd come to see Lottie a few weeks ago to tell her the story of Mr. Meyer's unexpected request and my later refusal to allow him to court Irene. It was so good to have a close friend to confide in, and she had more than shared my disgust. I was especially happy to report Irene had been horrified at the idea of "that old man" wanting to court her. Also, I had to give Mr. Meyer credit, for he'd been understanding and even gracious when I told him I thought Irene was too young for any man. I suspected that his affection for Irene had not been deep, and that made me even more relieved to have turned down his request. He just wanted to find a wife, but I hoped for any future Mrs. Meyer's sake, he'd wait until he found someone he could love as she should be loved. And that she'd be old enough and strong-willed enough to stand up to him.

That visit had been my first to Mrs. Vanderven's magnificent home since I was a young girl, and I had made the mistake of going to the back door. Lottie was appalled I'd thought I shouldn't use the front door.

"Mary Ellen, what were you thinking?" Lottie had gripped my hand once we were alone in her room and looked at me with both exasperation and something much too close to pity. "My mother needs to know you are my dear friend and not a tradesperson or servant who comes in through the back of the house. If she finds out, she'll think less of you."

"I just didn't want to cause any trouble, Lottie," I'd said, ashamed my reluctance to face Mrs. Vanderven's superior attitude had made me look foolish. Perhaps even cowardly. I'd resolved never to make that mistake again.

So, here I was, about to ring the doorbell of this imposing three-story home on Front Street in Wilmington. Daddy had some errands to run in town, and he'd promised me a good hour or two for my visit with Lottie. I had slid down from the truck's passenger seat, clutched my handbag, dusted off the back of my dress, and marched myself up to the dragon's lair. "Up" was the right word; I was already slightly out of breath from the steep climb leading from the street level. As I knew from past visits, the house was so high on this hill, a rarity in our area, an unobscured view of the Cape Fear River was clearly visible from the west-facing top floor windows where Lottie had her studio.

"Get ahold of yourself, Mary," I told myself silently as I heard footsteps coming down the darkened hallway. Like so many of us, Mrs. Vanderven kept many shades and curtains closed against the open windows during the long days of the hot months to help keep the inside temperature more bearable. I always thought it funny our houses in the South were probably much brighter inside during the winter, despite the shorter days, than the blistering summer months when we tried to hide from the heat.

Out of the dimness of the hallway, the figure of Mr. Simms, always just "Simms" to Mrs. Vanderven, appeared. Lottie's mother, as a young girl, visited a wealthy school friend whose family, being originally from England, called their butler by his last name. Mrs. Vanderven had adopted that custom when she married and acquired her own butler. There was no custom too grand for Mrs. Vanderven.

Mr. Simms opened the screen door and greeted me, "Miss Mary Ellen, it's nice to see you again." He had known me since I was a child, and I had always called him "Mr. Simms" even though I knew so many would only call him by his first name. My mother told me when I was very young that she could find nowhere in the Bible where it said to treat people with less respect if their skin happened to be darker than your own.

He had been out running an errand during my visit a few weeks ago, so this was the first time I'd seen him in many years. His cheeks rounded with his smile, and his eyes were warm. Since I'd last seen him, his hair had gone white, and he seemed shrunken with age now, but his deep, kind drawl was just as I remembered it.

"Mr. Simms! I'm so delighted to see you, too. I hope you've been well." I stepped into the hallway, my eyes slowly adjusting to the gloom.

He opened his mouth to say something when Mrs. Vanderven's sharp voice stabbed out from where she sat in the front parlor. "Simms! Stop gossiping and bring Mrs. Heath in here to say hello!"

No tiptoeing past the dragon then. Mr. Simms gave me a small smile and motioned to the parlor doorway immediately off the foyer. Overhead, I could hear rapid footsteps approaching the stairwell, but I knew not to dawdle by waiting for Lottie to appear. Best pet the beast and hope I didn't get eaten.

"Mrs. Vanderven, good afternoon." I tried to smile as I approached her. She perched on her ornate armchair of faded plum velvet. I wondered for a moment if that lady's spine had ever touched the back of a chair. Despite the heat, she wore a full-length dark dress with long sleeves and a tight, high neck. The only concession to the oppressive humid air was the black lace fan she wafted in front of her face. Not a trace of perspiration was there. No trace of warmth of any kind, really.

"Good afternoon, Mary. Please come visit for a while." She gestured to the settee. Turning to Mr. Simms, she murmured, "Tea, Simms." He left to get it just as Lottie appeared in the arched doorway.

"Well, Lottie, you are late to greet your guest, but do come in now that you're finally here. We're going to have tea before you young girls disappear upstairs." She indicated the settee where I sat, and Lottie slid into her place beside me, giving my hand a quick squeeze.

"Yes, Mama, I was just getting Bertie settled for his afternoon rest time." She turned to me. "He's adamant he no longer needs a nap, but I insist he has a little quiet time and just read one of his books. I can't understand how the heat doesn't seem to affect children, but I suppose we were like that, too, at that age."

"I hope you have him reading something other than those cheap adventure books he loves so much." Mrs. Vanderven sniffed.

"I think Mr. Mark Twain's books are of sufficient quality and reputation to please you, Mama." Lottie raised an eyebrow at her mother. I realized she was a long way from the young girl who'd been so cowed by this lady. I bit the inside of my cheek to avoid smiling.

Another sniff from Mrs. Vanderven, but before she could add any further objection, Mr. Simms brought in the huge silver tea tray. The tiered cake stand was there, as usual, with its buttered toast and little squares of sandwiches on the bottom, scones and jam on the middle, and charming petit fours and cake slices on the top tier.

I remembered all of this from the few teatimes I'd endured here as a young adolescent, including the imposing silver tea service Mrs. Vanderven probably considered part of her armor against the crude world. I sighed, thinking of how long this would take away from my time alone with Lottie, but gamely began with toast and gradually worked my way up the tiers, as Lottie had taught me years ago. Civilization would end, no doubt, were sweets to be eaten before the savory.

Mrs. Vanderven inspected the tea tray carefully and then curtly dismissed Mr. Simms. "You have to check their work, you know." She looked up from pouring our tea. "Lazy and careless, that's just to be expected, so you have to always be on your guard. You girls need to remember that."

Lottie looked down at her clutched hands. I stared at the carpet and took a deep breath, choking back what I wanted to say. This woman had such a good life, one of wealth and leisure, and yet she treated the people who worked so hard for her with such disdain. It seemed she needed to think of others as less so she could feel herself to be more. An entire race of people dismissed as lazy and careless. And her opinion was hardly uncommon. That was the truly sad thing. I couldn't see any sign of things getting better, either. But I'd teach my children better. I promised myself.

"Do you know," Mrs. Vanderven began after we were well into our tea, "some people would refer to this as a 'high tea?'" I could tell by her tone "some people" were sadly mistaken. Also, I'd heard this little lecture several times from her in my youth.

"Yes, I suppose they let the word *high* mislead them," she continued as a little self-satisfied smile flitted across her face. "But, of course, it refers to the height of the table being used, essentially a dining table. The lower classes in England had 'high tea' in the evening as their supper, not the sort of thing that *we* mean. A low table is used for an elegant afternoon tea, so it's really *low tea*, although it's never called that. 'Cream tea' sometimes, when clotted cream is served for the scones, but never, ever 'high tea.' Not by people of social standing." Again, the superior—and no doubt much practiced—smile. "We don't have clotted cream today. I only have my cook make it when I have special guests."

"Really, Mama, you should consider writing a book on etiquette. You have so much knowledge young people need to know." I made sure I didn't make eye contact with Lottie. I knew she was pulling her mother's leg, and I was not about to offend the lady by having a giggling fit. Even if she had made it clear I didn't fall into the "special guest" category. That comment had probably prompted Lottie's remark.

Mrs. Vanderven gave Lottie a suspicious look, but she seemed to decide Lottie was serious. "Yes, I've been told that a number of times by my friends."

Lottie choked on her tea. I patted her back, and looked at Mrs. Vanderven, "Yes, ma'am. I think Lottie is correct. Think how helpful that would be."

Lottie got a hold of herself, and we made it through the next fifteen minutes until we could escape to her room upstairs. I had asked her mother more about the book she might one day write, and the project I knew her garden club was working on.

Mrs. Vanderven didn't ask me a single question about myself, my children, or my plans for the future. I decided I didn't mind the absence of her interest.

Upstairs, the bedroom door shut behind us, Lottie turned to me. "I have no trouble believing her friends have told her to write a book. It probably means the same as 'go fly a kite.' To people of social standing, of course." We both doubled over, snorting with laughter.

Once we stopped laughing, I told her about the visit from Mr. Adams.

"Oh, Mary Ellen! An orphanage! And you never knew Tom's club was working on building one? I hardly know where to start with my questions. What do you think of it all?" Lottie had listened to my recitation of the lawyer's visit with amazement showing on every feature of her face. Even her breath kept catching in her throat.

Halfway through my account, she'd reached over and grasped both of my hands in hers. I don't think she could have looked more horrified if she thought the man was about to rip my babies from my arms and run off with them. "Mary, I just keep thinking of the type of orphanage that Charles Dickens would have envisioned!" She bit her lip, as if to prevent herself from saying any more.

Watching her reaction, I thought that was how I had looked during the meeting with Mr. Adams. Truth to tell, it was Jane Eyre that had shaped my views of orphanages, although I'd not realized it until just now. Lowood. The name of Jane's horrible institution popped into my head. I took a deep breath.

"Mr. Adams gave Mama and me a booklet that has more information about the place in Lexington. It has some photos in it. I've brought it for you to see." At that, Lottie looked at me in confusion.

"Mary, are you considering placing the children there?" I could tell she was trying to appear neutral, but she'd already shown her horror.

"No, no, of course not, Lottie. I just thought you'd be curious. I didn't even look at it until after all the children went to bed. Mama took it from Mr. Adams and brought it out for me to look at later. She said she just thought I'd be interested to see what Tom had been working on, which is what the lawyer had said. I was so put out with him for suggesting such a thing, I wouldn't even have taken it." I could feel my indignation rising. "Does he think I'm some lazy, horrible mother who wants to be rid of her children so I can have an easier life?" I blinked back the tears trying to come. Tears of anger, I told myself.

Lottie searched my face, took the booklet, and started looking through it after giving my hand a pat. I was sure she was letting me have a moment to calm down.

After a minute or two, without looking up from a photo of the main building, Lottie said, "Mary, I don't think he thought any such thing. The fact is so many widowed women simply cannot support their children. I think it's wonderful Tom's group has raised the funds for this. What a blessing it's going to be for the mothers and children who need it. And… well, I have to say, it certainly doesn't look anything like what I was expecting an orphanage to look like!" She kept turning the pages, looking at more photos.

Gradually, I calmed down. I moved over to sit by her as she looked at the photos.

"I didn't realize they just opened, Mary! This is all brand new. And look, they are going to have tennis courts and a swimming pool by next summer!" Lottie turned to me in amazement. "Tennis courts! Imagine!"

"It's not luxurious, Lottie, but they are trying to make it as nice as they can, Mr. Adams told me. They want to encourage the children to play outside and be healthy. Every child will be expected to have chores, too. Most of them are from farming families, so they'll be used to that. They are already starting their own farm. The boys, especially, are going to learn farming skills." I paused for a moment. "Like Tommy and Clarence would have from their daddy."

That was all I could say without wanting to wail. Clarence would never remember his daddy, and I doubt Tommy would have any clear memories of him, either. Poor Tom. He'd been so proud to have two sons after we'd had five girls. So proud and happy. He'd smiled and smiled on the days following their births, not caring for once that his front teeth were on display. Not self-conscious about his slight overbite for once, just full of joy.

He'd been delighted with each of our girls, of course, but he so looked forward to teaching his sons all the things he knew about farming. And about being a good husband and father, I was sure. Now they would only know him through the stories their sisters and I told them. Maybe from their uncles, his brothers, but I somehow doubted there was going to be a strong connection there. I'd heard very little from them since Tom died almost a year ago, although we spoke every few months on the telephone with Tom's mother, who continued to become even more feeble. Sis, Tom's sister, could tell them stories about him, but he'd been so much older than her. I resolved to talk about him more than I'd been doing. I had to keep his memory alive for them. They needed to know what a fine man he was and how much he'd loved them.

I looked up to find Lottie watching me. "Mary, what are you thinking about?" she asked. I knew from her soft tone my sadness was showing too clearly.

"About how I don't want the children to forget their daddy." I paused a moment. "Do you talk to Bertie about his father?"

Lottie's face brightened. "Oh yes, I do! All the time. Well, I guess I should say I do now. I don't think I did at first. I was too stunned by his accident, the suddenness. How unexpected his passing was. I know you understand what I mean."

I nodded my head. Stunned was a good way to put it.

"But as time went on, I wanted to talk about him. I wanted Bertie to remember him. I especially didn't want Bertie to think he couldn't talk about his daddy with me. We both needed to know he was still with us in so many ways. Still a part of our lives." She smiled.

All too soon, it was time for me to go down to the street to wait for Daddy to come by for me. The last thing I wanted was for him to have to climb up the hill from the street. Worse would be if he had to meet with Mrs. Vanderven. I wasn't sure which would be more harmful to his health.

As Lottie and I embraced goodbye, I realized, once again, how fortunate I was Lottie and I had reconnected. We'd been close friends as children; despite the differences in our circumstances and opportunities, we'd still found we had so much in common. The same was true now. I knew Lottie would never have to worry about finances and being able to take care of Bertie, but I had such loving, warm parents, whereas she had… well… her mother. Her home seemed like a palace to me, just as it had when we were young, with servants to take care of all the chores, but I know she would have gladly traded all that for the kind of home my children and I had now, one with joy, love, and laughter.

Still, I thought of the brochure. How was I going to provide for six children and myself? It was time to start looking for a job. Time to stop letting my parents bear the burden of seven others in their home. Time to end this limbo and move on to whatever waited for us.

❦

I finished telling Daddy about my visit with Lottie as we left Wilmington, with him chuckling over Mrs. Vanderven, but then growing quieter as I told him about my talk with Lottie. We were only a few miles from home when he said, "Baby girl, I think we need to talk about a few things."

I felt the immediate sick tightening of my stomach as I watched his profile. I was used to seeing him with at least a little smile on his face, and for a moment, his serious expression changed his appearance so much I felt I must be seeing him as a stranger would. Despite his weathered farmer's face and the hair that seemed to have gone from mostly gray to mostly white in just this last year, he was still a handsome man. Yet he seemed leaner; he'd always had a muscular frame, which went with a lifetime of farming, but now I could see that was no longer true. My mind skittered away from thinking he looked almost frail. Old.

He glanced away from the road ahead and saw me watching him. He gave me a small smile, transforming himself back into my familiar father.

Turning his eyes back to the road, he said, "You might want to think about selling Tom's truck. I've been driving it every week to make sure it's working fine and that no critters have taken up home in it anywhere, but I don't believe you're really interested in driving it." He glanced over again.

I shook my head, glad it wasn't a more serious issue. "Daddy, I just don't see me driving anytime soon. I need to find a job, and we both know that means Wilmington. I'll need to live somewhere close to where I work, and be able to shop in walking distance, too. I don't think paying for its upkeep is going to be something I can afford. Not with all the other expenses." I'd been thinking about the truck lately and wondering what I should do with it. "Don't you want it? Maybe sell yours and use that one instead?"

Daddy smiled. "No, but thank you kindly, baby. This here old jalopy and I understand each other, and I figure we both have about the same number of miles left in us."

I cut my eyes over to him. "Daddy, don't start with that." I gave his arm a little punch. But I didn't want to even joke about it.

"Well, anyway, I figure you could get a decent price for the truck if you sell it now. You can use all the cash you can get. I've been thinking I should have talked you into selling it right away, but no harm done. It's still fairly new, and it's in fine shape. Better to sell it sooner than later if you're not going to need it, though."

We talked about how to go about that, and it turned out Daddy had thought of several men who belonged to our church who might be interested. "I think any one of them would give you a fair price, Mary. Who knows, maybe we could get them to bid for it." He smiled. "Men do like to feel they've won and beat out even their friends when it comes to buying something they all want."

We reached the house as Daddy offered to talk to the men this coming Sunday. He drove us around to the back of the house, and there, parked right where he usually did, was a vaguely familiar dust-covered pickup. Daddy stopped and I could see he was trying to place it, just as I was.

"Oh, my mercy," I said. "I think Tom's brothers have come to call."

I stared at the truck, at the jumbled mess of tools, tarps, and trash in the back. I was sure it was one of the trucks I'd last seen right after Tom died, when Elim and Otis had visited to see what they could take of Tom's, including his children. Of course, farm trucks were used hard, but I'd rarely seen any that gave off such a wretched impression of neglect. If a truck could be downtrodden, it was.

Daddy must have been thinking along the same lines as I was. "If that truck was a horse, it'd already be in the glue bottle."

I glanced at Daddy as I gripped the door handle to open it. "I don't think we should mention deciding to sell Tom's truck. Not if there's any hope of getting a fair price."

Daddy huffed in agreement, and we both went into the kitchen to see what had brought on this visit. I didn't think it would be brotherly love. We walked in to find everyone sitting around the kitchen table, except Tommy, who was standing by Otis. Elim was holding Clarence, who immediately struggled to be released when he saw me. Elim set him down to toddle over to me, a skill Clarence was rapidly improving. I swooped him up and perched him on my hip, which only allowed a brief side-hug for Elim and Otis in turn, as they rose and walked over to greet us. I saw Daddy gravely shake hands with each of them, once again wearing that serious expression we so rarely saw. Mama had us sit as she poured coffee for us and refilled the cups for Elim and Otis. Irene looked over at me, and I gave a little nod.

"Girls, Tommy, let's go check on the animals and get those chores out of the way." Irene stood and patted Celeste, who was seated next to her, on the shoulder. "Come on." She grabbed Martha's hand, but Tommy dodged her reach as she walked by him.

"I wanna stay with Uncle Elim and Uncle Otis." He scowled at her.

"Tommy, go do your chores. Irene is in charge. I'll call you when you can come on back and visit with your uncles before they head back home." I wanted the children out of the kitchen. I also wanted Elim and Otis to understand they needn't hope to be invited to supper. They'd obviously been there for a while, judging by the empty cake plates still sitting in front of them. I just wanted to hear what they had to say and have them on their way home.

Irene marched Martha and Tommy along. Celeste shuffled out behind them, complaining to Leah in a low, resentful tone. Only Clarence remained, now seated in his grandmother's lap, his eyelashes drifting down as she stroked the dark waves away from his forehead. I was sure he'd missed his nap and hoped he slept, or we'd have a rough evening ahead.

"What brings you two out so far?" I hoped I didn't sound unhappy about them being here. After all, they were Tom's brothers and uncles to my children. I didn't want any hard feelings.

Otis cleared his throat and took another sip from his saucer. I tried not to stare at the beads of milky coffee that rimmed the bottom of his straggly mustache. Tom had always taken such care with his appearance, just as my daddy did, and he had had such nice manners. As always, I couldn't help but wonder how Mrs. Heath had managed to miss teaching her two younger sons to behave accordingly.

"Well, Mary Ellen, me and Elim happened to be in the neighborhood and…" He paused, and I saw Elim's eyebrows go up a notch or two. Guess that came as a surprise to him.

"Anyway, we wanted to see how you and the children was doin' these days." Otis nodded his head, apparently thinking that comment needed some support, and nobody else was going to supply it but himself.

"Sis says she and Mama talk with y'all every now and then on the telephone. That's got to be expensive, calling all the way to Tarboro just to talk." Otis paused again, and I wondered when he or Elim had last spoken with their frail mother. I also wondered if she minded. I was pretty sure Sis didn't miss them overmuch.

"Our wives write to them every now and then, don't you know, and they write back," Elim put in, almost the first words he'd spoken. Otis was clearly taking the lead, and I suspected that was the usual arrangement for them.

"Anyway," Otis continued, ignoring his brother's comment, "we heard you was living here now with your folks. Would have appreciated you letting us know sooner."

"Did you forget I'd said that in my Christmas letters to each of you and your families? I'm pretty sure I remember Sis saying you'd received them, but I might be wrong." I tried to keep my voice friendly as I wondered if they'd even listened to their wives read them all those months ago. I suspected Otis just wanted to make me feel wrong-footed before he got to why they'd made the trip out here. I didn't believe for one minute they'd just happened to be in the neighborhood, as he'd said.

"Well, anyway, looks like you're doing just fine. You planning on staying here permanent-like?" Otis leaned forward.

Daddy spoke up. "Mary's plans are still uncertain, but you're right. She and the children are doing just fine." Daddy's voice had a little edge that was as rare as the expression on his face.

"Well, we just want to make sure you know our offer to help you out with the children is still good, Mary." Otis kept his eyes on me. He seemed to deliberately ignore my father, not acknowledging he'd spoken.

"Help me out?" I asked, as if confused. I was not confused one little bit about what he meant. "That is so kind of you and Elim, but I can't take your money. You both have your own families to worry about. But that is so kind of you." Butter wouldn't have melted in my mouth, as we said around here. I could see Mama was trying not to smile. Daddy didn't try.

Both of Tom's brothers looked stunned. "No, no, Mary Ellen. That's not what we meant." Elim sounded a bit panicked.

Otis took a deep breath. "Elim's right. We meant about our offer to give the children a good home between the two of us." He paused. "We'd thought we'd each take us one of the boys and two of the girls. Even-like."

Before I could say anything, he rushed on. "Your girls are old enough to be helpful to our wives and won't be too long before those boys will be useful on our farms. Bet that little Tommy already is. So, you wouldn't have to worry about us being put out by taking them in."

"We'd raise them up right," Elim added.

My cup rattled in the saucer as I set it down. It felt like Mama and Daddy were holding their breath, waiting to see what I was going to do. I closed my eyes for a moment and promised myself those two men would be on their way home in just a few minutes.

"I'm so glad it wouldn't be much of a burden to you to each take three of my children and have them as…" I bit back the word *servants*, "…as *help* around your farms. What good brothers you are to Tom. But that isn't going to be necessary, so you won't have to make that sacrifice. But I thank you. And I know you need to get on the road so you can make it home in time for your supper and before it gets dark. Days are getting shorter, don't you think?"

Much to their apparent amazement, I stood and headed to the kitchen door. "Let's go on out so you can say your good-byes to the children and be on your way. Thank you so much for dropping by, and I'm so glad you didn't need to come out of your way to get here." Daddy coughed and turned his head away to hide his smile from Elim and Otis. He and Mama also stood and walked over to the door. Mama said how nice it had been to visit with them. In less than ten minutes, they were indeed headed back to their homes.

As they pulled out of our driveway, I gave that truck one last look. That was how they treated something useful to them.

CHAPTER 19

Black October

Friday, October 25, 1929

I watched the harvested fields go by as Lottie drove us back to my parents' home. Since late September, Daddy had brought me into Wilmington three times a week to look for a job. He'd drop me off downtown on Front Street and head back home to do whatever needed doing there as the growing season came to an end. I think he visited each collard plant and inspected every leaf for any insect that thought it was going to eat his prize crop. Those beautiful plants wouldn't be harvested until after the first frost. Daddy always said they wouldn't taste as good until then. And the sweet potatoes were now, in late October, laid out in many rows on the front porch, catching the afternoon sun to make them sweeter, as well. Every day Tommy, who had turned four on October 9, and Martha, would turn each potato over.

"They're getting a sunbath, Mama," she'd explained to me. I noticed she had her favorite dolls lined up beside them, also having sunbaths apparently. Unlike the sweet potatoes, they got to come in before the sun went down. "It's too chilly for my babies out here at night, but the swee-taters don't mind," she explained to Tommy, who had the young male's complete disinterest in the health and well-being of doll babies.

The first of October had been hard. It was a year ago we lost Tom. At supper that night, I had each of the children—except Clarence, of course—say their favorite memory of their daddy and the one thing they'd like to tell him about from our past year without him. Tommy's favorite memory of his father was just riding beside him in the truck, and I suspected I was right to fear he wouldn't have clear memories of his father after all. The older children had more detailed favorite moments about their daddy, and we all hung on those words. One child's story would spark the same memory in another child, a story they'd forgotten until then. Sometimes they were reminded of another favorite moment they'd almost lost.

And it was lovely to hear what event each child was eager to share with Tom. Leah thought he'd want to know about her new basketball and basket hoop, and how much she'd improved. Tom used to come in from the fields and overseeing the other farms, tired and dirty from a long summer's evening, and still he'd play some type of ballgame for a while with her and the other children.

Celeste loved how he looked in his Sunday suit when we went to church. Irene remembered how, when she'd been about Martha's age, he'd always listened to the Bible stories she'd just learned about in Sunday school. He always acted as if he'd never heard of Baby Moses in the bullrushes or Daniel in the lion's den. She knew now he had let her feel important by knowing something he didn't. I realized with a start Irene's kindness and care of her younger brothers and sisters was a clear reflection of her father's toward her. I'd never seen it that way before.

Even Mama and Daddy shared older memories of Tom, and the children were thrilled to hear about the two of us in our courting days. They laughed to think of their daddy as a nervous bridegroom. They basked in the wonderful things Daddy and Mama thought Tom should know about how each of them had been so strong and loving this past year. By the end of that supper, we all had tears in our eyes, but we promised ourselves that next year we'd do the same thing again. That night I felt we were bound together, and with Tom, even tighter than before.

That was the bright spot in the last month. The rest had been a disappointment as I walked from one business establishment to another in downtown Wilmington, asking if there were any positions available. Sometimes I got to speak with the owner or manager, but often there were no positions open, or they immediately decided I wasn't what they were looking for. Saleslady, receptionist, telephone operator, office worker   they wanted a young, single girl or an old matron, preferably one with more than a sixth-grade education. Not a widowed mother of six young children. Not one that had just turned thirty-one.

The owner of a smart ladies' clothing store just looked me up and down and shook her head. "Dear, you'd have to buy your wardrobe here. What you're wearing just wouldn't do with our clientele. Could you do that? Even with the employee discount?" I didn't need to answer, as she knew very well by the quality of my best Sunday outfit I couldn't.

I didn't know how to type. Or take shorthand. I also didn't wear the shorter dresses I saw on the young girls, probably not a one of them over twenty-one, who were pounding away on typewriters in so many of the offices I visited.

I was asked outright if I was pregnant. How many children I had. If I was getting married soon. With all those children, shouldn't I be looking for a man instead of a job? Or was that what I was really doing? One horrible old witch of an office manager told me that the men who worked there were happily married with children of their own, so maybe I should look elsewhere.

After the third week, I was more discouraged and desperate about my chances of finding a job than I had ever thought possible. Lottie and my parents tried to encourage me, but it was hard to pretend that I wasn't feeling frantic.

"Mary, I think there might be something else going on." Lottie glanced over at me as I slumped against the passenger door.

"What? What do you mean?" I half expected her to tell me I had some dreadful characteristic preventing me from having any luck in my search. Bad breath, perhaps. I turned my head away from her and blew into the sleeve of my dress, and sniffed. Smelled like starch.

Apparently, Lottie had caught that. "No, Mary." I heard the smile in her voice. "Nothing about you. Something my mother said she heard from her financial advisor the other day."

"Oh?" It sounded so important to think of someone having a financial advisor. Mrs. Vanderven really was well off.

Lottie's tone turned serious. "Yes, he said something about a man named Babson who gave a speech somewhere important up North early last month. I guess this Mr. Babson is supposed to be very smart about the business world. Anyway, he said a bad time might be coming soon. With the stock market and all."

"I don't see how that should make it hard for me to find work, Lottie."

"Well, if he's right and the stock market doesn't do well suddenly after so many years of booming, business won't do well. I guess it's all connected, down to what we pay for food and everything and how much buying people do. Or *can* do. My mother says if it were to get really bad, businesses would have to let people go."

"Let people go?"

"Fire them, Mary. If they don't have enough customers, they can't afford to pay their workers. Then those workers can't afford to buy things for their families, and even more businesses would have to cut back. Or go out of business entirely."

"Does your mother or her financial advisor truly think that's going to happen?"

"I don't think so. Mother was saying what an old worry wart Mr. Crawford is. She pooh-poohed it." Lottie slowed the motorcar as we neared my parents' house. "But what if other people are getting a little nervous? That might make them less likely to want to take on new office girls and new salesladies."

As we came to a stop in the driveway, I shook my head. "Well, that's more than I can deal with, Lottie. I'm just going to have to try harder." But a new worry was added to my long list.

Wednesday, October 30, 1929

Lottie and I walked the steep descent on Nun Street, from Front Street down to the Cape Fear River at the foot of the block. Ahead of us, Bertie raced, joyous to be released from his grandmother's austere house, no doubt.

"Bertie, slow down! Be careful!" Lottie's alarm wasn't out of place. A tumble here would have painful consequences, whether Bertie fell down the sidewalk or the bricks and cobblestones that made up this stretch of the street.

He reached the bottom of the riverside hill and looked back over his shoulder, sending us the cocky smile of the immortal seven-year-old boy. He picked up a stick and began poking in the shallow water lapping at the foot of the street.

Lottie and I both relaxed and continued down at a much more sedate pace, trying not to trip ourselves. I wasn't looking forward to the journey back up this street to our more usual flat landscape.

Once again, Lottie was going to drive me home after another disappointing day of searching for employment. I knew she had asked some of her friends if they knew of any suitable positions for me. She had even asked the women whose daughters took art lessons from her. Nothing had come of it, however, despite following up on each suggestion. I just wasn't what anyone wanted in a female employee.

"Lottie, you wanted to talk about something?" I had a feeling that was why we weren't already traveling out of Wilmington toward my parents' home. Bertie was going to come along and play with Tommy and Martha for a little while before they both joined us for supper, so it seemed odd she'd suggested this short walk away from her mother's house before we set out.

"Yes, Mary." Lottie lowered her voice, glancing at Bertie, who was absorbed in poking in a small puddle. "Something happened in New York City yesterday. Something that had my mother's financial advisor paying a visit after supper last night. That's never happened before. They talked in her parlor for almost an hour."

I could sense Lottie's anxiety and felt my stomach tightening without knowing exactly why.

"After they'd met for while, she called me in while Mr. Crawford—that's the financial advisor—was still there and told me something bad had happened in the stock market." She chewed her lip for a moment.

"Bad, Lottie? What happened?"

"I don't entirely understand what started it yesterday, but something caused stock prices to start falling. By the afternoon, many of the investors were completely wiped out. Wiped out, Mary! They lost everything in less than a day!"

I hardly knew what to say. I knew that owning a stock meant you owned a tiny part of a company, but it didn't seem real to me somehow. And it seemed incomprehensible to me anyone could lose all their money by investing it. But the feeling of dread was increasing. "Didn't you say some man had predicted something like this could happen? Is this what he meant?"

"Yes, Mr. Babson in New York last month. I think so. I really think this must be exactly what he meant. Anyway, my mother looked almost ill when she told me all this. Mr. Crawford let her do the telling."

"But she didn't lose any money, did she?" I caught myself. "Oh Lottie, please forgive me for asking. Please forget I ever said that!" I was horrified at prying into Mrs. Vanderven's business.

"No, no, Mary. Don't apologize. I'm not exactly sure. She wouldn't answer when I asked her. But she's told Mr. Crawford to sell everything today and get her money out of the market entirely." Lottie still seemed uneasy as she watched her son playing. "And I did the same thing."

I was confused for a moment. "You mean you've invested in the stock market, too?" Of course, I didn't know anything about Lottie's money. I just assumed between her husband's estate and her mother, she must be comfortably off. She certainly wasn't out going from business to business looking for work. She had what she called her pin money coming in from a few girls taking art lessons, and that, along with Bertie, kept her busy and happy. As far as I knew.

"Yes, Robert had some investments already set up, and Mr. Crawford added some more. He took over handling everything when I moved back here to be with Mother. Said I should put my money to work. Mother said we could trust his judgment. And you know she does love to read the financial and business pages in the newspapers she takes." Lottie looked away for a moment. "Those newspapers didn't have good headlines today. I can tell you that." She looked over at me and gripped my arm for a moment. "I'm worried. I can't afford to lose what I have invested."

I didn't know what to say, and before I could think of anything, she drew in a sharp breath, stopped walking, and turned to me. "Oh Mary, I'm an idiot. Please forgive me for going on about my situation when you are struggling with so much more. I forgot myself, and I'm right sorry."

I took her in my arms and hugged her tight. I felt her shoulders shake, and I just kept holding on. No one other than Bertie was around at this time of the afternoon, and I wouldn't have cared anyway. My friend was scared. I could only hope her situation turned out to be nothing to worry about.

I murmured in her ear, "This is probably just a temporary problem, and everything will be fine soon."

Lottie gave a little laugh and pulled away. Keeping her face turned away from the river, she wiped her cheeks before Bertie could see her tears. She took a deep breath and gave me a shaky smile. "I'm sorry you have to comfort me right now."

"Well, why not?" I smiled. "You've certainly been comforting me for months now—especially these last weeks."

"I'm sure you're right, Mary, I'll be fine. And so will you. It's all going to work out. Even if it's rough for a while, in the end, it will be just as the good Lord wants it to be. We just have to have faith."

Lottie was always far more devout than I ever was. She found so much comfort in her religion, and, for a moment, I envied her. But we couldn't fight our natures; I couldn't force myself to be like her. I could only hope and pray she was right.

I felt the Lord expected us to take care of ourselves and *make* everything work out if that's what we really wanted. For me, it would always seem more of a struggle than it would seem to Lottie, no matter what happened to each of us. It wasn't that she felt she could just sit back and let God take care of everything, not at all, but she was more trusting her efforts would lead to what she wanted, even after losing her husband so unexpectedly.

My nature was just several shades less relaxed about having a happy ending.

Later, around the supper table, my family once again made Lottie and Bertie welcome, and we laughed even more than we ate.

"I'm going as Harry Houdini for my class Halloween party tomorrow," Bertie announced at one point. He leaned forward and whispered, "Houdini *died* on Halloween, you know!"

"On Halloween?" Tommy's eyes bulged. "I heard about him. Are you going to be tied up in a big water tank?"

The older ones around the table smiled, but Bertie was kind to younger Tommy, thank goodness. "Nawh, Mama's just gonna tie some rope around me, and I'll carry some. Can't take a water tank to school, or I sure would."

Houdini had died only three years earlier, in 1926, and was still very much a legend. No doubt Bertie would not be the only little boy to dress as him this year. Like most mothers, Lottie was delighted a Houdini costume only required some lengths of rope. Tommy was entranced with hearing about the famous man's amazing escapes, and I planned to have Daddy talk to him about not trying any on his own.

The girls' school would have their usual Halloween party tomorrow evening, with families invited, everyone bringing treats to be shared. We were taking my applesauce cake and Mama's lemony sweet potato pie.

Tommy was going as a pirate with an eye patch I'd made for him and a charcoal beard. To Tommy's delight, Bertie was suitably impressed with the pirate laugh Tommy had been perfecting for the last week. My parents and I were looking forward to a pirate-free home in November, but for now all the children took turns giving their best pirate laugh. As Mama served dessert, her raisin-studded bread pudding with custard sauce, even Lottie tried. It would have come as no surprise that Lottie was not cut out to be a pirate, but she amazed us all with her robust pirate cackle. Somewhere inside her ladylike exterior still lived the daring young girl I'd known long ago. We all applauded her and decided she was voted "Most Likely to Become a Pirate." Tommy ran and got his eye patch for her to wear for the rest of dinner. It rather suited her.

Sitting there, I finally decided to set the new worries of the day aside. Lottie was right: everything would work out. She and her mother would be fine. And I just needed to increase my efforts to find a position. It was now a month since I'd started looking, so maybe returning to some of the places I'd begun with would be a good idea. They might have new possibilities that weren't available four weeks ago.

I felt myself cheering up as I listened to the lively discussion of what the girls planned to dress as for Halloween: Martha as a princess (cardboard crown), Celeste as a fortune-teller (headscarf and shawl), Irene as a nurse (an old button-down blue skirt as a cape and a folded-paper nurse's hat), and Leah as a basketball star (clearly an excuse to take her basketball to school).

"Mary, a penny for your thoughts." Mama smiled at me when there was a lull in the chatter.

I looked around the table at all those faces I loved so much and even little Toby, who'd parked himself by Tommy's feet, hoping for a deliberate or accidental droppage. "I'm just thinking about how we should all hold hands, close our eyes, and make a memory of this evening. How we feel right now, all together. How we look. How the table looks in the lamplight. All the wonderful dinner smells." I did this from time to time with the children. They were used to me saying, "Let's make a memory," and holding that moment in our minds for a minute or two to preserve it.

Mama smiled, and everyone clasped the hands of the two people next to them. Even Clarence, sitting in the worn highchair, stopped his chatter. Eyes closed, I took a deep breath and hoped I'd never forget this ordinary fall evening and all the dear ones sitting around the table. Thanksgiving might be in November, but that was my thanksgiving, right there, that night, when time seemed to stop briefly for a golden moment.

Even now, I am thankful I didn't know what was coming in just a few days.

CHAPTER 20

Friends in Need

Thursday, November 7, 1929

I slid left on the bench closer to my mother and put my arm around her shoulder. She didn't seem to notice my embrace and continued staring at the closed door in front of us, her face bleak. Lottie, to my right, was bowed in prayer, the traces of tears still on her cheeks.

We'd been sitting on this bench outside of the emergency room at James Walker Memorial Hospital for several hours as the doctors and nurses tried to help my father. Our nerves were stretched as tight as could be, and we longed for the door to open and to hear he would be well again soon. But we knew that might not be the news we'd receive, so we were also afraid for the door to open. We only knew as long as the door stayed closed, he must still be alive if they continued to work on him.

I kept thinking how lucky we'd been to have had Lottie at our house when Daddy collapsed. Once again, she'd brought me home after yet another day of job hunting and was just about to leave. Mama had invited her to stay for supper, but she wanted to get back home to join Bertie and her mother for the evening meal. The children had come out to say hello, happy to see her, but disappointed Bertie wasn't with us, and then said quick goodbyes at Irene's order to finish their homework so they could clear our kitchen table. They hurried in out of the damp chill, Celeste helping Clarence up the steps to the porch and along inside to the warm kitchen.

I'd noticed Daddy had seemed out of breath as he and Mama came outside to greet us a few minutes earlier, but didn't think anything of it at first. He was quiet as Mama and Lottie chatted for a moment, and then he said, "Ladies, I'm going to go make sure the animals are set for the night before it gets any darker. Miss Lottie, you be careful now, driving in the dark. You know a lot of critters will be out crossing the road, looking for their supper."

Lottie called her goodbyes after him as he and Toby started the walk down to the barn, just as he seemed to stumble. He caught himself, took a few slow steps, and then his knees gave out on him. I didn't understand at first what was happening as he crumpled to the ground and remained there, unmoving.

Toby whimpered and licked Daddy's face as Mama, Lottie, and I hurried to him, but, eyes closed, he didn't respond as we called his name. I ran to tell Irene her granddaddy was taken sick, and she would have to oversee getting the children fed and put to bed, and to make sure the animals, including Toby, were fed and bedded down. She understood not to get the younger ones worried, but just to say he needed to see the doctor. I grabbed Mama's coat and handbag and ran back to help lift him into Lottie's motorcar.

Mama sat in the back seat, cradling Daddy's head in her lap, as Lottie drove as fast as possible back into Wilmington to the hospital. I sat in the passenger seat, torn between watching out for any animals that might run into the road in front of us, and looking back to make sure Daddy was still breathing. From time to time, I heard Mama telling Daddy he was going to be all right. Otherwise, I didn't think anyone spoke more than a few words the entire trip.

It was full dark by the time we pulled up to the emergency entrance. I ran in to get help bringing in Daddy; two orderlies raced out with a gurney and whisked him away. I tried to help Mama fill out paperwork, but our hands were shaking so that Lottie took over and filled in the information we gave her.

As the hours ticked away, I kept thinking about how much worse it could have been. What if Lottie had driven away before Daddy collapsed? Or if Daddy had been driving me home instead of Lottie, and we'd crashed on some lonely stretch of country road? If Daddy lived, it might very well be that Lottie had made the difference.

If Daddy lived.

A few other people came through, mostly people with minor injuries. I heard one woman say her boy had been trying to slice an apple and had sliced into his finger instead. The little guy, only a little younger than Tommy, held a dishcloth around his hand and tried to blink back his tears. Later, a couple came in, the lady in labor. It was easy to see from the husband's frantic expression that this must be their first child. Within minutes, the lady was wheeled to the labor ward, and the husband was led to the waiting room for expectant fathers.

Other people's emergencies seemed so minor, even cozy, compared to ours. I would have traded with any of them that night.

It was after midnight when a doctor came out of the room and approached us. He knelt in front of our bench and smiled. "Mrs. Evans? I'm Dr. Gregory. I know you've been waiting a long time for news of your husband. Are these your daughters?"

Mama nodded her head. She was clutching her handbag so tightly on her lap her knuckles were white. "This is Mary, Mrs. Mary Heath, next to me, and next to her is our dear friend, Mrs. Lottie Lundstrom."

Lottie and I exchanged nods with the doctor as my mother tried to steady her breath. "Doctor, how is Bob? What's wrong with him?"

"First of all, I believe Mr. Evans is now stable. You ladies did the right thing to get him here so quickly. It seems he had a mild heart attack."

Mama clutched her own heart and sobbed. I tightened my arm around her and held her to me. Dr. Gregory patted her arm. "Mrs. Evans, please don't worry overmuch. We're taking Mr. Evans to his room now, and you can see him shortly for a few minutes. I believe he is going to be fine, although we're going to have to talk about some things that might need to change from now on. I was able to have a short chat with him, and he seems like a fine man, but I don't want to see him again in the emergency room. No, ma'am. I want him to live many more years and stay active. But any kind of farming or heavy work has to be out of the picture now. We'll talk about that in the coming days. Tomorrow, I'll have a heart specialist see him, and we'll go from there. Meanwhile, you can see him for a few minutes, but he's going to be asleep very soon with the medicine we just gave him. He needs his rest, and so do you. So, a quick visit, and then off to bed with all of you. He'll be busy with the heart specialist tomorrow morning, so don't expect to see him until around two in the afternoon, let's say. We'll know more then and can talk about the future. How does that sound?"

Dr. Gregory's tone was so confident and matter-of-fact that I don't think it occurred to any of us it could possibly go any other way. Even Mama seemed steadier. He shook our hands as he left to go back to the emergency ward, and we gathered our things together. A few minutes later, a nurse took us to Daddy's room, telling us in the hallway to be as quiet as possible so we didn't disturb the other three people in the room. The curtains were drawn around their beds, but obviously, we needed to take care not to wake them. Lottie motioned for Mama and me to go in, and she'd see him in a few days.

I hardly recognized my own father. He wasn't just pale, which I expected, but his features seemed altered, as if they'd crumpled in on themselves. He seemed at least a decade older. Mama and I each hugged him gently and kissed his cheek. I told him I loved him, and I'd see him later in the afternoon. I left Mama to have a moment alone with him. He managed a wink at me as I left, but it was clear he was exhausted.

Lottie and I waited outside in the hall, and I whispered how worried I was that his appearance had changed so dramatically in just a few hours. She was consoling me when Mama came out, wiping her handkerchief under her eyes. She gave a trembling smile and took turns hugging each of us.

"Lottie, I will always bless you for helping Bob when he most needed it," Mama said into her ear as she released Lottie's shoulders.

Lottie smiled and shook her head. "I think we know the good Lord was looking after Mr. Evans. And I'm sure He still is."

We started walking towards the exit to Lottie's motorcar. I could feel exhaustion and the release of tension making my steps drag. "Oh, Lottie, I'm so sorry you need to drive us back home!" I hadn't thought ahead to this problem. The shock had muddled my thinking even more than I'd realized.

"There's no need to worry, ladies. We're only a few minutes away from being able to relax. Our cook has left out some light sandwiches for us for a quick bite before we rest our heads since we missed dinner, and two guest bedrooms are waiting for you. I called home shortly after we got here to let Mother know about why I wouldn't be back in time for dinner, and she suggested you both plan on staying over."

"Oh, no, Lottie, Mary and I don't want to be any trouble for your mother or your cook," Mama started, but Lottie interrupted.

"Mrs. Evans, it's really a favor to me. I won't have to drive out into the country and then back alone in the middle of the night if we just wait until tomorrow morning." Lottie smiled. She knew we couldn't argue with that. She was very pleased with herself for thinking of how she could make it seem like a favor to her to stay at her mother's home. I gave her a knowing smile, and she had the grace to blush, but she didn't stop smiling.

"Oh. Oh yes, I see. Still, well, thank you, dear." Mama teared up again.

"And I called Irene shortly after we got here and told her we'd probably stay in town overnight. I told her to go on to bed, and we'd call first thing tomorrow morning. She is thrilled to help out by taking care of the children. She is so grown up, isn't she, Mary? I know she'll have to miss school tomorrow to stay home with Tommy and Clarence, but I hope that won't be a problem."

So going to make those calls was where Lottie had disappeared to shortly after we'd arrived at the hospital. I was so impressed with Lottie's clearheaded actions. I'd spoken to Irene on the phone later in the evening, when it was apparent we weren't going to be getting home before bedtime. I knew she needed to know what to do and how her granddaddy was doing, but she didn't mention Lottie had spoken with her earlier. She'd just said she had everything under control, and I need not worry about anything at home.

Mama sat in the front seat this time, and I rode in the back. It was a short drive, but I think I still managed to drift off while Mama and Lottie spoke quietly.

I'm sure we were all relieved Mrs. Vanderven wasn't still up when we arrived. We each quickly ate a few of the chicken sandwiches that had been cut into small squares as if for teatime, turning down the cake Lottie offered. Carrying mugs of warm milk, we went upstairs to the two rooms prepared for us. Mama had met Mrs. Vanderven years ago when Lottie and I were children, but never been in her home. "Lottie, it's like a palace!" Mama's eyes were huge as she looked around her bedroom for the night.

Ruffled pink material swamped the room, from the vanity and bedside tables to the coverlet and dust ruffle for the rice poster bed, and then on to the draperies of the two floor-length windows overlooking the river. On one wall, a cabinet held shelves of porcelain knickknacks. Only it and the large matching wardrobe beside it had escaped being swathed in pink.

"So lovely," Mama repeated, obviously so exhausted she hardly knew what to do.

Lottie smiled and scanned the room. "Well, Mrs. Evans, my mother does love to decorate. I've always thought this room must be very like my mother's childhood room. It seems so different from the rest of the house. Even my own room when I was growing up wasn't this… well, this pink. And ruffly. At least the wood isn't painted pink. It's burled walnut. That makes it a burled walnut whatnot cabinet. If you have trouble sleeping, try saying that ten times fast." She laughed, and even Mama smiled at her attempt to lift her mood.

Lottie continued, "Don't worry about getting up early. Breakfast will be on the sideboard after seven, since Bertie has school tomorrow, and we can help ourselves whenever we want to. I hope you'll sleep well tonight." She kissed Mama's cheek and left to check on Bertie before she went to her own bed.

I hugged Mama and wished her a good night's sleep. I noticed a nightgown and robe was at the foot of Mama's bed for her use, and I found the same in my room next door. I was staying in the room that had been Lottie's as a girl, and I was glad it felt so familiar. Before long, the warm milk, the day's miles of walking in Wilmington on my job search, and the terror of the evening pulled me into a restless sleep, with dreams I was glad to forget by the next morning.

Much to my pleasant surprise, Mrs. Vanderven was as cordial towards my mother at breakfast as I'd ever seen her be to anyone. She even offered to make sure Bertie got off to school on time so we could leave early for our home. I was anxious to get back home, even though I'd spoken to Irene first thing to reassure myself they'd made it through the night on their own quite safely. Lottie was going to wait at our house until it was close to the time the doctor had said to return. When we arrived back home, she drove Irene to school so she'd only miss the first hour or so of her class, as Mama insisted I stay with the children when she returned to see Daddy. After a light midday dinner, Lottie and Mama headed back into Wilmington. Lottie and Mrs. Vanderven both brushed aside any suggestion that we help pay for the gasoline for these trips or in any way consider their assistance as an imposition.

I felt ashamed I'd been so critical of Mrs. Vanderven in the past. While she still had many failings, her actions indicated a better heart than I had previously given her credit for. I set my mind to think of some way to thank both her and Lottie for their kindness, but settled in the meantime for writing letters to each one, expressing my gratitude. I knew Mama would do the same when things settled down.

There would be many thank-you letters to write in the upcoming weeks, as it turned out, as we learned at a deeper level just how many friends we had, especially friends from our church. Our minister, Mr. Prince, learned of Daddy's heart attack by chance on Friday, when he was making his usual rounds at the hospital, visiting several ill congregation members. He happened to see Mama walking down the hall to Daddy's room and came in to visit for a few minutes. Lottie had dropped her off and was planning on returning in a couple of hours, but Mr. Prince offered to take Mama home to save Lottie the extra trip. After that, from Saturday until Daddy was released the following Wednesday, different church members would take Mama to the hospital for visiting hours just after midday, run their errands in town, and pick her back up in a few hours for the trip home.

During the time Daddy was hospitalized, and even for the week or so after he returned home, we had so many kindnesses come our way. Every man who took Mama to the hospital to visit Daddy came with covered dishes from his wife, so the usual cooking workload was reduced as we took on chores usually done by Daddy. Several of the men, including Mr. Meyer, came by on the Saturday Daddy was in the hospital to make sure our little garden patch, the animals, tools, and sheds were all ready for the coming colder weather. Two of them made plans to take our hogs to Burgaw to be butchered early the next week and promised to go back for the meat when it was ready for pickup. Daddy would have no outstanding workload when he returned and no excuse to prevent him from resting.

That same Saturday, as the men worked outside, their wives (and Mr. Meyer's daughters) insisted on coming to help with a deep cleaning of the house. At first, I was a little taken aback by this, as I felt perfectly capable of maintaining the house, but they clearly wanted to be of help—and my older girls were delighted they would be spared a lot of heavy cleaning alone with me—that I could only relent with good grace. Of course, we worked alongside of them, and accomplished in just a few hours what would normally have taken days.

When Mama returned from the hospital late that afternoon, she was delighted to find her entire home smelling clean and fresh, with a vanilla pound cake just coming out of the oven. Shortly after, the men came in, and we all stopped for cake. We let the young ones have the kitchen table, and I was happy to see Irene having such a good time chatting with Mr. Meyer's daughters. We adults took our coffee and cake plates to the sitting room, so rarely used in colder weather, where Mama filled us in on how much better Daddy felt that day.

The company seemed to revive her spirits, and the smile stayed on her face for the rest of the evening after they'd left for their own homes and suppers. Even the girls were basking in Mama's repeated praise for their hard work. I bragged on them, too, for all four of them—even little Martha, who'd dusted every chair leg in the entire house—had worked with a good will, enjoying the company of the other women and the visible evidence of their own efforts. Tommy had been delighted to be with the men outside, Toby at his side. And, thankfully, he didn't cause any kind of accident. None I heard about, anyway.

It was Mr. Meyer who took Mama to the hospital on the day Daddy finally came home. When they returned, he helped Daddy up the back steps to the house and got him settled in his easy chair in the sitting room by the fireplace, where a cheery fire was already warming up the room. Mr. Meyer was his usual friendly self, and I was glad to see he didn't seem to hold any grudge about being denied permission to court Irene. The two men drank coffee and ate some cake, Daddy just picking at his slice. Then Mr. Meyer took his leave, but not before splitting several logs and stacking more wood for us.

I had telephoned my sisters and Janie's widowed husband to let them know about Daddy. Their letters started arriving a day or so after Daddy got home. Mama read them to Daddy and then again to all of us at supper each day. It was good to see the color that rose in Daddy's cheeks as he heard how dear he was to his daughters, sons-in-law, and grandchildren, whom he so seldom got to see. Over the next few days, Mama called one of them early each evening and said a few words, and then passed the telephone earpiece over to Daddy. Promises were made to come visit, if only for an afternoon, and I hoped this scare would prompt them to keep those promises. I was sure those letters and calls did as much as the new medicine to speed his recovery, although he still appeared much frailer than he had previously. I could see changes would have to be made, and I felt even more pressure to get my family settled in our own place so my parents could do what was best for themselves.

As we sat at supper on Daddy's first evening back home, Mama said, "I guess this is what they mean by 'friends in need,' isn't it?"

Irene nodded, but most of the others looked confused. "Friends in need of what, Grandmama?" Leah asked.

"It means we should help our friends who are in need, silly," said Celeste. "Your real friends are ones who need your help."

"Well, not quite. No name-calling, Celeste, please." Mama said gently.

"Sorry, Grandmama. Sorry, Leah." Celeste ducked her head. Leah huffed slightly in her triumph.

"'Friends in need are friends indeed' is the full saying," Mama continued. "It means friends who help you when you are in need, when you're going through some kind of problem or sadness, are indeed true friends."

I added, "Some people only act like your friend when things are going well for you. 'Fair-weather friends,' we call them. But as soon as you are in some difficulty, they disappear. They don't want to listen to your problems, much less help you out. But a true friend is there for you, whether things are going well or bad for you."

Celeste smiled. "Oh, I see now. *We* were in need, and it turns out we have friends indeed!"

"Exactly," my father said and patted her on the head. "Exactly."

CHAPTER 21

Visits

Monday, November 25, 1929

Thanksgiving seemed both busier and quieter this year. We were still receiving food gifts from our friends, so there was less cooking to be done for the holiday. Neighbors and friends continued to pay visits, always brief to avoid overtiring Daddy, and always bringing a cake or pie with them, so as not to deplete our pantry. They knew staying long enough to enjoy some hospitality on a plate was a ritual that couldn't be ignored.

On Saturday, my second-oldest sister Idella, her husband Frank, and their children arrived after breakfast and stayed for dinner, much of which they brought with them. Idella was on her best behavior, with little of her usual bossiness on display. I think Daddy's appearance, still so changed, affected her more than she showed. Just before they left, she flung her arms around him, a far cry from the quick peck on the cheek that was her usual goodbye gesture. He stroked her back, reassuring her as he must have done so many years ago when she was a little girl.

Her eyes had a glassy sheen as she pulled away from him and hugged Mama, who whispered something to her. Nodding, Idella motioned for her subdued children to say goodbye to their grandparents and the rest of us.

Just as they were loading up their truck, getting ready to swaddle the children in the quilts against the November chill, Jim, my oldest sister Janie's widowed husband, pulled up with his five young children. Greetings and more hugs were exchanged, but Idella and Frank needed to get back to their farm chores, and they drove off a few minutes later.

My children took Jim's four older children, already bundled in their coats, to visit the animals before coming inside to warm up and get their cake and milk. I suspected Molly, our old mule, would be giving rides once again, and I knew Irene would make sure everyone was safe. I joined Mama, who held a sleepy two-year-old Jesse in her lap, Daddy, and Jim in the sitting room for a few minutes to get Jim's news, but then went to the kitchen while it was still empty to start another pot of coffee and set up for our cake. I could hear the quiet tones of their conversation, but didn't follow the words.

I pulled on my coat and walked out to see if the children were ready to let poor Molly have a rest. Everyone who wanted a ride around on the old girl had had one, and they were ready to come in and warm up. We got Molly settled in her stall and rewarded with an apple for her efforts and patience.

"She wasn't a bit mulish about giving us rides!" Tommy crowed, showing off for his cousins. We all laughed at his little joke. It was probably a coincidence Molly huffed just at that moment, but I whispered in her ear I'd bring her another apple at the end of the day. I know I didn't imagine the gentle nicker as she nudged my shoulder. Molly the Mule was never, ever mulish, bless her.

I reminded Jim's children to be quiet in the house for their granddaddy's sake, my own having heard that caution so many times in the last week that it seemed second nature to them now. I was pleased to see they were happy but not boisterous around him.

Daddy was delighted to see so many of his grandchildren in one day, but it was clear he was tiring. Jim noticed and hurried the children along when the last cake crumb was cleared from their plates. Idella had insisted earlier on helping to clean up after our dinner before her family left, but of course no one expected Jim to volunteer for what we all considered to be women's work.

Once again, the children were wrapped up in coats and quilts. I made sure the colorful hats were pulled down over their ears. They were no doubt crocheted by their departed mother. The thought caused a catch in my throat as I kissed each of my nieces and nephews. Janie had always been so clever with sewing, knitting, and crocheting. I remembered her, almost thirteen years my senior, patiently guiding my own young hands as she taught me to crochet. It occurred to me then Tom's passing in October a year ago had overshadowed Janie's death that following December. Helping her children to bundle up, I felt a sharp sense of loss. Just as I worried about my younger children not remembering Tom, now I realized Janie would likewise be unremembered by at least Jesse and Henry, her two youngest. They sat in the truck's cab with their father, while the older three were in the truck's bed. I tried to shake off those thoughts as I said my farewells to them. At least they should get home before it got dark, and their housekeeper would have a good supper waiting for them. Maybe she would teach Ella Mae, Janie's only daughter, the skills her mother would have so patiently handed down.

Mama and I each held on to one of Daddy's arms, as he'd insisted on coming out to say goodbye to Jim and the children. Just before he backed out, Jim rolled down his window and leaned his head out. "Mama Evans, Pops, please think about what I said." He seemed quite earnest as he gazed at them. They nodded and waved, calling their goodbyes again.

As Jim drove off and we headed back into the warm house, I caught Mama's eye, but she shook her head slightly. Either they would tell me later what Jim meant, or it wasn't any of my business, but I couldn't help wonder what that had all been about.

Later that night, after everyone was in bed, I was sweeping the kitchen, and I thought about the whole "women's work" idea, along with the saying I'd heard all my life: "It's a man's world." I thought about how every bride promised to obey her husband. While I was married and had Tom right there, those weren't the kinds of things I spent much time musing on. I might have been occasionally irritated that women's work was considered less valuable than men's, but it just seemed that was the way of the world.

Even with women getting the right to vote just over nine years ago, nothing much seemed to have changed. I still had to look under "Jobs for Women" in the newspaper, knowing it was pointless to apply for the more numerous and much better paying "Jobs for Men." Wives who managed to have a paying job outside the home still had to do all the usual housewife chores as well. A man might come home in the evening tired from work, but he expected to spend the evening relaxing while his wife got supper ready, cleaned up afterwards, and took care of the children, no matter how hard she had worked during the day. As I had also always heard, "Man may work from sun to sun, but woman's work is never done."

I'd never really questioned the idea that the man had the head position in the family because he was the breadwinner and, if I believed what I was told, that was also how God wanted it to be. The problem, as I saw it, was I was now going to be the breadwinner, but earning the lower wages of a woman, assuming I could find a job at all, while also doing the housekeeping and childcare chores. I smiled to myself. I needed a wife. And a decent-paying job.

"Good luck, Mary." I sighed aloud, causing Toby, who was checking under the table for food crumbs before they were swept away, to look up with a quizzical expression. I laughed. "I see you are hard at work, too, Toby. You don't get enough credit either."

He gave me a hopeful grin and walked over in case my tone of voice meant a little treat might come his way. Thanks to the biscuit-and-molasses dessert I was still nibbling on as I cleaned, it did.

I was sure my situation had played more than its share in Daddy's heart attack, and I suspect Mr. Prince realized it was weighing on my father's mind even more, now he wasn't fit to make the drive to and from Wilmington so I could continue job hunting. Although Lottie had insisted she could take over that task entirely, Daddy worried about putting all the burden on her, and of course, I felt I continued to impose on both. Selling Tom's truck had been necessary, but I'd started berating myself for not finding the time to learn how to drive better, although Daddy's old truck seemed to respond only to him anyway.

Apparently, Mama or Daddy had mentioned my difficulty to him, and Mr. Prince offered to take me to Wilmington on the two days a week he usually drove into town to visit patients at the hospital. I accepted his offer, grateful for his kindness and that it meant only a slight detour for him to pick me up and drop me off at my parents' home.

On December 2, the first Monday of the month, I was once again visiting the various departments of the Atlantic Coast Line Railroad. I'd read in the newspaper they had over 2200 employees. Apparently, they didn't think they needed 2201. At least, they didn't seem interested in *me*. But I kept checking in with the managers, just in case. One of them, who always seemed more sympathetic than most, took me aside as I was leaving his office after another fruitless inquiry.

"Miz Heath, I don't want to worry you more than you already are, but if I were you, I'd put all my attention on finding some kind of position as soon as possible." He tugged on his shirt sleeves and cleared his throat.

I felt a jab of irritation. That was what I'd been trying to do for months now. What was he thinking to say such a thing to me? My expression must have conveyed something of what I was thinking, because he added, "You cannot say you heard this from me. You hear?"

I nodded, now a bit taken aback.

"You see, there's word going 'round some of the big bosses—very high up, you know—are worried about what happened in October with the stock market up North. Right worried." He gave me a meaningful look.

"But… I thought that was all over. And I thought it was just some rich people that lost money." I hadn't heard much about it since late October. It occurred to me Lottie and I hadn't talked about it again, either. I wondered if her mother had lost much money. I prayed Lottie hadn't.

I really needed to stop thinking only about my own troubles.

"No, ma'am, if the bosses are right, it might wind up making a difference to everybody. If the rich get scared, it's going to work its way down to us eventually. Maybe sooner than later. Anyway, we've been told to hold off as much as possible on hiring new people. We're just replacing people if they leave for some reason. They want to wait and see what happens. If a company this size is doing this, won't be long before little businesses in town start doing it."

I took a deep breath. Now I understood why he said to get a job as soon as possible—while there might be any to be had.

He added, "And let's just pray to the good Lord we don't have to start letting people go. If people decide they should save their money rather than travel to visit their old Aunt Bessie or Cousin John, you know, that's going to affect our passenger business. And if people can't buy as much because prices go up or they lose their jobs, that's going to hit our freight business."

He sighed and looked through the glass window of his office into the big open room outside his office. There must have been twenty desks there, where men worked on stacks of paper or adding machines and office girls typed at amazing speeds. The dings, clicks, and clacks of those machines filled the room every bit as much as the cigarette smoke that wafted up from each man's desk. It was hard to imagine any of that work could just go away.

"Anyway, Miz Heath, just to be on the safe side, get your foot in the door. If you find any kind of job that will do, take it, is my best advice."

I thanked him and turned to go. "Miz Heath, remember what I said about not hearing that from me."

I nodded, thanked him again, and headed back down to the lobby of the three-story office building. Even though I wanted to continue checking on jobs, I needed to stop for the day, as it was only an hour or so until it would be time to meet up with our minister to head back home, and there were no businesses left at this end of town I hadn't already visited today. Mr. Prince was to pick me up outside the railroad depot across the street from the Atlantic Coast Line business offices, and I certainly couldn't keep him waiting. I felt wobbly for a moment as I thought about what I'd just learned, so I walked over to the well-maintained depot waiting room, where no one would object to me sitting for a time.

There were few people in the main waiting room, although I could see the much smaller "Colored" waiting room was crowded. It seemed a shame they had to be so uncomfortable while many seats in this room were empty. A distant memory popped in my head of my mother asking my father, "Do people honestly think there is going to be a 'whites only' heaven?"

Daddy had just said, "People are idiots, Ella. You know that." Sounded right to me.

As I sat down, I decided I'd spend my remaining time alone planning where I'd go on my next trip into Wilmington and to try to think of some businesses I hadn't gone to before. There couldn't be many left. Although I hated to impose, maybe I needed to ask Lottie to come for me early in the morning so I could have a full day in town next time, and then get Mr. Prince to take me back home at the end of the day. I felt a new sense of urgency and a deeper sense of dread. I hoped that manager's warning turned out to be just a brief scare.

After a while, it occurred to me to make use of the ladies' room before the ride home. A few minutes later, I finished washing my hands before leaving when a cleaning lady, probably in her late forties, walked in with a bucket and a collection of mops and rags.

"Oh, good afternoon," I said to her. The room was empty save for us, and it seemed impolite to act as if she wasn't there.

"Good afternoon, ma'am," she responded, clearly surprised to have been acknowledged.

As she started to enter one of the stalls to begin cleaning, I said what I'd been thinking for the last few minutes. "It's wonderful how well you keep this restroom looking, what with all the ladies who must be in here throughout the day. And the floors of the entire building, the offices as well as the waiting room, well, they always look like they were just scrubbed and waxed every time I've been here."

At that, she set her bucket down and smiled. "Thank you, ma'am. That's right kind of you to notice, much less to say so. There's a crew, of course, not just me, but we all work together to keep everything looking the way it should."

"But how do you keep the floors so nice? What with all the traffic in and out? Come to think of it, I've never seen anyone working on the floors. I believe you're the first cleaner I've ever seen."

"Yes'm, most of us cleaning ladies work at night when the offices are closed, and the last trains has come and gone for the day. But the bosses want the passenger restrooms checked and cleaned throughout the day, so that's me—at least, this week it is. Us senior cleaners kinda take turns so we have a week of day shifts every now and then, you see."

"Well, you all do a wonderful job. Reminds me that I need to do some work on the kitchen floor at home."

We both laughed a little. Then much to my surprise, she used the very phrase I'd been thinking about recently. "Well, you know what they say, ma'am: Woman's work is never done."

We exchanged cordial goodbyes, and as I returned to the bench in the waiting room, it occurred to me that if there was one thing I was qualified for, it was cleaning. I could clean as well as anyone else. After thinking about it for a while, I got up and walked back to the ladies' room. The woman I'd spoken to earlier was now cleaning the sinks, and she looked up in surprise as I walked up to her.

I worked up my nerve and blurted, "I need a job." She certainly wasn't expecting me to say that, and her expression moved from startled to compassionate as I continued. "My husband passed away a year ago and I have myself and six children to support. I've been job hunting for several months, and I'm not having any luck with dress shops or offices, and a waitress's wages wouldn't begin to cover what I need for my children. I never thought about being a cleaner… that someone might pay me for cleaning. Do you think there could be some kind of opening here?"

She reached out and patted my sleeve. "Oh, ma'am, I'm right sorry for your troubles. I hardly know what to say. This sure ain't a high-paying job, but if you really mean it, I can tell you who to go talk to. At least then you'll know. If you got time right now, let me just finish up in here. I'm almost done, and I'll walk you to the basement where my boss's office is. It's a rabbit warren down there, so it's best I take you. That suit you?"

I sighed with relief. "Yes, thank you so much. At least he's someone I haven't talked to yet, so you never know. By the way, my name is Mary Heath."

She smiled. "I'm Lizzie Green. Nice to meet you, Miz Heath."

It was only a few minutes before she came to get me. She was right about the rabbit warren basement, but we arrived eventually at the closed door of a Mr. D. Malpass. Under his name on the pebbled glass door were the words "Maintenance Department."

Mrs. Green nodded towards the door, and then quietly wished me luck. She went back the way we'd come as I lifted my hand and knocked.

"Come in, come in." Judging by the irritated growl, Mr. Malpass wasn't having a good day.

I opened the door to find a middle-aged man standing behind a desk littered with stacks of papers he kept shuffling, lifting, and stacking in unstable piles. "Can't find my dern spectacles again," he grumbled, not looking up.

"Good afternoon, Mr. Malpass. I'm sorry to catch you at a bad time." I looked around. "Could those be what you're looking for on the windowsill behind you?"

Mr. Malpass looked up as I spoke. Going by his expression, he'd been expecting someone else. A heavy-set man in his fifties, I judged by his iron gray hair. He was in his shirt sleeves, but he grabbed his dark plaid jacket from the back of his chair, shrugged into it, and tightened his tie. Giving me a quizzical look, he turned to the window behind him. Snatching them up and putting them on, he immediately took them off to peer at me more closely. "Well, thank you, Miss…" he started.

"Mary Heath, Mr. Malpass. Mrs. Mary Heath." I tried to keep my nervousness under control. I just had to make this work.

"Well, have a seat, Miz Heath. Just move those papers over to… well, anywhere you can." He sat as well. "What can I do for you now? You sure you in the right place?" He picked up a half-smoked cigar, damp and chewed on one end, from an overflowing ashtray, looked up at me, and immediately set it back down. Judging by the aroma and haze in the room, it was usually lit. I was glad the radiator in the corner wasn't working very hard.

I explained my desire for employment, giving the same short explanation I'd given Lizzie Green earlier. No need to go into more detail than anyone wanted to hear, I reminded myself.

It seemed to be my day to astonish people. He sat back in his chair, picked up his unlit cigar again, and put it in the corner of his mouth.

"Ma'am, I'm not too sure how you found me down here, but this here is Maintenance. I do handle our cleaning staff, that's true, but you cannot seriously mean this here is the kind of job you want."

"Mr. Malpass, it is the kind of job I think I am qualified for. It seems I don't have the kinds of skills or attributes other jobs require. But I grew up on a farm and was a farmer's wife for fourteen years. I know about hard work because it's all I've ever done. You need reliable workers. I'll be reliable because that's how I was raised, and now I have six children to raise by myself. I do *want* this job because I *need* this job." Here I faltered. "That is, assuming there are any jobs to be had in your department, of course."

I had to make myself add, "And that the wages are agreeable." I had never once in my life been paid for any work I'd done. I had never asked or expected to be paid, for that matter. It seemed unreal that I now had to do so.

He continued staring at me as he chewed his cigar stub. I wondered how his wife liked kissing him. I almost shuddered at what that must taste like. As I realized how inappropriate my wandering thoughts were, the telephone on his desk abruptly shrilled. I hoped he didn't notice I'd jumped. He answered, had a brief conversation, and hung up. He sighed, stood up, and walked back and forth behind his desk. Then he sat down and sighed again.

"Yes, I do have an opening in the cleaning crew. At least, I will have one starting in January. I have a gal who wants to work until then, but after that she's moving to—well, I forget where—to help take care of her old mama. So, there's that. But Miz… uh… Heath, I just don't think this is the job for you. It's midnight to eight in the morning, six days a week. It's hard work. Real hard. The cleaning gals gotta scrub all these floors, see? We're talking what's probably miles of linoleum, what with all the floors of the office building and then here in the depot. They're scrubbed every night, including Sunday night, and every few days, the old wax gotta be stripped off and new wax put on. All that is on their knees, Miz Heath. And all the other cleaning that's gotta be done."

He leaned back and let me take all that in. Then he added, "And it sure don't pay a fortune, I can tell you that. I don't see how it could be enough to make it worth your trouble, much less 'agreeable,' as you say. See here…"

He wrote some numbers on a piece of paper and handed it over the leaning stacks between us. He was right. It wasn't a fortune. At all.

I looked up at him. "Mr. Malpass, if I decided that this was the job for me, are you going to offer it to me?"

He stared at me for several minutes. I waited for the cigar to be shredded by his constant chewing. "I'd give you a two-week trial, starting in January. If it don't suit after all for either one of us, that would be that. But I'm willing if you are."

I tried very hard not to sigh with relief. It was my first job offer, no matter how uninspiring. As I started to answer, he said, "I think you should know there's only one other white lady. If that might bother you."

I blinked. "No, Mr. Malpass, that doesn't matter to me at all." I bit off anything else I wanted to say as I thought of Lizzie Green's kindness just a few minutes earlier.

"And I can't be having you missing work every time one of those six children gets sick, no, ma'am. And you need to think about not being there at night for them, not to mention you needing to get your sleep during the day, when they're going to be up and about. Think real hard about that." He squinted at me. "You got a telephone now?"

I gave him my information and got his telephone number in exchange. "You call me by, let's say, by December 16, to let me know what you've decided. That'll give you two weeks to think about this. I'll need to look for someone else if you back down, which I fully expect and recommend you do. I'm trying to do you a favor by saying that, by the way, and I mean that."

I nodded, stood up, and reached across the wreck of a desk to offer my hand. He stood also and shook my hand. "I gotta get back to these repair orders now. You take care, you hear?" He started patting the piles of paper again.

"You put your spectacles in your vest pocket, Mr. Malpass."

He clutched the pocket and pulled out his eyeglasses. He chuckled and put them on. "You going to be able to find your way out of here?"

"I'm good at finding my way, Mr. Malpass. It takes me a while sometimes, but I always get to where I mean to go." I felt buoyant. Despite the grim picture he'd painted, I wasn't dismayed. I just had to figure out if it would be enough money and how to make sure my children were safe while I was working. But it was the first real hope I'd had in so long. And the very first job offer of my entire life.

Mr. Malpass nodded, and I noticed for the first time he had kind eyes. "I have that idea about you, Miz Heath. I look forward to hearing from you in a couple of weeks."

His tone was so nice I felt a little bad for having my harsh thoughts about his cigar habit. I was sure Mrs. Malpass liked kissing her husband just fine. Probably.

Riding back home with Mr. Prince, I was still excited I finally had a job offer, but I started worrying about what it would pay. I knew I needed to sit down and see what kind of budget I could come up with. I needed to find a place for all of us in Wilmington, and I really had no idea what that might cost. I needed to talk with Martha. Not my little girl, but my sister I'd named her after.

My older sister Martha, her husband, and their four children were living in what was most of the second story of a house on North Fifth Avenue in Wilmington. Martha and her family had visited us to check on Daddy the Sunday after Thanksgiving, and she regaled us with stories about the old lady, Miss Avery, who was very particular and set in her ways.

Miss Avery, who had never married, had lived there her entire life with her younger sister, also a spinster, and the two Miss Averys lived on the money left to them by their father, who'd been a merchant ship captain. Her sister passed away a few years ago. Finding her fortune running out, or so Martha assumed from the rather shabby state of the house, and since her knees were giving out, making access to the second story too painful, Miss Avery had decided to rent out the upper floor. There was one small apartment (two small rooms, really) and the larger one rented by Martha's family. Miss Avery now used what had been the back parlor as her bedroom, so most of the first floor remained her domain.

Clarence, Martha's husband, was a mechanic for the City of Wilmington, and worked at what was still called the City Stables. There were fewer horses there these days, he once said, and more trucks and motorcars, so maybe they'd get around to changing the name one day soon. He made needed repairs to Miss Avery's house in exchange for reduced rent. I assumed a similar arrangement was in effect as Martha took over the kitchen downstairs, and Miss Avery joined the family for meals. Martha was responsible for the kitchen and upstairs housekeeping, and Miss Avery's long-time maid took care of the rest of the downstairs.

It seemed the arrangement more or less suited them all. Even if she sometimes complained about Martha's children walking too heavily on the floorboards above her head, Miss

Avery must be glad to have other people in the house, especially at night. The location was ideal for Clarence to walk to his work and for Martha to walk to the shops. I hoped I could find something in the general neighborhood, to be near family still and now that I expected to be working at the railway company, which was about five blocks from there. And Martha said it was a safe neighborhood, which was important, especially as I'd be walking to work alone late at night.

So with a lighter heart, I thanked Mr. Prince as he pulled up to our house. I was at the steps when Mama came out, shut the door behind her, and whispered, "Mary, I need to talk with you, and I don't want anyone to overhear us." She came down to me and pulled me away from the house.

She handed over an envelope addressed to me. "I got one of these today, too. It's from Tom's sister in Tarboro. I guess she wanted to make sure one of them got through in case one got lost. She said in my letter she didn't want to discuss this over the phone, knowing about how things get out on a party line, but she wanted to let us know as soon as possible." Mama was gripping my wrist at that point, clearly upset. "Go ahead and read your letter, honey."

"Mama, I'll read it in my room later. It's getting so dark out here I doubt I can see the writing well enough. Just tell me. Is it Tom's mother?" I dreaded hearing she'd passed away, but I didn't see why Sis would worry about that getting out on the party line.

"No. It's Tom's two brothers. Elim and Otis. Sis heard from Otis's wife they are talking about going to a lawyer and seeing about taking the children. They think they can make a case you can't support them. Otis's wife seemed to think this wasn't just talk, either. She wanted to write you, but she was afraid Otis would see the envelope addressed to you and have a fit and insist on seeing it. Sis called her after she got the letter and told her she'd let you know 'all her news.' So that explains the two letters to us. Sis is worried they really mean to do this. After all, they're her brothers and she knows what they're like. She's thinking they might have a good chance of finding a judge who would agree with them." Mama looked so pale. "We can't let your father know about this. It might truly worry him to death."

As soon as I was able, I read Sis's letter alone in my bedroom. If anything, Mama had downplayed Sis's concern. She said she knew Otis was the ringleader, as usual, and he was always determined to get his way. That he was willing to pay a lawyer to get this done was the part that worried her most, because he had to really want something to part with money to get it.

After over a year of feeling as if I were trudging through some limbo land, events whirled by like a picture show being shown at double speed. I had no idea how much my life—and the lives of my children—would change in the space of just one month.

CHAPTER 22

Hard Choices

Thursday, December 19, 1929

I stared straight ahead, through the windscreen and down the country road. I just wanted my mind to go blank for a little while. It wouldn't last long, I knew, but I needed a break, a spell of emptiness, with no thoughts whirling around in my head, no emotions squeezing my heart. Lottie and I had not spoken since we left Sis and Mama Jo standing in their front yard in Tarboro, waving to us as we drove away. That had been over an hour ago, and we still had several more to go before we'd be back at my parents' home. The fields we passed by were empty, all brown mud and gray stubble, as the rain that had been with us since yesterday continued to come down. Everything looked as forlorn as I felt.

Finally, I looked over at Lottie. "You are the best friend in the world to do this for me," I said. I barely had the energy it took to be heard over the engine, the splashing tires, the rain, and the windscreen wipers. I reached over once again and wiped the moisture off the windscreen so she could see better. The rag I used was sodden, so it smeared more than anything else. I shivered despite the stream of heat that Lottie's fancy motorcar puffed out from under the dash.

She shot a glance at me. "Oh, come on, Mary, you'd do the same for me. I'm just glad I could help."

In the days following the receipt of Sis's letter, so many things had unfolded. After I told Lottie about Elim and Otis's plan, she first helped me to figure out if the cleaning job was going to pay enough to support the family. That meant I needed to talk to Martha, as I had never lived in the city. Lottie brought me into Wilmington to visit my sister at her home. The three of us sat down and worked out some numbers. Martha gave me an idea of what she and her husband had to spend each month on room and board for their family of six. I knew I would have to have a smaller apartment than they had, but it gave me a starting point to work from. As we talked about how my salary would need to stretch, it became clear very quickly the cleaning job would never stretch that far. I would need double that amount, probably. Then Clarence, her husband, came home from work and added a few things we'd not thought about. I felt my euphoria of earlier in the week melt away as I looked at what I needed. I'd been so focused on just finding any job at all, I had not done what I should have done long ago. I finally admitted to myself I'd known the chances of being offered a job that would support all seven of us were so low that to face that would have led to paralyzing depression. I had hidden from the truth without realizing it, but I couldn't hide any longer.

As Lottie drove me back to my parents' house, I finally gave up and simply wept. I felt I was at the end. My own sisters all had large families that were ever increasing in size. The only relatives who were in any position to offer us a home were Elim and Otis, for the children, at least. I truly believed splitting them up between those two brothers would be the same thing as sending them into indentured servitude, if not worse. They wouldn't be sent to school, they'd become laborers for their uncles, and their lack of education would lock them into that life. The boys wouldn't inherit any land, so they'd never have farms of their own. They would literally be dirt poor. As for the girls, I kept thinking about my poor cousin Mamie, and I did not want that kind of life for my girls, to grow up and live as adults in a home not their own or to marry early to escape. It wasn't that I thought Elim and Otis were evil, but I knew their priorities and how they went through life. I wanted my children to have more options. My girls and my boys.

And the option of continuing to live with my parents was not possible. I knew that despite everything, we'd been a drain on their savings, although they denied that, as well as adding to their worries. Mama's arthritis and Daddy's heart condition were not going to suddenly improve. The day after Sis's letter arrived, after Lottie brought me back home from the meeting with my sister Martha, I cornered my mother and asked her what Jim had meant for her and Daddy to think about.

She tried to brush me off, but I was determined to know. I was sure it was something important. I was right. Jim had asked the two of them to come live with him and his children. His housekeeper still lived there, so he wasn't trying to get Mama to take over housekeeping for him. He said he'd been thinking about them for some time, and he knew Janie would want him to help them. He'd already drawn up plans to convert his large back porch to a bed and sitting room for the two of them. The additional expense of them living there would be minimal, he claimed, and of course, they had the rental income from their farmland. By moving out of the big house, they could also rent it or even sell the entire farm.

Mama said he'd felt terrible about not being able to take in me and my children, but there was no way he could build on to the house enough to accommodate all seven of us as well as the two of them. Naturally, Mama and Daddy felt they couldn't decide as long as I needed a place for my family, but I realized this would be the perfect solution for them. They'd have their own space and yet still be with family, without any pressure on them to do manual labor.

Jim had even discussed this with his housekeeper, who seemed delighted to have the children's grandparents there, and no doubt having another woman close to her own age would be welcome company.

I was sure it was only misplaced guilt that prevented them from accepting Jim's offer immediately. We brought Daddy into our discussion, and it was agreed they'd call Jim to let him know they were going to accept. There was no rush for him to complete the carpentry work, but in a few months, they would decide if they wanted to sell the farm or rent it all out, and then make the move to Jim's house. There was plenty of time to decide what to do with the animals. Toby, obviously, would go with them, and I was sure old Molly would be welcome in Jim's barn. They tried to hide their relief, but it was clear this was the best path for them to follow. And what a blessing it would be to Janie's children, having gone a year without their mother, to have their grandparents right there to help ease the empty space that remained in their hearts.

After many tears over that sleepless night, I called Mr. Adams, who had come during the summer to tell me about the orphanage that Tom's civic group had recently completed in Lexington. He spared us having to get a ride into Wilmington and came out to the house while my four older ones were at school. Tommy played outside with Toby while Clarence had his afternoon nap. Daddy wanted to be included in the meeting, so he and Mama joined us.

I had studied the brochure Mama had kept from his first visit, so I was ready to ask every question I could think of. Mama and Daddy asked good questions I'd not thought of. Once again, Mr. Adams emphasized the Home (as he always referred to it) was committed to ensuring the children remained in school until they either graduated or turned eighteen, as they could only stay until they were that age. Boys would also learn farming skills, but not at the expense of their schooling, on the Home farm. Girls would likewise learn the housekeeping skills they'd need as wives. Some of those skills, such as sewing and cooking, could also help them gain employment when they left the Home.

It was almost time for the children to get back from school when Mr. Adams said, "Mrs. Heath, would you like to visit and see it for yourself? We have a couple of rooms we're keeping available for just this purpose, so you'd be able to stay overnight and see everything. You'd have a chance to meet with the superintendent and with the matrons who take care of the children, and even speak with some of the children, if you like. You can see what kind of place it is, and I think that would put your mind at rest that you're doing the best thing possible for your family, if you choose to do so. Would you be able to do that? It would be an overnight trip on the Atlantic Coast Line. There's no direct route, so you'd change trains in Florence, South Carolina, for Lexington. And you know they stop at every little town along the way, so it's not a fast trip. But it will get you to the Lexington depot, and the Home will have someone there to pick you up. Your folks could come, too. I'd just need to check to see when the two rooms would be available and so forth."

I was stunned. It was so far away, farther than I'd ever been in my life. But I knew I could never do this without seeing with my own eyes, if I could ever send them away at all.

But how to get there? Train tickets were so dear. I looked at Mama and Daddy. "Would you want to come?"

Mama looked over at my father and sighed. "Honey, I don't think that would be a good idea for your daddy just now, and I don't want to leave him on his own. And we need someone to stay with the children, of course. But," she thought for a moment, "what about Lottie? She has a good head on her shoulders, and I think it's a good idea for you to have a friend with you. You'll both notice different things. Do you think she could leave Bertie with her mother for a few nights?"

Mr. Adams got back to us in a couple of days. He'd arranged for us to stay there in two weeks, on Tuesday, December 17. Lottie suggested we drive. I half suspected she knew I would want to pay for her train ticket from my dwindling bank account, and she saw a way to avoid that issue. Of course, that left gasoline to pay for, but I hoped she'd let me take on that small expense. We looked at a map to plan our route, and I realized Tarboro was the midway point between Wilmington and Lexington. A phone call to Sis and it was agreed Lottie and I would break our long journey to and from the Home with her, her husband Clyde, and Mama Jo. I was delighted with the idea of not only seeing them again but being able to discuss the situation. Mama Jo and Sis would be powerful allies if they thought the orphanage was the best option for Tom's children. I knew I was going to need strong allies against Elim and Otis, no matter what I decided to do.

I spent the next week and a half searching harder than ever for a job that would allow my family to stay together. Twice I stayed over at Lottie's house so I could leave early in the morning to pay visits to establishments that opened before most of the businesses, and to stay later than I would if someone had to drive me back to my parents' house. Every extra minute I could use on my search seemed as if it might make the world of difference for all of us. I only needed one, just one, decent-paying job offer, and it would change the course of our lives. Equally, the thought of being away from my children one minute more than necessary, when I might soon lose them entirely, was enough to make me panic. No matter which I chose, I felt I should be doing the other.

Nothing offered even a whisper of encouragement. Just the opposite. Several of the owners and managers I spoke with said until "that dern Yankee stock market problem," as several referred to it, got settled, they weren't taking on any more employees. I got a sense of something I couldn't put my finger on at first, but gradually realized it was fear. Genuine fear.

"Why now? Why now?" I asked myself over and over. If only I could have started looking for a job a year ago. Why had I waited? I'd start berating myself as I went from office to office, only to finally remember a nursing mother would have had no chance at all finding a position, and that was why I'd had to delay. Still, I knew part of the problem had been the denial I was clinging to. Had part of me hoped last summer Mr. Meyer would be the solution to my problems? I could feel my cheeks burn with shame. I should have realized I had to rescue myself, not hope for some fairytale ending.

Monday, December 10, was my mother's sixty-seventh birthday. At thirty-one, I couldn't imagine what that age must feel like, although Mama's arthritis was so bad I knew sixty-seven for her would be even more painful than sixty-six had been. Still, I wished I was now at her age, with all these problems behind me, and solved somehow. That all my children would be around my kitchen table, eating birthday cake with me. I'd much prefer painful joints, I told myself, to the pain I felt now at the possibility of losing my precious family.

The week passed, and no job offers came my way. On Monday morning, December 16, I called Mr. Malpass as I'd promised to do. I accepted the job as a cleaner. I could tell he was surprised. He told me to come in on Friday, January 3, to sign my payroll papers. I'd start to work at 11:00 pm on the night of January 6, 1930. I hung up the telephone handpiece and sighed. My options were narrowing down.

As it turned out, staying overnight at Sis's each way had unexpected benefits. Not only did we avoid passing a night trying to sleep in uncomfortable seats, as I'm sure any seat would be after so many hours, as the train stopped and started over and over on the route, we had the chance to hear what they thought about my options. On the first night we stayed with them, on our way to Lexington, they listened carefully and suggested more questions to ask at the Home (as I was beginning to call it in my mind). Even Mama Jo was pragmatic about the alternatives open to me, and less emotional than I had feared.

"Honey, I know you are going to do the right thing. I don't have one little worry about that. And I know Tom would feel the same way," she'd said after supper that first night, squeezing my hand across the kitchen table.

I looked around at the sympathetic faces of my family and my dear friend. "But I always wanted to be a good mother. Someone who took care of her children, not someone who would ever think of putting them in an orphanage. I wanted to be someone people respected. I wanted to do the right thing. If I were to do this, how could I even live with myself? What will happen to my babies? What will they think of me and how will they ever believe I love them?" I had to stop before I started sobbing again.

Sis raised her head. "Mary. Think about what Mama just said. You *are* going to do the right thing, whatever you decide, because that is who you are. You have to look at all your options and choose the best one for your children. The best one that is truly available to you. Maybe this orphanage won't be it. Maybe it will be. You'll find out tomorrow."

Mama Jo, still holding my hand, said, "Sometimes we have an idea in our head about what is right and what is wrong. Sometimes things are just more complicated than that, Mary. You think being there and raising your children is the right thing, and that would mean you were being a good mother. But maybe being a good mother is making choices that are so painful it takes your breath away. Even rips your heart out."

Lottie nodded in agreement. Clyde, a deacon at his church, murmured, "Amen to that."

"Maybe being a good mother is living with the fact that your children don't understand your choices, but you know it's the best decision. Do your children think you're a wonderful mother when you make them take some awful tasting medicine when they're sick? No, I'm sure they don't. But you know better. And when they are older, they will understand about the choices you had to make when they were too young to see your reasons. Hear what I'm saying and believe it, Mary. Those children will always know you love them. And even if other people think you've made the wrong choice, or your choice means they think less of you, you have to remember the most important thing: you made the best decision you could for your children's sake. I have faith in you. You need to have faith in you, too." I looked at Mama Jo, and for a moment it seemed I was looking into Tom's eyes again.

The next morning, Lottie and I set off early so we could get to the Home by noon if we were lucky. My jitters were gone. I didn't know what I'd see at the orphanage. It didn't seem real I might even be considering this path, but I felt calm and determined to find out everything I needed to know. I was resolved to be open to this possibility. And to the possibility that being a good mother didn't consist of only one right way to be.

After looking at the black-and-white photos of the brochure, it seemed a little startling to see the main building of the Home in color. Or, at least, as much color as early December allowed. Although rain clouds seemed to be coming in from the west, the sun was shining brilliantly on the red bricks of the stately building as we pulled up in Lottie's car, the patch of sky behind it a clear blue for the moment.

"Oh my, Mary. I would never think this was an orphanage. It looks more like an expensive school or college, even." Lottie stopped the motorcar to gaze at the two-story building I remembered was in the Colonial Revival style, according to what I'd read. Everything looked fresh and new, being only two or three years since construction had been completed. We parked to the side of the building and followed a sidewalk around to the front entry, passing under the limbs of a massive oak tree off the corner of the building. Somehow, it seemed important to me to know they'd not cut it down to make the building process easier, as happened so often. Maybe I was looking too hard for a comforting message in that, but I hoped it meant they could build for the future without needing to destroy the past.

Up the steps and into the warm foyer, we went over to a glassed-in reception window. The lady there smiled as she heard our names and came out into the foyer to greet us. She suggested we get settled in our rooms and then join the superintendent in his office. He planned on taking us to the dining hall for lunch, as she called it, and then we'd be given a tour of the entire premises.

All three of us walked back out to the car, and she directed Lottie the short distance to the building where we'd be spending the night. Lottie and I had decided to stay together in the same room. We knew we'd have a lot to talk about, and we also didn't want to put them to any more trouble than necessary. We parked by the smaller building, in the same red brick style as all the buildings seemed to be, and went into a comfortably warm hallway leading to our room. The door opened to a plain but pleasant room with two twin beds, each with a white coverlet and a woolen blanket folded at the foot. The receptionist waited for us to set our luggage down, freshen up in the washroom down the hall, and then walked with us back to the main building to meet with Mr. Shuford, the superintendent of the Home, who turned out to be exactly the sort of man I felt I could trust with my children.

Twenty-four hours later, we were headed back to Tarboro. The rain had arrived during the night, and poor Lottie had to strain to see through the downpour. We finally arrived at Sis's house, where they were eager to hear what we'd found out. Given all my earlier misgivings and expectations of an orphanage that would feel familiar to a reader of Charles Dickens or Jane Eyre, I had not a single negative thing to say about the Home created by the members of the Junior Order.

Lottie and I had not only met with the superintendent, Mr. Shuford, but many others of the staff. We met with Mr. Leonard, the head of the Home farm, where the boys would learn farming skills; Miss Owen, the head matron, along with three of the other seven matrons; Miss Link, the nurse; Miss Winn, the on-site teacher who taught the little ones the basics before they went to the public school with the older children; and Miss Daley, the seamstress. Mr. Shuford and Mr. Leonard lived on-site with their families, as did the man who kept their electrical generator, boiler, and radiators working (at least, as I understood his job to be). All three men had children, and I saw several of them playing happily with some of the Home children.

I got to meet with many of the women working there, including Mrs. Shuford, who joined us for supper that evening. Without exception, the women seemed dedicated to the children in their charge. Some seemed more maternal than others, whereas some had a brisker approach, but the overall feeling I got, and Lottie agreed, was one of benevolent care. I was glad to see there was no overt pity displayed, and the general tone was not different from the one I tried to create in my own family.

Maybe it was so different from my expectations because I'd never heard of an orphanage created by a group of men who saw it as a possible necessary refuge for their own children. Mr. Shuford mentioned, as had Mr. Adams in our initial meeting in the summer, the Junior Order had chosen that course of action after realizing how vulnerable, and perhaps even destitute, their own wives would be if anything happened to them, the sole breadwinner of the family. The Great War and the Spanish Flu had driven in that message.

Wednesday evening, Lottie and I took turns telling Mama Jo, Sis, and Clyde about what we'd seen. It was true that two tennis courts had been put in, and construction on a swimming pool had been started. The children seemed like any their ages, with the excitement of Christmas coming adding to the mix of happy voices calling to each other as they played outside. The hallways of the administrative building, as well as the dorm building where the children lived, were festooned with colored cutouts of ornaments and drawings of what were or might be construed to be manger scenes, depending on the age and ability of the young artist. The children were currently working on making ornaments, again paper cutouts and strings of popcorn, for the trees that would be cut down closer to Christmas.

Mrs. Shuford and Miss Owens assured me each child would have a Christmas stocking with an orange, a peppermint stick, a toothbrush, a pair of socks, and nuts in the shell, along with a wrapped gift from Santa, courtesy of the Junior Order. They discussed how the children were given new shoes and also new clothing, usually made by the seamstress, Miss Daley, and her more senior sewing students, as needed throughout the year. I could not begin to imagine what it would cost to provide for the 200 children in their care, and I was proud of Tom for having belonged to such a fine organization. I still wished he'd told me more about it, but I had to resign myself to never really knowing why he hadn't. Maybe he felt it would sound like bragging.

Mrs. Heath and Sis looked more and more relieved as we told them about the Home. Saying grace that evening at supper, Clyde thanked the Lord for the many fine men who had made the Home, and for the fine men and women who now ran it. As we said "amen" at the end of his prayer, I felt the uncertainty that had loomed over me for more than a year finally dissipating, but the sorrow of the reality of my choices was just beginning.

As Lottie battled the wet windscreen and drenched roads as we drove home the next day, the enormity of the task that lay ahead threatened to undo me: I had to tell the children.

Lottie interrupted these thoughts. "I'm glad I could be with you, Mary. I would never want to go through what you're going through all on my own. I don't think I could do it. So there's no way, if I can help it, you're going through it alone. Not as long as I'm able to be here for you."

There was something about the way she said it that seemed odd, but I was too tired and distracted to figure it out.

Lottie continued, "There's one other thing I'd like to say. I don't know if it will seem even remotely helpful, but I've been thinking about this a while now." She glanced at me. "And especially now that I've seen the Home, it seems more like sending your children off to a boarding school. You know about boarding schools, right?"

I nodded. "I've read about them in novels, I guess. But aren't they where rich people in England send their children?"

"Well, yes, and here in America, too. My grandmother wanted to send me to a girls' boarding school in New England when I was ten or so, but Daddy wouldn't hear of it." Lottie smiled. "I think my mother wouldn't have minded, though."

I tried not to smile, but I was sure Lottie was right about her mother's feelings. Then I thought about what Lottie was saying and added, "I appreciate you trying to make me feel better, but it's not the same, Lottie. The parents don't give up their rights to their children at a boarding school. The children come home on holidays and vacations, don't they? Well, unless they're like the young Ebenezer Scrooge and have a horrible father."

Lottie wrinkled her forehead. "I never thought about it before, but boarding schools and orphanages in Mr. Dickens's novels seem a lot alike, don't they? Maybe we shouldn't pay him too much mind. If you ask me, the Home seems a lot closer to a nice boarding school than an orphanage. Anyway, it's just another way to look at it, isn't it? If you think of it as an orphanage, it seems sad, but as a boarding school, it's a wonderful opportunity."

I stared out my rain-streaked window at the gray and brown beyond. Lottie was doing her best to help me. She had a point, but I knew which one I would really be choosing by sending my children to the Home. I wasn't going to sugarcoat it just to make myself feel better.

Several more miles went by in silence, except for the slap of the wipers and the pounding of the rain. On the other hand, thinking of the Home as similar to a boarding school could benefit my children. I was so terrified that they'd think I didn't want them anymore. If I could just help them see all the good things in this choice. "I do thank you so much, Lottie. I do. I can't imagine doing this without you. I keep thinking I'm on my own, but that's ridiculous. My parents, Mama Jo, Sis and Clyde, my sister Martha and her husband, my church, and so many others have helped this past year. And you, my dearest and oldest friend. You."

Lottie teared up, but gave me a quick smirk. "Hey, I'm not so old, you know."

We laughed, and I tried to clear the windscreen once again for her. This time I used my glove. Better. Much better. Sometimes it just took time and effort to see clearly.

CHAPTER 23

Christmas

Tuesday, December 24, 1929

We were all in the front sitting room. The children gazed with joy at the Christmas tree they'd just finished decorating. Mr. Meyer was once again the hero, for it was he who had offered to cut down and bring a tree from his own property, knowing Daddy would try to do it otherwise. He'd come by that morning and set it up for us. A little over five feet tall, it was big enough to satisfy their dreams of the perfect Christmas tree, yet short enough we could easily decorate it. He had some of Mama's famous fruitcake before he headed back to his family. I smiled, thinking of all the brandy soaked into that cake, and hoped he'd had a substantial breakfast. The brandy, carefully hoarded since the beginning of Prohibition, was the only alcohol my mother ever allowed, and only for our Christmas fruitcakes. We walked Mr. Meyer out to his truck and sent him off with shouts of "Merry Christmas!" He really was a decent man, and

I hoped he'd find a good wife one day soon. A strong, highly opinionated one. Maybe Santa would bring him one.

"What are you laughing about, Mama?" asked Irene as we turned to go inside. The cold air had put roses in her cheeks. She continued to grow into the beautiful woman she was going to be.

I took her arm. "Nothing, sweetie. Just wondering what Santa is planning to bring tonight, is all."

She didn't seem entirely convinced by my answer, but put her arm through mine and smiled as we went up the steps and back inside.

Now it was Christmas Eve night. The children, dressed for bed, were waiting in the kitchen with their grandparents, the door to the sitting room closed. Toby was at my feet. Even he seemed to simmer with excitement as I took the box of matches and began lighting the clip-on candles one by one. When I finished, I blew out the one lamp I had lit in the room and gazed at the tree in all its glory for a moment. I wanted to savor every minute of this evening and tomorrow. Not rush anything. But I knew my children were about to burst with excitement, especially Martha and Tommy, so I first glanced at the two buckets of sand sitting near the tree in case of an accident, then went over to the door. "Children, close your eyes. No peeking. Tommy, I really mean it!" I cracked open the door. "Your grandmama and granddaddy are going to lead you in here. You keep your eyes shut until I tell you to open them. You know how we do this." Tom and I had started this tradition when Irene was just a toddler. Although the children had decorated the tree that morning, seeing it lit with all the candles at night was a completely different experience.

With much giggling, they lined up in front of the tree. Mama, holding little Clarence, who was exempt from the closed-eyes command, of course, shut the kitchen door again, so the only source of light was the tree. I picked up Toby and joined my parents and Clarence behind the children. "I'm going to count to three… one, two, three!"

A second of stunned delight, followed by gasps and exclamations. It really was beautiful, with the flickering candlelight and the scent of the tree filling the room. Leah clapped her hands and bounced on her toes, as Celeste and Irene pointed out favorite ornaments to Martha. Tommy went to touch something on the tree. "No, Tommy, back away. You know how dangerous it can be with candles lit. Find a seat, everyone. We'll sing a few carols, and then we have to blow out the candles. Let's enjoy them while we can."

Daddy sat in his chair, and I put Toby on his lap. I didn't think Toby would bother the tree, but the candles might attract his attention, and it wasn't worth the risk. I took Clarence from Mama and let her sit on the settee. When we were all settled, we sang our favorite carols. I had thought we might do two or three, but the children kept begging to do one more. With an eye on the length of the tree candles, I agreed.

It wasn't in me to deny them anything tonight. The thought that this would be the last Christmas Eve we would all be together for years, but perhaps forever, just kept droning on in my mind. Could that be possible, I wondered, that we'd never be all together again on Christmas Eve?

"Mama, are you all right?" Irene was looking again at me, and I realized my eyes were brimming with tears.

"Honey, you know how sentimental I get listening to Christmas carols. They're just so beautiful." I tried to make light of it. "What do you want to sing next? Whose turn is it to choose?" I saw Irene continue to look over at me through the next songs, and I tried to just think of this moment.

I looked at each of my precious children, then at my mother. And my father. His face was glowing with happiness, but he still seemed so weak. Out of the blue, I thought of the *Christmas Carol* story by Mr. Dickens, and for the first time truly understood why the most frightening of the three ghosts was the Ghost of Christmas Yet to Come. As a young girl, I couldn't understand why the future would be the scariest. Now I understood.

"Children, you know the sooner we go to sleep, the sooner Santa will come. But before we go to bed, guess what I want us to do?" I asked, as the candles were finally getting too short for my comfort.

"Oh no, Mama. That's for sissies." Tommy rolled his eyes.

"No, Tommy," Daddy spoke up. Tommy whipped his head to look at him. "Not at all. Let's close our eyes and make a memory. Concentrate real hard. Let's make one to last forever." He looked over at me and smiled gently.

And we did.

The day after Christmas, I went to Mr. Adams's law office in town to give up most of my legal rights to my children going to the Home. Lottie had insisted on driving me to meet with him. Mr. Adams went through all the conditions and limitations I would have as of January 1 regarding my children. I was allowed to visit them, but that needed to be no more than twice a year without special permission. I knew one of the few benefits of working for the railroad would be an employee discount on travel. I just prayed I could afford to go twice a year.

There was one matter I had to make sure of. "Mr. Adams, I do not want my children adopted by anyone. Not anyone. I don't want them split up. At least they will be together there. At least until they each turn eighteen. I don't want people I don't know raising them. I'd worry they'd be working in some tobacco field somewhere."

"No, ma'am, you don't have to worry. That isn't the purpose of the Home we've created. We don't let strangers adopt the children. That's why our membership has gone to such expense to make it a true home for the children. This way, we know exactly what kind of conditions our children will be raised in should the worst happen, and they need to go there."

"But Mr. Adams, what about family members who might show up to take them? It was my mother-in-law who thought of this, of her two sons, the ones I've told you about, getting it into their heads they could drive up there to Lexington and take them away. You understand, as their uncles, just take the children. Maybe tell Mr. Shuford they were going to give the children a home with their family, or maybe just grab them when they were playing or something like that." I was grasping my gloves so tight it was a wonder I didn't split them apart.

Mr. Adams smiled. "I can assure you they would have a wasted trip. And they'd probably spend at least a night in jail, Mrs. Heath. Mr. Shuford would never agree to let anyone at all get any of the children there in his care. And he'd not hesitate to call the sheriff on them if they tried to go around him. You met him. And Mr. Leonard and maybe Mr. Johnson, too?"

I nodded, and he continued.

"They're all right there at the Home, and all three of them are big men. I'm not sure they would even need to call the sheriff to… well… to discourage those two. Children are always watched by several matrons while they are outside playing, too. No, Mrs. Heath, you don't have to worry about that. Even the very worst-case scenario, where they snatch the children, would be an easy problem to solve because we know where their farms are, don't we? But I'd bet my last dollar it would never come to that. The children at the Home are well protected by their caretakers and by the law. Put your mind to rest."

Lottie sat beside me as I signed my name on the documents.

"Mrs. Heath, if you have any more questions, I'm giving you my home telephone number, and of course, you have my number here at the office. In the envelope are instructions for what to pack for each child. Remember everything has to fit into the chest at the foot of their bed. I'm sure you saw the limitations for storage there when you visited."

I took his card and saw the number written on the back.

"Mr. Preston, one of our Junior Order members, is going to escort your children on the train. His wife will be with him, as I mentioned. He will have the tickets with him. I plan on being there myself, just to see them off with you."

"That's so kind of you. I… I just wish I could take them to Lexington myself." I bit my lips and reached for my handkerchief. Lottie had been blotting her eyes since we got here, although she tried to hide it.

"I understand, I really do, Mrs. Heath. But we've found this is the best way to handle things, so please trust me. It won't be easy to say goodbye at the train station, but it's best for the children. And they will settle down at the Home faster than you will believe possible. They'll have new children to play with and so many new things to occupy their minds. At the end of their first week, they'll write to you and tell you all about it. The matrons will help the little ones, and then you'll see everything is going to be all right. It will take time, of course, but did you see any children there who looked unhappy?" He looked at me searchingly.

I thought. "No. No, I didn't." I turned to Lottie. "Did you?"

She shook her head and reached over for my hand. "No. Not a single one. I think Mr. Adams is right. We have to trust they know how to handle this in the best way possible for the children."

Mr. Adams added, "They're leaving on New Year's Eve, and they'll arrive at the Home on New Year's Day, Mrs. Heath. Think of that. The first day of a new year. The first day of a new decade. I think that's a sign, don't you? A good sign."

I could only hope he was right.

We shook hands with Mr. Adams and left his office. Lottie took my arm and led me to a café a short way down the street. It was early afternoon, but after the midday rush, so there were only a few customers scattered around the room.

"I thought we could use some coffee or tea before we head back to your parents' house," Lottie said, glancing at the menu. "And I want a little something to eat. You need some sugar, I bet. I'm sure I do. Let's have some of this chocolate cake."

I went along with her suggestion, although I hardly felt like eating anything. Maybe the sugar would settle my stomach, though.

We were almost through our slices of cake when Lottie said, "Mary, I have some news of my own." I noticed then she'd pushed more of her cake around the little plate than she'd eaten.

I looked up in alarm at the tone of her voice. "What? Has something happened? Is something wrong?"

She took a deep breath and looked out the café window. "It turns out Mama lost quite a bit of money that first day the stock market fell off so much. You know, the day all those people killed themselves in New York because they lost all their money. Well, Mama was even more heavily invested in the market than I realized. She lost a lot. Not everything, thank goodness, but… well, enough to make a difference." Another deep breath. "And I lost money, too. Also, not everything, but more than I want to think about." She still didn't look at me, but kept staring out the window.

Once again, I felt awful. I'd never followed up with her about her or her mother's situation. In part because I didn't want to pry, but I knew the larger part was my own self-centeredness. I was so focused on my own worries.

"Lottie, I'm so, so sorry to hear this. And that I haven't been a better friend to you. I'm sorry I've been so wrapped up in my problems I forgot you might be in trouble."

Lottie just shook her head. "You have every reason to focus on your own problems, Mary. I've deliberately held back from letting on there was a problem. I should have waited anyway until the children… well, until the children and you were all settled down in January. I guess I just couldn't go any longer without letting you know."

"No, you didn't need to wait, and I'm glad you're telling me. What are you going to do? And your mother? And tell me to mind my own business if you don't want to say any more." I felt sick. Chocolate, grief, and guilt were a worse combination than I'd realized.

"We have to retrench, as Mother says." Lottie managed a little smile. "Very Jane Austen, don't you think? Like in *Persuasion,* I think it was. 'Retrench.'"

"But what does that mean, exactly? I know the definition, but… what does that mean she's going to do?" I wondered if their poor servants were going to be let go, but then I realized Lottie and her mother could hardly take over maintaining that mansion themselves.

"She's going to sell the house. At least, that's what it looks like. And now she's thinking she better try to sell it sooner than later, before no one is willing to give her a fair price. Or before no one is even *able* to give her a fair price. She thinks we are in for hard times, Mary. Really hard times. That's one reason I've been so supportive of the Home. They are going to have everything they need. Those Junior Order men will make sure of that. They are safe, Mary. I just hope I can keep Bertie that safe." Her voice cracked, and she fumbled for her handkerchief. It was a day for tears.

I hardly knew where to start, and I did not want to push Lottie. I knew what it was like to have "what are you going to do?" thrown at me when I had no idea myself. I just said, "Yes."

She took a moment and then said, "I'm sorry for being melodramatic. I've got to stop that. The truth is we are not destitute. We aren't. We just… can't live as we've been living."

"Do you think your mother will buy a smaller house in town?"

Yet another deep breath. "No. No, I don't. In fact, my grandmother—Mama's mother in New Jersey, you know—sees this as her opportunity to get us to move back closer to her. Really close. In her house. Her estate, as Mama and Grandmama always call it. She wants us to sell up here, come to New Jersey, and move in with her. And not in that order, either. Grandmama thinks the house here might be on the market for a while, so we should just move in with her immediately. I think she wants us to move there before we can think of some alternative, really." Lottie gave a little laugh that had no humor in it.

"How does your mother feel about this?" I tried to sound neutral. I was so sorry for Lottie and stunned to think I might lose her if she had to move so far away.

"Oh, I think she's coming around to the idea very quickly. She wasn't thrilled at first, but I think she started…" Lottie broke off. "It is so disloyal to my mother, but frankly, I think she started thinking about how old my grandmother is, and how sharing the estate with her wouldn't be something that would go on for very long."

We sat quietly for a few minutes. Lottie took a few bites of her cake. She looked up. "I guess getting that out has made me feel better. It's been hard not telling you. But I'm so sorry to add to your worries."

I waved that aside. Lottie took a sip of her tea and continued, "Anyway, to sweeten the deal, Grandmama says she will pay for Bertie's education. And that includes setting aside money for his college and law school if he wants to go into law. I bet she's had that set up since Robert passed away, but obviously, I can hardly say so. Still, I'm not sure I have a good alternative. Nor does my mother. She could afford to live very modestly on her own, I don't doubt, but she's never lived even slightly modestly in her life, and I don't think she plans on doing that at this stage."

Lottie huffed and added, "It's not so much the money as it is the status, you know."

"But… when, Lottie? When do you think this is all going to happen? Leaving Wilmington, I mean."

"Mama said last night how pretty spring is in New Jersey. Really? As if it isn't beautiful here?" Lottie's temper was flaring, which was easier to watch than her despair. "I'm sure she doesn't want to move up there in winter, so I imagine late March at the earliest. Maybe April or May." She looked over at me. "And don't you worry. Mr. Simms has already told my mother he needs to retire, and she has an annuity set up for him to live on. Our cook will probably be fought over by every household in Wilmington that can afford her, as will the other servants. Everyone knows anyone who could please my mother enough to remain employed by her must be a treasure."

We both laughed at that. I was especially relieved for Mr. Simms.

Lottie reached over for my hand. "I don't know how I'm going to do without seeing you so often, Mary. You are going to have to visit me."

I tried to imagine taking time off my floor-scrubbing job to visit my friend at her estate in New Jersey. "Well, we'll see. One way or another, we won't lose touch again, will we?"

Lottie smiled. "Never again. I think we learned our lesson there."

As Lottie finished her cake, I thought of one of my remaining problems. "Lottie, may I ask another favor, if we have time?" I hesitated.

"Of course. What is it?"

"Could we go by my sister's place? I think I need to see if I can rent that small apartment on her floor. I thought it was too small when I thought I'd need a place for the seven of us, but…" I couldn't go on for a moment.

Lottie nodded. "I understand. Let's go see what that old lady wants to charge for it. I'll help you talk her down." She gave me her wicked smile.

Later, having come to an agreement with Miss Avery that even my paltry paycheck could handle, we headed back to my parents' house.

"I think Miss Avery realized what a wonderful tenant you'd be, especially as she knows your sister. That's going to be a blessing to be living right there with Martha and her family just down the hallway." Lottie smiled. I knew she was pleased she'd convinced Miss Avery to lower my rent for those very reasons. It was clear the old lady thought a lot of my sister.

"I agree, and you were wonderful talking to her, Lottie. I'm not sure I could have gotten her to go so low on the rent."

"Because you wouldn't ask, or at least, not push as hard as I did. You're wonderful standing up for others, Mary, but you need to do that more for yourself, too."

"You know, I named my little Martha and Clarence after my sister and her husband. Tom thought the world of them, too, of course."

Lottie raised her eyebrows. "I guess I assumed that about Martha, but I hadn't thought about Martha's husband and your little Clarence having the same first name."

Speaking of Martha and Clarence ended the brief contentment I'd felt at settling my problem about where to live. Lottie, who no doubt sensed the change in my mood, started telling stories of her grandmother's absurd pretensions. I suspected she was also hoping to lift my spirits, at least for a short while. I knew we were both thinking of the news I had to break to my children. As we pulled into the driveway, I decided I was going to wait until tomorrow.

We'd have one more night together as a family before I broke their hearts.

CHAPTER 24

New Paths

Friday, December 27, 1929

Irene and I walked away from the chicken coop and back toward the barn where Molly waited. Her breath clouded the air as she hung her head over the stall, reaching for the apple Irene offered to her. We stood a moment and watched our sweet-natured girl enjoy her treat, apple juice spraying out the sides of her mouth. Finally, Irene turned to head back inside, and I reached out to hold her sleeve.

"Irene, I need to talk with you about something. Something serious." My tone alarmed her. She knew whatever I had to say wasn't going to be good.

It wasn't. But she listened to me as I explained what was going to happen. Despite hardly sleeping the previous night, trying to figure out how to tell the children their world was about to be upturned. Destroyed. At some point in the early hours, I'd finally accepted that the worst thing I could do was make it sound like a tragedy. For their sakes, I had to believe, so I could make them believe, this was a new adventure for them. An adventure that had a big price to pay, but one that would turn out for the best in the end. I hoped I could do that for all our sakes.

So, I told Irene about her grandparents no longer being able to take care of this house, much less handle even the few animals and small vegetable garden they would need. About their Uncle Jim offering them a good place to live, with him and their cousins.

Irene nodded. That made sense to her, but, "Mama, are we going to live here without them?"

"No, baby, no. Your grandparents need to sell this farm, so they have something to live on. They don't want to depend on Jim's charity. He has his five children to raise, and he has to pay his housekeeper, you know. And all the expenses of running a farm, besides."

"Is Grandmama going to take care of his house and all? I don't see how that's better than working here."

I explained about the housekeeper staying on. We both knew my mother would help out as she could, but her days of hard housework were behind her, just as farming was over for my father.

"So, where are we all going to live, then?" Irene was hugging her arms as the damp, chill air wrapped around us.

I told her as quickly as I could about my job, and about the apartment in the same house as her Aunt Martha, Uncle Clarence, and cousins. And I told her the rest. The Home. Her brothers and sisters. Her own near future.

She just looked at me as if I'd lost my mind. She grasped the stall gate and swayed, trying to get enough air to say something.

I reached over to hold her, but she jerked away. Her blue eyes filled with tears as she gave me a look I will never forget as long as I live. I'd betrayed her. Twice over.

"No. No. No. It can't be like that. No. It's not fair. It's not fair to any of us. No," she repeated over and over.

"Irene. Listen to me. Listen. If there were any other way, I'd take it. I would. I have tried to find another way, one where we could all stay together. I've tried for months. But this is the very best I can do for all of you. I've explained why. I know it's going to take a long time to accept this. I feel the same way. But this is what we've been sent to deal with." I was trying so hard not to break down. Irene was just the first child who would hate me today. I was sure of that.

This time it was just a whimper. "But it's not fair." And the tears came. Finally, she let me hold her.

When she was cried out, I said, "Remember what Daddy and I always told you? We need to be as fair to each other as we can, but we can't expect life to be fair to us. We have to take it as it comes. I know it doesn't seem I'm being fair, but I'm doing the best I can. I love you. I love all my children. You know that."

Irene shuddered and pulled away. I handed her my handkerchief. She wiped her face and blew her nose. She nodded. "I know it's not you, Mama. But… it's so hard."

I stroked her dark hair away from her face and cupped her cheeks in my hands. "It's going to be harder for your brothers and sisters, Irene. I need you to help me tell them. I need you to reassure them we are still going to be a family, and they are going to be all right. Can you do that? Can you help me? I know it's a lot to ask. You can wait out here if you can't do it. I need to go tell them now."

I waited while she turned to Molly, who sensed something was wrong and snuffled into Irene's hands. After a moment, she gave Molly's ears one last stroke and turned to me. "Yes, Mama. You know I'll always help you."

We walked slowly back to the house. Mama, Daddy, and Irene, holding Clarence on her lap, were all at the kitchen table when I sat the other children down and told them about the Home. Martha and Tommy didn't seem able to take in what I meant at first. Celeste and Leah were silent and stricken, and they kept looking from me to their grandparents and Irene. Mama also tried explaining to them. Gradually, one by one, they started to absorb how their lives were going to change, and tears flowed. I cuddled Martha in my lap, and Daddy held Tommy as he shook. Irene had an arm around Celeste on one side and Leah on the other, as all three sobbed. Even Clarence, not understanding anything but the sadness all around him, wailed.

Her tears slowed, and Celeste turned to me. "Even Clarence? He's just a baby, Mama."

"No. Not yet, at least. The Home will only take children who are old enough to be out of diapers, so Clarence won't be going at first. He's only a year and a half old, you know, so he's going to be in diapers for a good long while. Tommy was almost four before he got into his grown-up underdrawers, you know."

Tommy lifted his head from his granddaddy's shoulder and glared at me.

"Anyway," I continued, "he'll be coming to be with you as soon as he's a big enough boy. You will have to show him how to do there, you know. He'll be depending on his big sisters and brother to watch over him." I was hanging on by a thread. I couldn't start crying again.

Irene let go of Celeste and Leah, and they sat back down in their usual chairs. Martha asked, "Will Irene be the boss of us now, Mama? She'll be like our mama at the Home?"

I helped her blow her nose before I answered. "No, sweetheart, no. Celeste is going to be your biggest sister there. She's not going to be your boss or like your mama. The nice matrons who are there will take care of you. I met them, and you are going to love them. I just know it." I waited for the shoe to drop.

That went over Tommy's head, and he just cuddled his body closer to his granddaddy. But Celeste and Leah looked confused. "Me? What do you mean, Mama? Why did you say I'll be the biggest sister there?" She looked over at Irene, who held her head down.

I took yet another deep breath. This would be the last of it. I just had to get through this part. I prayed this was as bad as it would get.

"Irene isn't going to the Home. She's staying here. She'll have to take care of Clarence when I'm off at work."

All four of the other children stared at me as they tried to understand what I was saying. "Mama? We have to go to the Home, but Irene gets to stay with you and Clarence?" Celeste was incredulous. "No. No, that's not right."

"If Irene can stay, why can't we?" wailed Leah. Irene tried to put her arms back around Celeste and Leah, but they pulled away and kept staring at me.

I started to explain, but Celeste stood up, her face getting redder by the moment as her tears dried and anger took their place. "Irene is always your favorite, Mama! Always! It's not right!" Her entire body was shaking. "Why does Irene get to be the lucky one?" She whirled on Irene and yelled at her. "Why are you *always* the lucky one?"

At that, Irene's head snapped up. "Lucky one? You think I'm the lucky one? You all are going to some fancy new home. Mama just told you about all the nice things there. Do you think I'll be getting nice new clothes and shoes as soon as I need them like you will? Do you think I'll be going to a swimming pool or playing tennis next summer? Do you think I won't miss all of you and wonder what you're doing and if you even remember me? Do you think I want to be responsible for Clarence and be in some tiny apartment all alone with him every night? In a few years, even Clarence will be gone, and I'll be all alone with Mama. I'll be all alone, Celeste! And you really think I'm the lucky one?"

We were all shocked at Irene's outburst. I think even Irene was shocked at herself. She pushed her chair out from the table, stood, and ran to her room.

The silence continued for a moment. Celeste sat back down and mumbled, "I'm sorry, Mama."

My mother stood up, walked over, and handed a squirming Clarence to Celeste, and took Irene's chair. As Irene did earlier, she put an arm around Leah and Celeste. Softly, she said, "Let's let your mama explain why Irene isn't going to go with you."

I waited until they all were looking at me, even Tommy and Martha. "Irene is *not allowed* to go to the Home. It's their rules. Remember how I said Clarence can't go until he's completely potty trained? That's their rule. Well, another rule is that only children under the age of thirteen are allowed to be at the Home. That is, they have to be under thirteen when they first start to live there. Irene is already thirteen, so she's just too old to go there. They won't let her. It's not my choice, and it certainly is not Irene's choice—or fault."

I continued, "I think someone might see you, Celeste, as the lucky one." Celeste looked at me. "Yes, you. You're getting to go live in a place where you are going to make lots of new friends and have fun adventures. And from the very beginning, you'll have two sisters and a brother with you. In a few years, it will be two brothers. They'll be looking up to you now. You'll get to go to a nice school until you graduate, if you study hard. You'll learn how to sew on the fancy new sewing machines I saw there. If you get sick, they have a nurse to help you get well. In fact, I talked to her about all of you, and you, Celeste, are the one she's a little worried about."

Celeste's eyes widened. "Why, Mama?"

"I was telling Nurse you are so much thinner than Irene was at your age. Even Leah has more meat on her bones than you do, and it's been worrying me for a little while. Anyway, Nurse says she's going to pay special attention to you and make sure you get light chores and maybe an extra afternoon snack to help build you up." I wasn't going to tell Celeste that her thin body might make her more susceptible to tuberculosis. The nurse was going to make sure that didn't happen. A silver lining in a very dark cloud.

"Oh, I see." Celeste paused a moment and preened—just a little. The thought that she didn't mind receiving special attention almost made me smile. "I didn't mean what I said about Irene being your favorite. And I didn't know about having to be under thirteen and all. I'm sorry."

Leah nodded agreement. She hadn't said anything, but it had been clear she had also resented what she saw as Irene's unfair good fortune.

"I'm sure you're both going to go tell Irene that in just a moment," Daddy said before I could respond to Celeste. They both nodded, shame on their faces at having to hear that from their dear granddaddy.

I turned to Leah. "Baby, you're going to be glad to hear they already have a girls' basketball team. How about that?" I was right; she looked excited.

"Why don't you two go say sorry to Irene." I motioned to Celeste and Leah, and they raced off to make amends after Celeste handed a dozing Clarence back to Mama.

I looked over Martha's head at my mother. "Could you talk with Irene later? And… well, you know…" I looked down at Martha and then Tommy. Both had nodded off, too. The emotions of the afternoon had worn everyone out.

Mama nodded and looked at Daddy. "We'll make sure we talk with each of them, honey. Don't you worry. We want this to be as easy as it can be, though we know it's going to be hard on all of us. Your daddy and I have gotten so used to having all of you with us." Her tired voice cracked, and Daddy leaned over and took her hand.

He said, "Don't worry, Mary. We're going to get through this. You and the children are going to be just fine. So are we." He gave a little smile. "It's just a little hard to see that right now."

That was Friday afternoon, December 27. From then on, I dreaded marking the date on the wall calendar in the kitchen. We had so much to do that the days passed more quickly than I would ever have expected. But the blessing was we didn't have time to dwell too much on our imminent separation. Christmas decorations came down to make room for the piles we made for each child to take to Lexington. I had to decide what I would need at the tiny new apartment.

On Sunday, several congregation members came to bring us to church. Mama had spoken with the minister and let him know about what was happening and why. Months ago, I would have so dreaded being judged as a bad mother, I probably wouldn't have dared to show my face, but somehow, I was finally set in my mind I *was* being a good mother by doing this for my children. I held my head up as we arrived at church, and much to my pleased surprise, I was met with nothing but kindness and good wishes. The children were surrounded by well-wishers who expressed only happy anticipation for their upcoming adventures, and my children started looking as if they were indeed fortunate. It didn't hurt that some of the younger children even seemed a little envious. Irene was praised for being such a help to me, and she took on a pleased glow.

All in all, I was struck again by how true it was: we could decide if we were going to dwell on the good or on the evil that befell us. We weren't going to escape missing each other or wishing we could all still be together. We couldn't escape sorrow entirely. But we could choose to spend much more of our time thinking about all the good things that came our way.

I just hoped I could hold on to that thought in the days to come. And, most of all, that my children could.

Then Mr. Prince, our kind minister, gave his sermon. He looked out into our congregation until he saw me, and smiling right at me, he began telling the story of Baby Moses, and how his mother saved his life by placing him in a woven basket and floated him on the Nile where the pharaoh's daughter came to bathe. The Egyptian princess had her serving woman bring her the little boat from the bulrushes. As the princess exclaimed over the baby, Miriam, Moses's older sister, came out of hiding and offered to get someone to nurse the baby. And so his mother nursed him until he was old enough to go live in the palace as son of the princess.

As he spoke, I reached over for Irene's hand.

Of course, every person in our church knew that Bible story. We had all grown up with it. But this Sunday, I think we heard it in a new way. Mr. Prince talked about the bravery of the mother and sister of Moses, and how they had sacrificed their own happiness to ensure Moses would not only survive but have opportunities they would never experience. At the end of his sermon, Mr. Prince smiled again at me and then at Irene.

I think there were very few dry eyes in our church that day.

On Monday, December 30, Mr. Prince and two of the deacons came by right after breakfast to take all of us to see the new apartment. It was Mr. Prince's idea it would be good for the children to be able to picture us in our new home. I was so grateful, for I couldn't imagine how we could have all traveled there otherwise. Mama and Daddy came as well. The men dropped us off to see the apartment and visit for an hour with Martha and her children, who were home, as it was still Christmas break. Clarence had arranged to go into work a little late so he could see everyone, too. The children walked through our two rooms, eyes big, and then went off to play with their cousins. Fortunately, the older ones understood about being as quiet as possible for Miss Avery's sake, so I didn't worry much about that.

Irene had stayed with us and joined in the discussion about what pieces of furniture we'd need to bring with us. We hoped to be moved in completely by the weekend, as I had to start work the following Monday. Clarence and Daddy talked about getting the furniture from the farm, and it seemed Clarence had already enlisted the aid of a few friends to help convey everything on Saturday. I thought about how some people had to do everything on their own, and again, I decided I needed to keep being grateful for the many people who had helped my family this past year and continued to do so.

All too soon, it was time to meet our minister and deacons outside. The younger children hugged their aunt, uncle, and cousins, promising to write to them about their adventures yet to come. Irene heard them and gave me a little smile. "I'm glad they're feeling better about this, Mama. I'm feeling better, too." I suspected that last part wasn't entirely true yet, but I could only hope it would be soon.

Tuesday, December 31, 1929

Just before two o'clock the next day, New Year's Eve, we stood on the platform, looking at the billowing train that would take the children to Florence, South Carolina, where they'd change trains for Lexington. Mr. and Mrs. Preston had introduced themselves and now stood chatting with Tommy and Martha. I could see they'd take good care of the children on the trip, and I was glad at how friendly they were with them.

All four children kept looking over at the train. Their excitement about their first rail trip was helping to bolster their grief at leaving. I was glad they had that distraction to help ease them into their new life.

Mr. Adams, who had found this haven for my children, was there just as he had promised, as were Mr. Prince and the deacons, who, along with Lottie, once again had brought us into town. The men each had an enclosed car, rather than a truck, which kept everyone warm for the trip. I certainly didn't want the children to get sick, and especially not to arrive in Lexington having become ill on the train.

Mr. Prince's wife was back at the house with Clarence. His ears were prone to infection in cold weather, and I didn't want him out here on the train platform. She had volunteered to stay with him, which relieved at least one worry. The children had each held him before leaving for the station. Baby Clarence didn't understand what was going on, but basked in their attention. Just in time, I caught myself from saying, "You won't recognize him the next time you see him." I hoped we'd be able to visit Lexington before that truly became the case.

Earlier in the day, Mr. Meyer had transported the children's luggage to the depot. My parents and I took turns hugging and talking with the four children who were about to leave us. Irene and I took turns holding Martha or Tommy in our arms, even though they were both getting so big I knew we'd be sore the next day. I kept sniffing their hair, their necks, memorizing their scent. I wanted to take them back inside me and keep them with me forever. Leah and Celeste kept trying to hide their tears as they wrapped their arms around my waist or Irene's.

Much too soon, passengers were called to board. After bright, cheery talk for the last few hours, we faltered. The last hugs and kisses were wet with tears. Even Mr. Adams and the deacons had brimming eyes. Anyone with a heart would have.

Mr. and Mrs. Preston finally took the hands of the four children and led them up the short set of steps. A few minutes later, those little faces were pressed to the windows by their seats, their breath clouding the cold glass. Martha held her doll, Miss Muffet, up to the window and waved her hand for her. The train screeched, shuddered, and spewed diesel fumes as it slowly lumbered away from the platform. Irene and I had our arms around each other as we waved them out of the station. Lottie came and put her head on my shoulder as we stood there, watching the caboose disappear in the distance. I could see Mama and Daddy wiping their eyes, still waving.

"Mama, I'm ashamed. I'm feeling so sorry for myself. They're the ones who are having to leave," Irene sobbed. I knew she was still hearing Celeste tell her she was the lucky one, because she got to stay with me. I didn't want any guilt or resentment to grow in her tender heart.

"Oh, baby, it's natural to feel that way. I think it must always be harder to be the ones who are left behind. The ones who are going might be sad to leave, but they have something new to look forward to, even if it's just their first ride on a train." I held her to me even more tightly. Tonight, I would wonder who was holding my children, for I knew that was when their tears would come. But for now, I tried to set that thought aside for Irene's sake.

"This is a good thing, Irene. We're going to make it a good thing." I pulled her more tightly to my side.

Our friends and family on the platform were entirely silent for a few moments. Then we turned to walk back to the motorcars. Surely, this New Year would be better to us than the previous two years. "We're going to *make* it a good year," I said to no one in particular, as we walked toward 1930.

Epilogue

Tuesday, December 24, 1946

"Mama!" Martha's dark-blonde head snaps up. "You didn't really say that, did you?" She looks over at her husband of three months, who just laughs and shakes his head.

"Oh, Mother, you had better be more careful. Someone might have done something awful to you!" Celeste stops feeding her six-month-old son and glares at me. Poor girl, her Navy husband is back at sea somewhere, even though the war ended over a year ago. Apparently, he is going to make a career of it, and the separation, especially with an infant to care for, is wearing on her nerves. I'm glad she's agreed to move in with me until Bennie gets home. As always, her dark hair is beautifully coifed, and her figure is as slender as it was when she first married.

I recently moved into this house, so similar in design to the one I lived in with Tom all those years ago, and not far from where it stood before being torn down during the war to make way for newer homes on what had once been farmland. So much larger than that pokey little apartment in town, this home has plenty of room for Celeste and her baby, as well as Tommy and Clarence. My boys are on leave for the Christmas holidays.

Leah, expecting her third child in April, walks back into the room from changing Johnny's diaper, with five-year-old Jimmy in tow. Pushing her dark curls away from her face, she asks, "What happened?" She looks around in surprise at the shocked expressions on her sisters. The menfolk are trying not to laugh, although they aren't trying hard enough, in my opinion.

"Mama took on the men at the fishing pier a few months ago, it seems, Leah." Tommy smiles at her.

"What Tommy means to say is our mother is one tough… um… lady." Clarence grins and winks at me. I swanee, I think that good-looking boy just naturally winks at anything in a skirt so often that now he's winking at his own mama.

"Please tell me Mr. Walters was with you, Mama." Irene looks over at my husband of ten days. "Please say she wasn't alone out there and saying that to those men." My Pete, whose light blue eyes are swimming with tears of laughter, just shakes his head. I frown at him. He laughs harder.

Pete inherited this house about a year ago from a bachelor uncle and started fixing it up for us. It isn't one of the new ones, just an old farmhouse that has withstood its share of storms and needs some loving care. The day after our wedding, he took me to the courthouse to add my name to the deed. Although I never said a word about wanting that, he knows my family was left homeless when Tom died. He wants me to never worry about that happening again.

"Would somebody please tell me what happened?" Leah is getting more alarmed.

"I'll tell you, sweetheart. Sit down now. One of you men let her put her feet up on your chair." Clarence hops up and gets his sister settled while Tommy brings in a chair from another room. Pat, Irene's eight-year-old daughter, her hair as blonde as Irene's is black, goes to get a pillow for Leah's feet. Tommy still has such blond hair, so I suppose it runs in the family somewhere.

Now we are all crowded around the kitchen table, except for Irene's George, who, as a butcher, feels only he can carve the turkey and ham to his exacting standards. He's probably right. He stops sharpening his knives and turns to hear my silly little story again. Also missing from the table is Leah's Howard, who should be back from the store any minute. Judging by the wonderful scents filling the entire house, we are about to have a feast. Martha and Irene insisted on doing most of the cooking, and they are both gifted in the kitchen. I smile as I notice the little tray of baby biscuits ready to be baked at the last minute for Pat and Johnny.

The real surprise in the room is Jack, Martha's new husband. At twenty-three, Martha is still as pretty as she was as a little girl, and now always elegant in her stylish clothes. In October, she married her coworker at the Atlantic Coast Line, where she is a secretary. Jack is a telegraph operator. He's fifty-one and bald as an egg. And one of the nicest men I've ever met, thank goodness. Still, the man is three years older than I am, which I find a little hard to get over, although I'll never admit that to anyone. I can only wonder if losing her daddy at such a young age led her to be drawn to Jack. Whatever the reason, they seem to have a strong and loving bond.

For all I know, people might wonder about Pete and me. Tom was almost half a foot taller than me, but I am several inches taller than Pete. Tom was lanky; Pete is stocky. Not fat, just stocky. We're the same age, at least. But none of that really matters. I thought I'd spend the rest of my life alone, but there was a different future waiting for me. Who would have thought I'd be a bride at forty-eight? A very happy bride.

Clarence went to the Home to join Tommy and his sisters when he was four. Irene and I lived at Miss Avery's house until Irene got married to George in 1935, when she was nineteen. I continued living in that apartment for years, and that's how I met Pete. His first wife passed away two years before we met, and he moved into an apartment several houses down from mine. We'd see each other out and about and sitting on our front porches on summer evenings. Over the years, we started saying more than a quick hello and got to know each other slowly. And now I'm Mrs. Walters.

Pete operates a big sawmill at a lumberyard, and often has little curls of fresh wood in his silky gray hair when he comes home. He's quiet and seems to love to hear me talk. He's a gentle soul.

He's also very patient. I wouldn't walk out with him until all my children had returned from the Home. It didn't seem right somehow. The girls came back to me as soon as they could and found jobs. We lived together until each one married, so Martha was with me until recently. The boys went straight from the Home into the war. They both left early, before they were eighteen, and enlisted, Tommy in the Navy, and Clarence in the Coast Guard, although the war was winding down by the time he joined up. Those two boys are both tall like Tom, but otherwise so different from each other. Tommy, much to my surprise considering how he was as a little boy, is quiet and thoughtful. He's learned to be an electrician in the Navy, and I am sure he'll do well when he leaves the service. Dark-haired and "as good-looking as any movie star" according to Celeste, Clarence is ever the ladies' man and can talk anyone into anything, I do believe. I hope he'll go into sales and make a fortune, although he says he's thinking about making a career out of the Coast Guard. For now, though, they are still enlisted, and they both look so handsome sitting at the table in their uniforms.

Irene has had her share of sadness as well as joy. She delights in Pat, who could not be a more loving and sweeter child. But last year, she lost her second daughter, who wasn't quite five months old. Pneumonia. The same as took my little Alice all those years ago. Irene and I, having gone through those years in that apartment, have always been close, and her baby's death has drawn us closer still. Just lately, she seems to be coming out from the cloud of grief, and I suspect she'll have another little one sometime next summer. I'll wait for her to tell me, though.

As I look around my kitchen, I spot the Christmas card from Lottie I'd been reading earlier. Lottie and I have stayed in touch over the years, as we promised each other. She's come to visit me in Wilmington several times, and we still sit up and laugh over our youthful adventures. She remarried a few years after she and her mother moved in with her grandmother and now has two daughters in addition to Bertie, who is an attorney in Washington, DC. Both her grandmother and then her mother passed away shortly after her marriage. I know Lottie loved her mother, but I think she truly bloomed without constant critical monitoring. Pete and I are planning on visiting her for the first time in the spring. I can't wait to see her children and her husband again.

There are others who aren't here, of course. My sister Martha, who helped me so much in those years when Baby Clarence, Irene, and I lived across the hall from her family at Miss Avery's house, passed away of a heart attack in July 1935, just a month before her fortieth birthday. Three weeks later, Daddy had his last heart attack at seventy-four. Mama followed him seven years later. Even now, I am sometimes overwhelmed by my need to speak with them just one more time.

One of the few good things that came about as a result of Tom's death was that the children and I got to spend those fifteen months with Daddy and Mama. I came to know them as I had not had the chance to before my early marriage, and as an adult I was able to realize how fortunate I was to have such loving parents, and my children to have such wonderful grandparents.

Tom's mother, Mama Jo, passed away the same year as Daddy and Martha, leaving Sis and Clyde, still childless, on their own in Tarboro.

I hope all my departed loved ones are together. If they aren't, I don't want to know.

Until her death, Mama Jo defended my decision to put the children in the Home, despite Elim and Otis telling me on more than one occasion that Tom was turning in his grave knowing what I did. At one point after the children had been in the Home for almost a year, I made a special trip to Lexington to speak directly to Mr. Shuford, the superintendent, about their repeated threats to come get the children. As he had on our first meeting, Mr. Shuford assured me that Tom's brothers would never be able to take the children away. Over the years, and especially after Mama Jo's passing, I stopped hearing from Elim and Otis. I'm happy to say Sis and I are still close and visit each other when we can.

I bring my thoughts back to the present. "Well, here's what happened, Leah. I don't know why your sisters are making such a fuss. You know how Pete and I love to fish off the pier at Kure Beach a little ways from here. Well, he went into the snack area to get us a soft drink. We'd been there a little while, but the blues were running, so we had to keep fishing."

Heads nod. Everyone knows you don't just walk away from a good run of fish.

"Anyway, I'd noticed some of the men out there on the pier had been drinking from brown paper bags. I'm sure you know what I mean." My girls look disapproving. The men seem to find something amusing.

"That was none of my business, of course, as long as it didn't get out of hand. But after a while, I started hearing foul language every now and then. While Pete was in the snack shop, it picked up and got louder, and there was more of it."

"Yes, Mama?" Martha looks worried again, even though she's already heard me tell this earlier. For a moment, I see her as that little girl who wanted to hear the same stories over and over.

"Well, I'd finally had it. I wasn't about to put up with that. So, I reeled in my pole, turned around, and let them know I didn't want to hear another man take the Lord's name in vain again. That I was a lady, and they needed to behave like gentlemen. That I was trying to have a nice time fishing, and I wasn't about to listen to cussing. They could stop it or go somewhere else to fish."

Leah's mouth drops open. "Oh, my mercy, Mama. Oh my. What happened then?"

Pete leans forward in his chair. "I can tell you that part. I was just starting back with our soft drinks, and I could see my Mary all lit up like the Fourth of July. Hot under the collar. You know how she is. She had her hands on her hips, and I only got the last sentence or so she said, but I can tell you—you could've heard a pin drop when she finished. Well, you could've if the ocean had been quiet for a moment, you know. Anyway, all of a sudden, these men took their hats off and apologized. I'm not sure I've ever seen a man take his hat off on a pier, now that I think of it. Your mother said something like, 'I hope I don't have to tell you again' and turned back to her pole. We were there another couple of hours, and I can assure you there was absolutely no more foul language on that pier. We haven't heard any since then, either."

George looks over at Pete. "Well, I guess you know you better be careful, too." The men chuckle.

"Apparently, 'I swigger' is about as bad as I can get away with, fellas." Pete tucks his chin against his chest and smiles.

"Mother, honestly, do you not see that one of those men could have hauled off and hit you?" Celeste is still irate.

"Honey, thank you for worrying about me, but I don't think I was in any danger. One man on his own might have wanted to talk back to me, but most of them knew very well I was right, and they shouldn't talk like that. And I don't think rolling your eyes is very attractive, missy."

Celeste huffs a little. "Mother, I just don't think you understand. What are people going to think about you? That's not how ladies are expected to act."

Poor thing, she seems so upset about this. I sense her disapproval and her fear that she will have a mother that other people look down on.

I look around at my family, all waiting to hear my reply. From their expressions, I think they expect me to be angry with her, but I'm not. I remember only too well worrying about the same thing all those years past—especially afraid people would think I was a bad mother and a betrayer of Tom's memory.

"Celeste, I had to stop worrying about what people think of me a long, long time ago. There are always going to be people who criticize you, no matter what you do or even what you don't do. You have to think carefully and then choose what you believe is the right thing, whether anyone else agrees with you or not." Celeste nods, but I can tell she's not happy about my answer. I try to lighten her mood. "But don't worry, I don't intend to go around correcting everyone I disagree with. Probably just Pete from now on."

Pete's eyes go large, and then he laughs, along with everyone else. Bless his heart, he thinks I'm kidding. I smile at my new husband fondly and know that he's right. Mostly.

Tommy stands up. "Well, is it about time to eat? We've got a load of Christmas presents to open up, don't we, Pat? You think so, Jimmy?" The two youngsters bounce on their toes. "Gotta eat first so we have strength enough to get through them." Vigorous nodding from the children, who race off to wash their hands.

We are all having Christmas Eve dinner together, and then tomorrow, Irene, Leah, and Martha will each be in her own home. I know it's natural that they want to have their own Christmas traditions, and I'm just hopeful that being here on Christmas Eve will become a tradition, too. In addition to Celeste and her baby boy, Tommy and Clarence are staying over with us until they have to report back to their ships, so Pete and I will have a busy Christmas Day this year.

As the girls start putting the food into serving bowls, Howard returns from the store with the extra milk for the children and George brings the platters of turkey and ham to the table. I look at my family, my children and all the new additions. Even over the delicious aromas coming from the kitchen, I can smell the Christmas tree in the front living room. The large bulbs glow red, blue, green, and gold. So different from our candles from our last tree before Celeste, Leah, Martha, and Tommy left for the Home.

Thanks to the awful war, this is the first time we have all been together on Christmas Eve since then. Seventeen years.

So much heartache and loneliness for all of us, but also joy. All five of my children who went to the Home always speak of it with real love, even Tommy, who tried to run away in the first few months to get back to me. He didn't make it very far, of course, and he eventually settled in and thrived. Irene and I got to go see them twice a year, which helped all of us. I am truly blessed that eventually, each one of them understood that sending them there was the very best I could have done for them. And they had each other while they were there. If anything, my heart aches sometimes thinking of the years Irene missed with her brothers and sisters. Our life together was hard during the Depression, but at least she has found happiness with George and now her dear Patricia.

And I've found happiness, too. All those years of scrubbing floors on my knees, all the hardships of the Great Depression and the war years, all those things fade away as I look around me. I hope Tom knows how our family has turned out. That we got through all of it, and now we are spending Christmas Eve together.

Diamonds, Tom. I have so many diamonds.

THE END

Mary Ellen

Photo taken 1940s

A GIFT FOR YOU

Thank you for reading *A High Courage*! Please scan the QR code below or go to my website to access "Behind the Book: The Historical Truth of A High Courage." The album contains photos of my family members who inspired this story—Mary, Tom, Mama Jo with her dog Teddy Bear having tea, along with the six children at the Home and as adults.

www.gailpiner.com/book-bonus

Acknowledgments

So many people have helped turn the dream of this book into a reality and have all, in one way or another, been the best of teachers. Endless thanks.

To my cousins—Carol Caldwell, for always being excited to listen to parts of our grandmother's story and laughing at your dad's imagined boyhood; Patricia Rackley and Gerald Holland, for sharing memories of your lovely mother and encouraging me along the way (and for being your sweet eight-year-old self in this story, Big Sis); and John (Johnny, as you'll always be to me) T. Robbins, for telling me about your mother's love of basketball and for appearing in this novel—in diapers. Robyn Holland, wonderful cousin-in-law and fantastic artist, for sharing your dad's WWII prisoner-of-war autobiography and inspiring me to get on with this book. Also, thanks for moving from Australia to keep Gerald in line; no one in this country could manage it.

To Carol Georgen, for being hard to please, because when you said you liked this book from the beginning, I knew you really meant it. You're the best must-be-a-sister-from-a-previous-life I could hope for or, at least, that I'm going to get.

To Betsy Krakauskas, your warmth and encouragement have been unwavering, and I think we need a trip to Southport soon. Also, Katie Pogo expects to see you more frequently now.

To Tori and Joe Uhler, your support and excitement for this book have helped keep me afloat during the challenging times of writing. Tori, your own family-history book reminded me how fascinating someone else's family can be.

To Isla Wesner, for a lifetime of friendship, laughter, and adventures (some remembered better than others).

To Alice Canup, for your insights and encouragement that have made all the difference. I really have no words for all the ways you've helped me. Heartfelt gratitude, Alice. Heartfelt.

To my fabulous writing group—Andie Biagini, Marie-Claire Lander, Megan Mabee, John Roper, and Linda Velte. You have been with me through almost every word of this book, offering many suggestions and endless encouragement that my grandmother's story was interesting and worth telling. Without the support of you five, I don't think this book would have been written. No doubt I should have taken even more of your suggestions.

To all the advance readers. Your time and comments are so appreciated!

To my wonderful team at Paper Raven Books. More than anyone, you folks know how unlikely it would have been for me to get this book from my laptop to the world on my own. Special thanks to Brandy Lay for fielding so many questions (even on weekends, at your daughter's soccer games, and when you had the flu), and to Abbey Ryan, Charlotte Zang, Colleen Tomlinson, M.A. Hinkle, Ray Harvey, and Stef Gilmour for your expertise, patience, kindness, and, let's face it, psychological services on a few occasions. Thanks to the very talented Antonio Cesar of 99Designs for my beautiful cover; it's even better than I had imagined it could be. Morgan Gist MacDonald, you've created a great company. All of you went above and beyond. It's been such a pleasure working with you!

To Katie Pogo, for your insistence every few hours that I get up and attend to your demands, thus no doubt saving me from some health-related crisis brought on by sitting too long while writing this book. You are proof that a lot of attitude and love can be packed into a mere nine pounds. Who's a good girl? You are, you are.

Author's Note

It seems universal that children take their family circumstances for granted. Certainly, it seemed normal to me that my mother, brothers, and I went to visit Grandmother every Sunday afternoon, while knowing that our mother had grown up in an orphanage with her younger siblings—always referred to as the "Home"—during the Great Depression, and that her older sister had stayed with Grandmother during those years. My mother, aunts, and uncles spoke casually about the Home, while showing their mother nothing but love and appreciation. As I got older, of course, I began to realize how unusual my family was; at least, none of my friends had a similar situation.

I'm glad I asked my mother for her memories of her life at the Home and my Aunt Irene about her time during that period. I also had conversations with my grandmother and so learned more about the situation she was in after my grandfather's death. I especially recall her face as she told me of his brothers' reactions to her decision to send the children to Lexington, of their claims he was turning over in his grave and she was disgracing his name, and her fears they would simply take the children and use them as unpaid farm laborers. She was so frightened in the months following their move there that she made the long trip to Lexington to speak with the director in person, who told her there was no way the uncles could legally take the children. Would they really have treated the children as she feared? I can only say that she believed they would.

I wish that I'd asked many, many more questions of all of them, as I didn't realize how little I knew about the details of their lives until I started writing this book. Even so, many of the facts and stories contained in this novel are true, especially the family history details both sad (infant deaths and the death of Janie and her unborn child just before Christmas 1928) and humorous (yes, my grandmother did indeed toss an undercooked drumstick at a church picnic and accidentally hit the minister in the head—and never confessed, I believe, until she told me the story more than fifty years later, laughing as she did so). The beach trolley in Wilmington, North Carolina, existed for decades, and my mother loved to reminisce about taking it from Front Street to Wrightsville Beach in the late 1930s and early 1940s.

Some of the stories are true but happened to other people, such as the ill-fated horse ride and the little girl standing up in church to suggest it was time to go home (both of those were me). Great-Aunt Mamie really did tell those stories from the Civil War on a moonlit summer night on Grandmother's front porch, but to my two young cousins and eight-year-old me, and Grandmother made her stop before she could get to the "even worse ones."

As for the truth about Aunt Mamie's circumstances, the bare facts are true, but I have invented the parts about her being treated poorly by our family members because of her marital status as a way of illustrating the situation that no doubt faced many "old maids" of the time. I don't know how she was treated by those on whom she was dependent for her entire life, as she was an elderly lady when I was a child and knew her as an infrequent visitor to my grandmother. I hope she was loved, which is likely given that her grave marker reads "Aunt Mamie."

And some are of questionable truth, such as the rituals for girls to find out which man they would marry; my cousins and I couldn't get past the don't-laugh requirement. Prone as I was to headaches as a child, I was subjected to the burnt-toast and the vinegar-and-brown-paper-bag remedies several times at Grandmother's house; I do not endorse them.

Although many of the characters are based on real people, some are entirely fictional, such as Lottie, Mrs. Vanderven, and Mr. Meyer. I just wish they had existed. Of course, most of the day-to-day events are entirely fictional; I certainly never had a discussion with my grandmother about her wedding night.

I have tried to envision what life might have been for my family during those fifteen months and to understand the dynamics that were in play. I have felt much like a detective as I tried to imagine how one event led to another and why it might have taken fifteen months to reach a resolution.

Many books have been written about the history of Wilmington, North Carolina, and photos of the Lumina (and its movie screen set in the surf) can be found online. For those who might prefer a novel, *Lumina,* by Mary Flinn, brings to life Wilmington and Wrightsville Beach during the late 1920s, especially the social classes more affluent than my grandmother's family of farmers. I like to think her elegant characters would have been kind to my grandparents on their (imagined) honeymoon evening at the Lumina Pavilion.

The orphanage in Lexington, NC, was the second one constructed by the Junior Order of United American Mechanics (usually referred to as "the Junior Order"), a fraternal organization that originated in Philadelphia. Initially, only orphaned children of Junior Order members were accepted. At the time my family members went there, children had to be out of diapers and younger than thirteen to be admitted, which is why Clarence, at eighteen months old, didn't initially go with his four siblings, and Irene (thirteen) never did. Still in operation, but now called American Children's Home, it accepts children from birth to twenty-one through Social Services and offers residential housing as well as foster-care placement. It holds regular fundraisers and accepts donations. It certainly made a world of difference to my family.

In 1999, I took my mother to visit there, only the second time she'd been in Lexington since she left the Home in 1936. She was so excited to stand by the door to the North Carolina building, the dorm she and her siblings slept in during their years there. Mother pointed out the huge oak tree still in the front of the Administration building; much to her dissatisfaction, her assigned chore was to sit under its leafy boughs on summer days, watching the younger children play, and then she was required to go to the kitchen to get an extra sandwich midafternoon, as they tried to increase her weight to protect her from developing tuberculosis. All those years later, she was still miffed they hadn't let her do what she thought would have been more fun—working in the sweltering laundry. As you may have gathered, my mother was Celeste.

The staff members were so welcoming to us during that visit, even going to the trouble of finding the seventy-year-old ledger that was filled in when Mother, Leah, Martha, and Tommy arrived. That was the first time I learned they had arrived on New Year's Day, 1930. Mother had forgotten that detail, remembering only the tearful departure from the train station. Seeing their names and ages written in that ledger made all the stories I'd heard growing up more real to me than I would have thought possible.

I think it is to the credit of my mother, aunts, and uncles that I never heard one of them complain about how their lives were changed by the death of their father. They seemed to understand that their mother had made the best decision that was available to her, all for their sakes. Far from feeling they had had tragic childhoods, they felt they had been fortunate compared to so many during those dreadful Depression years.

For years I thought about my grandmother's bravery as a young Southern woman in the 1920s, raised to be obedient and deferential to men and the expected norms of the time, to stand up and resist that pressure—both familial and societal—to ensure the safety and well-being of her children. I am very proud to be her granddaughter. I can only hope that I've honored her memory as she deserves.

Author Bio

After almost forty years of wandering in the deserts of Virginia, upstate New York, Colorado, Texas, and Illinois, Gail Piner retired from academics and returned to her hometown on the coast of North Carolina, a mere two miles from the house where her Grandmother lived and most of this story takes place. She now spends most of her time dodging hurricanes, procrastinating on paperwork, wishing she'd started writing nonacademic fiction much sooner, and, most frequently, acting as a domestic servant to her nine-pound Maltese/Bichon rescue pup, Katie Pogo, who has a surprising gift for sarcasm. This is her first novel, based on the true story of her family.

author@gailpiner.com

9 798988 116110